T0058026

Praise for Paul Lisicky's *Lawnboy:*

"The sexual awakening of a gay teenager leads to a peculiar, short-ranged rebellion in Paul Lisicky's moody, thoughtful first novel. . . . *Lawnboy* recalls standouts of the genre."—*SAN FRANCISCO CHRONICLE*

"*Lawnboy* is, quite simply, the real thing, a novel of mystery and great beauty. The appearance of a writer like Paul Lisicky—a writer who deeply respects the complexities of love and desire, who can find tragedy and transcendence almost everywhere he looks—is a rare event. I read this book increasingly slowly, dreading the moment when I would have no more of it to read. Now that I've finished, all I can say is that I hope Paul Lisicky is hard at work on another one."—MICHAEL CUNNINGHAM

"This novel is to young gay men growing up in the 1980s and 1990s what Edmund White's *A Boy's Own Story* was for gay men who grew up in the 1950s and 60s. It's the best gay coming-of-age novel I've read in a decade, written with a wonderfully crisp prose. This story concerns a young man trying to find a family anywhere he can; he drifts from situation to situation in South Florida until he finally makes peace with himself. This writer could be the next David Leavitt or Michael Cunningham."—*BOOKSENSE 76 NEWSLETTER*

"Nobody writes about hilarious longing the way Paul Lisicky does. Some writers manage to be funny and sad in turn; in *Lawnboy*, Lisicky manages to be both at the same time. His characters are lovable and fallible; his prose is gorgeous. *Lawnboy* is a tribute to the endless series of life's first loves: your parents, your siblings, your best friends, your childhood fears. It's beautifully written, it's beautiful."—ELIZABETH McCRACKEN

"Savvy enough to recognize the importance of buzz cuts and sleeveless shirts in gay identity formation, Lisicky is also smart enough not to rely on hackneyed consumer-culture signifiers, resulting in a lushly emotional, romantic and tragic pursuit."—*PAPER*

"Lisicky's prose shines, at times hilarious, at others entrenched in sorrow and longing, but always gorgeous to read. . . . The reconciliations between the characters are moving and earned, graced with compassion and vitality."—BRET ANTHONY JOHNSON, *BOOK*

"What distinguishes *[Lawnboy]* is the depth of humanity that flows into Lisicky's cascade of crisp, fresh sentences. . . . Lisicky never ceases to be funny, ironic, and surprising. . . . *Lawnboy* scythes a remarkably touching journey."—*LAMBDA BOOK REPORT*

"This adventure-of-the-heart takes place in as evocative a landscape as any you'll find in fiction, its Floridian decay and lushness the perfect setting for a story dense with eroticism, disillusionment, and the surprising grace notes of renewal."—BERNARD COOPER

"*Lawnboy* re-landscapes the front yard of American fiction."—CAROL MUSKE DUKES

"The power of this book is its ability to touch you on so many different levels."—*HOUSTON VOICE*

"Lisicky charts Evan's conflicting emotions deftly. . . . Humorous and moving . . . hitting musical notes of insight and wit."—*AUSTIN CHRONICLE*

"Reading this often brilliant novel makes a critic want to apply the cliché 'promising,' which doesn't do justice to this accomplished and highly readable excursion into human emotions and the choices that we make, or have made for us."—SUITE 101.COM

Lawnboy

Also by Paul Lisicky

Famous Builder

The Burning House

Unbuilt Projects

The Narrow Door: A Memoir of Friendship

Later: My Life at the Edge of the World

Lawnboy

❖ ❖ ❖

a novel

Paul Lisicky

Graywolf Press

Copyright © 1998 by Paul Lisicky
First published by Turtle Point Press

Publication of this volume is made possible in part by a grant provided by the Minnesota State Arts Board, through an appropriation by the Minnesota State Legislature; a grant from the Wells Fargo Foundation Minnesota; and a grant from the National Endowment for the Arts, which believes that a great nation deserves great art. Significant support has also been provided by the Bush Foundation; the McKnight Foundation; and other generous contributions from foundations, corporations, and individuals. To these organizations and individuals we offer our heartfelt thanks.

Supported by the Jerome Foundation in celebration of the Jerome Hill Centennial and in recognition of the valuable cultural contributions of artists to society

Published by Graywolf Press
212 Third Avenue North, Suite 485
Minneapolis, Minnesota 55401
All rights reserved.

www.graywolfpress.org

Published in the United States of America

ISBN-13-978-1-55597-448-0

Library of Congress Control Number: 2005938154

Cover design: Kyle G. Hunter
Cover photograph: © Corbis

for Mark

And so it was I entered the broken world
To trace the visionary company of love, its voice
An instant in the wind (I know not whither hurled)
But not for long to hold each desperate choice.

HART CRANE, *"The Broken Tower"*

Ching-a-ling-a-ling
Ching-a-ling-a-loo . . .
If you love me like
I love you
No one can cut our
love in two.

CHARLES LUDLAM, *"Eunuchs of the Forbidden City"*

Prologue

We stared up into the dark, flamboyant branches, waiting for the wind to pick up. All it took was the slightest push, and there it was: crimson blossoms swaying above us like bells. We stood beneath its heavy canopy, gazing up its trunk, quiet, motionless. The air thickened with its fragrance. And then, as if in gratitude, the tree released itself, little red pieces falling now, coating us, sticking in our hair like blessings.

We walked further into the park. Peter grasped my hand, reading aloud the names on the signs. Soursop. Gumbo-limbo. Frangipani. Sugar apple. He spoke these words precisely, with the slightest thrill, as if they tasted dangerous. Could we be any happier? Our parents, to our surprise, had encouraged us to come here by ourselves, and it was that dry October morning when the heat finally breaks, when people tired of humidity and air-conditioning finally throw open their windows.

I pointed to a flower. It faltered between a lamppost and a ditch, nameless, forlorn. "Look," I said.

Peter smiled, crouching down beside it. "Pretty."

I knelt next to him. I pulled in a breath: he'd always be older.

I was five then, an age I'd resisted, while he was thirteen. How I wanted to grow like that, to go through three different shoe sizes within a year.

I drew closer to the flower. I touched its leaves—crenellated, yellow—its dusky muscular stem. I squeezed shut my eyes. I saw it growing somewhere else, someplace better, in silence and beauty, craning its face toward the light.

I picked it. I twirled its stem between my fingers, listening. Do it. Don't do it. Do it. Don't. No. Then stuffed the whole thing, root and all, in my mouth.

Peter's face tightened. He jerked me up by the arm. "Evan—"

"What?"

"Spit it out!"

"But—"

"You heard me."

I turned my head away, holding my flower inside. The petals tickled the back of my throat; my tongue contracted. The earth blurred, warped. Grapefruit, I thought. My flower tastes like grapefruit. I swallowed, smiled, looked up at my brother through hot, hot tears.

"What if it's poison?" He nodded, once, twice, tensing his bottom lip. "Think about poison."

I curled tighter into myself. The woods smelled cold. My forehead burned. Skull and crossbones: would that be me? Bottle of iodine? Alive, I was alive.

Part One

Chapter 1

There were things nobody knew about me. They didn't know about my old train set in my bedroom, complete with Cape Cods, hotels, signal crossings, and papier-mâché palms, a set that I tinkered with until the ninth grade, then smashed—to my uttermost sorrow—after a fight with my father. They didn't know I could recite a handful of psalms—the 13th, the 23rd, the 42nd, and the 53rd—completely by heart. They didn't know about my deep interest in Greek myth, my faith in the shifting weather, my fascination with Saturn and the outer planets. They didn't know that I spent hours at a time inside a concrete pipe, a cool, cramped cylinder in the middle of a field, whenever I needed to get away. They didn't know about the morning in my thirteenth year when out of sheer boredom, I stitched my fingertips together with needle and thread, making an intricate basket of my hand and giving myself a tremendous infection. They all thought I was good-natured, upright and responsible, generous, affectionate, and kind, and of course I could be those things, but there was much more to me than that, a side that unnerved even myself, and this side included William.

William. William the pigeon-toed, William the conqueror. His name, though banal, still conjures up an otherworldly thing, not a being of flesh and blood. For a while I kept him hidden from everyone—my mother, my father, Peter. It even took me months to tell my best friend Jane about him, though she thought she knew me. Well, she didn't.

I liked to keep him that way: my secret path, my own private joy.

I was mowing my parents' lawn. He was standing in our yard between the joewood and the carambola, mopping his tanned forehead with a blue rag. He was watching me, hard, and I made an effort not to notice. He'd been around forever; he had to be almost as old as my parents: forty, forty-two. I'd never even given him a thought. I only knew that he worked the camera for Channel 7 News, had a gentle greeting for my folks whenever he walked his Dobermans, and had the most profound and beautiful travelers tree I'd ever seen (like me, he loved plants). That was it. He meant absolutely nothing to me, until he stepped forward, then I started noticing: jaw, eyes, hair, smell, hands, feet, mouth. There was a kind of buzz about him, a field of hissing electricity that jerked with my ions and electrons. I felt myself getting hard. I thought: now you've really gotten yourself into trouble.

"Lawnboy," he said, mocking me. "Lawnboy, Lawnboy."

I pulled back on the lever. The motor silenced. "Is there a problem?" I said, with some irritation.

The hush overwhelmed. Above, dry palm fronds clattered in the heat.

"Can I help you?"

He nodded, shyly. He tucked in his shirt, a striped Haitian thing patterned with yellow parrots. "My lawn mower's broken. My place is a mess. Would you be interested in cutting my lawn?"

My expression dulled. I reacted as if he'd been asking to tap my spine.

"I'll give you twenty bucks. Twenty bucks, an hour a week. No weeding or mulching."

I frowned. I felt simple, my tongue swelling fatly in my mouth. Befuddled. I glanced up at the shocked treetops and saw a sun shivering in a glazed sky. When I looked back at him, his eyes, blue with sprinklings of gold, were watching mine. I thought I detected some fear in them.

"I have to ask my parents," I announced.

I loped through the side door. I crouched in the living room, pressed my nose right down into the quarry tile so I could almost breathe in the dust. I was seventeen years old. Of course my parents didn't need to know. If anything, they'd be thrilled that I'd finally stopped moping around the house, dreading the resumption of school. I stood, watching the second hand of the clock make three complete rotations. I peered through the slats of the Bermuda shutter. He was shifting his weight from foot to foot. I reached into my pants, gave myself a firm and brutal yank. When I looked down, I noticed the trembling of my hands.

"What did they say?" William called out to me.

I bounded down the walk. I tried to seem matter-of-fact, reckless. "They said fine. Fine. When do you want me to start?"

"Tomorrow." He grinned, his shoulders drawing imperceptibly backward. "So we have a deal then."

"Deal." I extended my hand to him.

But he didn't take the hand. Instead, he placed his palm flat over my face, then pushed up, and as I started the mower, I decided he was probably the creepiest, most disgusting individual I'd ever met in my life.

◇ ◇ ◇

That night I lay in bed, listening to the house. Ice maker, pool motor, air conditioner, computer, oven cleaner. Everything but voices. It was the fourth day in a row that my parents, Ursula and Sid, hadn't spoken. I should have been used to it by now, but their silence only seemed to have gotten noisier, so shrill I pictured it puncturing a hole, the size of a meteorite, through the ceiling. I couldn't be safe from it, not outside, not in my room. I suspected it would follow me everywhere, even after their deaths, till my own death. I glanced at the digits of my clock radio. 10:04. Boy, am I seeing the world.

They shouldn't have gotten married. They couldn't stand each other. Anyone could see it in their eyes and their clipped, joyless mouths. Once, seeing intimations of these same expressions in their wedding photos, I thought, with relief—*ah*—so it isn't my doing. Still, it maddened me that they kept holding on like this. They never dealt with anything. The same way they couldn't deal with me. I mean, I didn't mince or prance. I didn't weave, I didn't dot my "i's" with circles or curlicues, but my eminent faggotry should have been obvious to them. Hello, Ursula. Hello, Sid. Knock, knock. Anybody home?

I fooled with my armpit hair. I thought of his face: the mussed-up brows, the deeply cut eyes. He carried a smoky smell about him, as if he were burning deep from inside.

"So where are you going?" Ursula said the following morning. Her voice sounded upbeat, despite the goings-on with my father. At least she'd gotten herself dressed today.

I stuffed a banana muffin in my mouth. "Beach. I'm going with Jane. I'll be back before dinner."

She pressed the small of her back into the countertop. She held her pale, slender arms tightly over her chest. "You're not going to the beach," she said with a knowing grin.

Crumbs caught in my throat. Did she know? She couldn't know. "Why do you always have to accuse? You never believe me. You always think I'm plotting, Mom. I think you despise me."

"Are you going to start with me again? I made a simple psychic assertion. You're a lousy liar. You can't hide a damn thing from me."

"Oh yeah?" I laughed, and slammed out the door.

I stood outside William's at 8:54 a.m. I was early, but wanted to get it over with. The door opened, and he stood there in a robe patterned with marine flags, a mud masque on his face.

"Lawn mower's in the garage," he said with a husky rasp.

I pulled up on the door handle. The mower hunkered beside the pool chemicals—a nice one actually, with pretty green paint and detachable grass catcher. Unlike our lawn mower, a piece of shit that was constantly leaking gas, this one started first try.

I bent over, stretched. The grass, a high-quality Floratam, was pleasantly spongy. I worked up and down, sidestepping sprinkler heads, guarding the tender young trunks of the palms. I started making up a song. I frequently made up songs and sang them aloud, almost yelling them up to the trees.

Lenny, the lusty Lawnboy,
Cuts the yards and makes them sizzle.
Everyone who sees him needs
His moisture-seeking love-hard missile.

I studied the sliding windows of the house and realized I wasn't going to have sex with him. I didn't know where the warped idea had popped into my head anyway. Once again, I'd allowed myself to get all worked up about someone who was unavailable to me, foreign as the workings of a nuclear power plant. I looked up at the window again. He was just a regular fellow. Lonely. Dumb. A little fun.

I finished up in record time, forty-three minutes. The yard was smaller than I'd expected. I stepped through the gate, sat, and took in the reeking trees: flame vine, soursop, wild cinnamon. My fingers smelled of gasoline, fertilizer. The lawn, green as mouthwash, glittered in the morning heat. Above me, the sky bubbled and fried.

"Nice tune," William said, stepping outside.

"What?"

"I said I liked your song."

My stomach folded in on itself. "I wasn't singing."

He cuffed the top of my head and laughed. "Do you want to come inside for breakfast?"

My words came out sludgy, like juice squeezed from a freeze-damaged orange. I told him that I had to leave, that I needed my payment, please, but he kept scrutinizing me. I tasted a fresh filling deep in the corner of my mouth. Finally, he reached into his rear pocket and pulled out three ten-dollar bills.

"But this is ten dollars too much."

"Take it."

"It's too much."

"Just take it. Buy yourself some candy."

"I don't need any candy."

"Whatever."

I shrugged. For some reason I felt myself welcoming, letting down the defenses, when I noticed the fractures of light in his eye. I went off. I imagined him capable of all sorts of things. Hangings, slayings, snuff films. Whole freezers filled with kidnapped boys in body bags stacked according to height, weight, race, creed.

"So would you like to come in?" he asked again.

"Sure," I said, and followed.

◇ ◇ ◇

Something disturbing and immature in my nature wanted to startle people. Perhaps it was because I was essentially unstartling in appearance. I slumped through the corridors of my school, Coral Gables High, a quiet, mealy kid with Dumbo-like ears, in flannel shirts, racking up B after B, even though I was most likely a genius. My fifth-grade teacher, Mrs. Edge, had extracted me from the class and said, "You're too good for us. I'm going to recommend to the principal that you be passed on to the sixth grade." And she did it, easy as the snap of a finger. These achievements continued until Peter—crying, stoned—left the house for good after an all-night fight with my father. I'm not sure what happened after that.

William and I sat at the kitchen counter. He told me about his ex-wife, Lorna, his daughter, Poppy, at Rollins College, his years in the Episcopal seminary, and his preparations for the priesthood. I was bored out of my skull. I picked up an empty mayonnaise jar. The same image kept drifting across my tired eyelids: a hole in the clouds, torn like a bullet wound, with the sky on fire behind it.

Then I thought about Jane. We were supposed to have gone to the beach. She had to be pissed by now. Or worried. She was always worried about me. Sometimes she told me that if

I wasn't careful, I'd be one of those people you read about in papers, carved up like a Christmas turkey, lying in a ditch. She could think what she wanted. But I knew I was protected. Something, somewhere, was watching, keeping me. God. An angel. I could walk through fire, thrive through sickness, pass through the harshest danger, and come out alive.

I looked up. William was smiling. "You haven't listened to a word I said."

"What?" I put the jar down. The tabletop was littered with the scraps of the peeled label.

"Tell me about yourself. How's school?"

I shrugged. I wasn't going to give in to him. He thought he had something. He thought I was innocent, powerless, that I was going to lie down and take it. He was wrong. I pictured him lying on his stomach in a warm dark cave. A bowl full of liquid beside his head. How easy it would be to lift the bowl in his moment of peace and kill him.

We were in his room. He sat on the bed while I swayed above him. He unzipped my pants and felt for my dick—a hard, red, glistening muscle. He gripped it, cranked it around. "Beautiful," he rasped, gazing up into my face.

He started sucking me off. It wasn't like I'd expected. I mean, I'd fooled around before, but it wasn't serious sex—not in a bed or anything—and this, I supposed, was serious sex. I wasn't particularly excited. Maybe I was bored, even disgusted. I concentrated on the motions, trying to pinpoint the smells in the room. I thought: bleach, weeds, sweat, funk, hair.

"Good?" he asked, taking a breather.

"Yeah."

We continued. We rolled around on the bed, when a thought, a full sentence, occurred to me: *He is getting younger, while I am getting older.* I didn't know what it meant. I thrust out my leg, kicked over the lamp, then rolled him over on his back, even though he was the stronger. I hiked his legs onto my shoulders, and to my astonishment, started fucking him.

"That's it," he muttered. "Fuck your old man, boy. That's it. Keep fucking your daddy."

"Shut up," I whispered. "Just please shut the hell up."

A thin cord of electricity quavered up my spine. I realized: this is what I'd always wanted. All at once I departed from myself, turning above the bed like a huge ticking wheel, watching us pushing against each other. My breath was sticking in my throat. I leaned over and kissed the harsh sandpaper of his face. I returned to myself, felt him clenching and relaxing around me, then pulled out, coming across his heaving stomach.

I stood before the bathroom mirror. I stuck a coated finger in my mouth, pushing it around my gums, feeding myself. My body felt new: the blood enriching my face, the muscles sharper as if dug by fine tools. I had something. I had a power all along and hadn't even known it.

But when I walked into his bedroom, I was only the mealy high school boy again. I eased under the covers, punching him softly on his broad freckled back, waiting for encouragement, or something returned, when he only swung away and rolled on some basketball socks with holes in them. His head appeared to be swimming with thoughts. His Dobermans jumped up on the bed, panting, licking at my bare skin.

"Get dressed, kiddo," he said. "Your parents are going to be worried."

"But can't we do it again?"

"No, that's enough for me. " He laughed softly. "Get dressed. It's time for you to go."

"You sure?"

He nodded.

So that's it, I thought. That's what you do. I picked up my clothes from the sweaty heap on the floor. He kissed me dryly on the mouth. I left. On the way home I kept repeating: *I went to the beach. I went to the big beach with my friend Jane and saw palms and sand and girls carrying buckets full of tulip shells. I took a swim and ate a snow cone.*

Chapter 2

Years ago, Jane had wanted me to be someone else. Or at least myself with one big difference.

We were sitting inside the South Miami house of Gwen Marino, the upper-level art teacher. We loved Gwen Marino, her tangle of hair and trailing black scarves and the many Bakelite bracelets she wore on each arm. Not only because she talked openly about the possibility of sex in our paintings ("What these beach roses need"—she'd step back, pulling at her lip, clenching her brow—"is more *foreplay*"), but because she invited us—only *us*—to babysit her daughter Saga, and that very opportunity bestowed on us a stature that all the other lowly worshipers in her cult could only dream of.

Jane was wearing a chopstick through her hair, her deep red lipstick setting off her pale skin. Gwen was out for the evening, on a date with Roy Panner, the industrial arts teacher whom we'd decided was not good enough for her. Saga had long been put to bed, and we sat on the couch, staring occasionally at the film canister of pot and the aqua bong on the end table. Something told us that this had been deliberately left out for our partaking and pleasure, and soon enough we were taking hit after hit, giggling hysterically, staring at the homemade pole lamp as its beautiful pieces revealed themselves to us: discrete, then whole again.

"God, I'm horny," I laughed. "What the hell's in this stuff?"

"Yeah," she said, biting into her lip. "It's funny. I was just thinking the same thing."

Instantly I regretted my admission. Casually, Jane pushed the tips of her fingers into the waistband of her jeans.

"What are you thinking?" she said, smiling.

"Nothing." Then my laughter broke apart as if shattered by a BB.

"You want to fuck me, don't you?"

"No!" I said, still laughing.

"Yes, you do. You want to throw me on my back, you little beast, and fuck the living shit out of me."

If at that moment we'd been distracted by a ringing phone or a distant radio, the urge would have passed and our friendship would have remained just that—something effortless and self-contained. Instead, I leaned over and kissed her wetly on the mouth. Her tongue felt slippery and hot, like my own. I needed to see whether I could pull this off—that is, sex with someone of the other gender. I thought, why not? Why the hell not? She's my friend, and we care about each other. No one's going to get hurt here. Why not?

I lay my weight on top of Jane. I unbuttoned the top two buttons of her shirt, then started kissing her, reaching inside for her breasts. Was I doing this right? Was I giving her what she wanted, the reassurance and the strength? I looked down into her face, her open shocked face, and she back at me, and before I could assess, something had changed: I felt foreign to myself, more remote than I'd ever felt before. I was nothing short of a liar. I hadn't yet told her the truth about myself, for the secret seemed to be enormous. She'd walk away, I knew it. I'd be telling her I wasn't the person she thought I was, and didn't we tell each other everything? Didn't I know about her cramps and her lies and her fights with her parents?

Paul
Lisicky

Didn't I know about her doubts, her rages, her fleeting depressions concerning her little sister, Anna, who'd fallen back, thrown up, and died to the dread of her kindergarten as she scissored through a sheet of blue construction paper and constructed a George Washington hat? And didn't everyone—Gwen Marino included—assume we were a couple just waiting to happen if they didn't think we were already together?

She reached into my fly. I felt a quick high panic, thinking that she'd think my dick was mediocre, when it wasn't mediocre, not when I had an erection at least. I pulled back and folded my arms. Even when I'd imagined this scene, it had never been so clumsy.

"What's the matter?" I said.

"You think I'm fat."

"No," I insisted. "I don't think you're fat."

"You're not attracted to me. You think I'm disgusting." She pulled at the excess skin of her thigh.

"Stop," I said, reaching for her shoulder.

"Don't touch," she said, and curled up with a pillow. "Go away. I feel like being alone now."

I waited a week to explain the truth about myself. When I told her, though, in the school cafeteria, within earshot of the entire girls' ensemble (who were working out the kinks in Benjamin Britten's *Ceremony of Carols*), she reacted with the slightest hint of condescension, as if it weren't news to her, before walking to the ice cream machine to buy a Buddy bar.

What happened next was more complicated. In the latter months of spring, she began dating a sophomore, DeMarco Huff, who'd been transferred to our school from the suburbs of Memphis. If you could call it dating—what it essentially amounted to was a series of quick trysts behind the Dumpsters of the Coral Sea Garden Apartments, where DeMarco lived in a two-bedroom with his mother. In any case, Jane had never been crazy about him. He wouldn't talk to her, and they had not one single thing in common, but he was black, and she loved black men, and he had the loveliest, tiniest waist, with the prettiest belly button she'd ever seen.

"Are you sure this is a good thing?" I asked her one day.

"Sure." She tried out a grin, looking not entirely convinced.

"Is he nice to you? Does he treat you well?"

"Of course. He's the sweetest little piece on the planet. He's just horny is all, and that's all I want right now." Her eyes were dried out, miserable. "God, I love to get fucked."

Jane and I still managed to call each other from time to time, though we saw each other less and less. An occasional wave in the hall outside Gwen's ceramics class—that seemed to suffice. We were always running somewhere. Then one day I received a call from her, not three seconds after I'd arrived home from school.

"I need you to go somewhere with me."

"Go where?" I wasn't in the mood. I spread a thin, gritty layer of peanut butter on my sandwich bread.

"Don't ask. I'll tell you later."

She picked me up in her parents' Vista Cruiser, a faded green station wagon from 1968, which we'd nicknamed the Flintstone-mobile due to its salt-corroded floor. It was amazing that her father had kept the car running, keeping a place for it beneath the palms, refusing to give it up while it still had some life left in it. The thing had embarrassed the hell out of Jane, and she'd never driven it alone before, but her face looked urgent and necessary as if its ramshackle appearance were the least of her worries.

"I'm getting an abortion."

"You're what?"

"Shut up. I'm getting an abortion, and I don't want you to stop me. You're my assistant here. Your job is to keep me safe and protected and calm."

"Are you scared?"

"Of course I'm scared. What do you think this is, some kind of party?"

"Don't yell at me!"

"I'm sorry," she said quietly. She raked her fingertips once down her forehead. "Why am I so mean to you?" she asked. "You who I love so much. Tell me why I'm so mean to you."

I gazed out the window at the sand pit, the lawn-ornament yard with its Marys and Buddhas. Beneath my feet Route 1 scrolled through a hole the size of a pie plate.

"You didn't tell your parents?" I said.

"Are you kidding?"

"You really think it'd bother them?"

"They'd kill me. Especially if they found out about DeMarco."

I squinted. "Are you saying your parents are prejudiced?"

"No. Not in the conventional sense. Let's just say they'd do everything in their power to stop a KKK rally from happening on their street. But they'd be funny about DeMarco. They'd just think I was trying to get back at them."

She parked outside the clinic, a yellow, stucco-coated building near a microwave tower topped with a strobe light.

"Do you see any picketers?" she said, glancing around.

The parking lot was vacant. I shook my head.

"Just wait here for me."

"Can't I come inside? I want to come inside."

"No," she insisted. "Stay right here. It'll be over in an hour."

I did what she said. I focused all my attention on the door, awaiting her return. A woman in white stockings came out, regarding me briefly, warily, before hurrying down the block to her hatchback. I wondered whether Jane had been more upset than she'd let on. Two weeks ago, against the advice of Mrs. Wash, the health teacher, she'd given an oral report about the right to safe abortion—admittedly the most hackneyed of topics—but the class had actually listened. Her words were rational and tough-minded, so who could have assumed that getting an abortion would have been a big deal for her?

I stared for five minutes at the door. I hoped they weren't hurting her.

When we were at our most inseparable, Jane came up with the notion that she'd one day like to have a child with me. And if we couldn't have that child, we'd have an imaginary child. He'd be a boy. We'd call him Nico, after the Velvet Underground's lead singer. He'd be the perfect child. He'd be fluent in many languages. We'd take him everywhere with us—Paris, Goa, Crete, Amsterdam—where everyone would ask, who is that child? Who is that stylish, witty, extraordinary child? Ours, we'd say humbly. Nico.

God knows why I was thinking about that now.

A half hour later, according to schedule, the door opened and Jane walked toward the car. She appeared neither relieved nor distraught, a little pale maybe, the hint of raccoon rings beneath her eyes. Her breath smelled faintly of orangeade. I wasn't sure how I was supposed to behave. Was I supposed to hug her, comfort her, speak words of wisdom, or act like she'd just been to the dentist's, like nothing significant had happened? I stared at the blue bruise beneath my fingernail. I felt less assured than I'd felt in a long time.

So I asked, "How did it go?"

The corners of her mouth were filmed with white. "I don't want to talk about it, okay? Just don't let me talk about it."

"Do you want me to drive?"

"Nn nn." She pulled out a Kleenex and wiped off her mouth. "I'm feeling a little woozy. Did you eat?"

I shook my head. I was ready to do anything she wanted.

"Let's go to Burger King. For some reason I'm really in the mood to go to Burger King."

It was the silent time between lunch and dinner, and we seated ourselves away from the windows to keep ourselves out of the direct sun. My skin felt chilled and hot at once. Jane stared down at the tabletop, eating onion rings with one hand, propping up her jaw with the other, twirling a piece of hair between her fingers. She hadn't spoken in a full ten minutes.

"Poor Nico," she mumbled.

"What?"

She smiled, exhausted, a watery glaze in her eyes. "He would have been the best." And as if in slow motion, she pushed over her Coke, watching its contents fizzing on the tile floor.

I tossed down some napkins to cover it up. A uniformed boy walked toward us with a mop, but I waved him away, kneeling down to take care of it myself.

I glanced up at Jane. I said, "Don't talk like that. We're not kids anymore."

"It was just a joke," she said in an exceedingly hurt voice. "Don't be so hard on me, okay?"

I held her close to me for the longest time.

We left. Jane dropped me off, and I went to bed early that night. She came back to herself in the next few days, but our friendship seemed strained and uneasy after that. We'd crossed some line. We knew too much. The thing was, I believed it was possible now to know too much.

◇ ◇ ◇

Once a week, I went to William's house, mowed the lawn, weeded the garden, and had sex. I gradually began to understand him, his silences and quirks, how he couldn't stand when I nicked the flesh of the century plant or splashed gas near the bird feeders. I learned when to talk, I learned when to be quiet. I also learned not to be resentful whenever he ignored me afterwards. We had a pattern. We knew exactly what to expect from each other. No hurts, no disappointments. Not much talking. Sometimes, if we finished up early, he'd take me to the Speedboat Restaurant in Fort Lauderdale and I'd order exactly what I wanted: hamburger, salad, fries, dessert, soft drink. We might have been any other father and son. No one suspected a thing.

One afternoon I saw both of my parents sitting across from each other in the living room, silent. It was unlike them to be together in the same room. I couldn't tell whether I was grateful or frightened. Then it occurred to me that one of them, most likely my father, had cancer.

"Sit down," my father said grimly.

"I already have."

My eyes drifted to the baseboard heaters. It was a murky afternoon, threatening rain, and Ursula flipped on the lamp, which depressed me. Lamps are for night, I wanted to say. Their silence somehow amplified things: the clicking of a palmetto beetle, the pressure of the palms against the window glass. A stray nerve kept pulsing in the small of my back. I knew what was coming. I wanted to pick up and run down the street.

My mother finally sat forward on the sofa. "You've been spending a lot of time away from us."

Silence from Sid. He slouched low in his seat, curled the edge of his hand over his brow.

I nodded solemnly. "You want me to help out more?"

My mom nodded, then wagged her head. "I'm surprised."

I smiled, because I couldn't contain it any longer, but neither of them smiled back. "I don't understand."

"People are talking."

"Huh?"

She whispered, "Why are you spending so much time with that man?"

I raised my chin. Always what the neighbors thought. "So what?"

My father sprang to attention. "Don't talk to her like that. That's your mother."

My eyes smarted. Did I know them? All my life I'd come and gone as I pleased. All my life I'd taken care of myself. Even when I was younger they'd never asked for report cards, never taken an interest in my hobbies or projects. I was the kind of five-year-old you saw circling the shopping-center parking lot on his bicycle, dodging cars, bewildering the parents, years before the other kids. And I wasn't complaining, okay? But there seemed to be a tacit agreement that they completely stay out of my business.

"What's this have to do with Mr. Parsons?" I stood up now.

"You sit down," my father demanded.

I didn't sit. They'd never talked to me this way before, and it wasn't going to start now.

"Do you see how he listens?" my father said to my mother. "Just like his brother."

"What's he have to do with anything?"

She ignored the question. Her lips hovered over the rim of

her cup. It seemed that I'd frightened her. "What have you been doing with that man, dear?" she asked shyly.

I stood. My mother reached into her sundress pocket and showed my a piece of wadded-up paper. The printing was mine. I'd covered the entire page with the same phrase, in columns, using the tiniest of letters: *I love to fuck I love to fuck I love to fuck I love to fuck.*

"I found this in your notebook. I know I shouldn't have gone through your things. I know it was wrong, but when you started withdrawing from us, I didn't know what else to do."

I wasn't withdrawing from anyone. "You had no right, Mom."

"Have you been sleeping with that man?"

"What makes you keep asking these stupid things?"

She nibbled at the corner of her mouth. She recognized the truth in my eyes. "We're having that bastard arrested."

"Don't talk about him that way."

That did it. My father went for my arm. He didn't punch me; he didn't do what any regular father would do. Instead, he drew me to him, somehow rolled me over his knee like a puppet, and—get this—started spanking my clothed butt for a good half-minute or so. I was seventeen years old. It was such a comic thing that I let him do it until we both filled up with shame.

"Happy, buddy boy?" I said.

I laughed all the way up to my room. When I lay face-down on my bed, minutes later, I was still laughing. Fools. I took breaths, many deep breaths, breathing, breathing, calming myself down, then reached for a pen, a red ballpoint, and started punching it in and out of my right palm, deft and precise as a sewing-machine needle, until I was looking down at a smear, a little red star on my hand. It was beautiful to see. The house stilled, and I fell fast asleep holding my beating hand to my face.

Chapter 3

I wished I'd had more courage. I wished I'd held onto my anger, letting it fuel me, giving me the beauty and strength of the supersonic, but in the weeks that passed something happened. I learned that I was nothing more than a coward. My parents kept looking at me as if I'd crossed a bridge over a steaming fjord and had become a stranger to them. I became flat, an outline, weightless. One afternoon, coming home from school, I overheard my father talking about removing my name from his will. I didn't care about his money. But this erasure from their lives startled me, like an unexpected punch in the neck. I'd thought they'd get over it after a while, that we'd be the family we'd always been, fixed in our silences and resentments.

So I gave them what they wanted. I avoided William. I stopped picking up the phone and answering the door. I even shirked my gardening duties. I didn't even pass William's house, and imagined his lawn grown mangy and foul without me. On my way somewhere, I'd take the long route, around the park, through the college gates, just so I wouldn't bump into him. I lived in great fear of bumping into him, at the drugstore, at the motor vehicle registry, of seeing the worn-out expression on his face: *Why have you done this?*

I helped with the garbage, manicured the hedges. I even scrubbed the mold from the side of the house, something that should have been done years ago. I made it quite clear, without saying it, that I no longer had anything to do with William, or with people, for that matter. My parents started treating me with kindness. They actually talked with me, asked my opinions, discussed current events. They'd finally gotten a good son, whoever that was, and he was gradually becoming an exemplary young man. I had only one more year of school, then I'd get out, hungry and loosed upon the world. I watched my soul shrink then shimmer to a tiny point.

I began studying all night long. I began achieving perfect grades, throwing off the curve for the entire class. My teachers were amazed by me. Princeton, Stanford, Swarthmore, Michigan—all of them wanted me by the end of the year. I kept on going. I was giving myself up to the powers. I swam, I ran, I beat off constantly, sometimes so much that it stung to pee. I was burning, a saint, purifying myself in these blaring fires. A dream would often come to me, and I'd force the dream, force myself to watch it, though it made me sick. I'd be standing over my young self, the sweet, boyish, optimistic self, punching his face until his mouth fell open.

We were eating dinner one Saturday night. My mother stepped out, then back in the kitchen, holding a cake rimmed with candles. My father handed a wrapped present to me. Then I realized it must be my birthday. I'd completely forgotten all about my birthday.

"We're so proud of you, Evan," my mother said blankly. "You're doing everything right."

My father added: "I'm so glad you've changed."

I nodded, smiled. I unwrapped my present and stared at the watch in the box. It meant nothing to me. I should have broken it right in front of their needy eyes.

"Thank you," I said, and kissed them. Their foreheads were dry. I might have been kissing the brows of the dead.

Months passed. Jane and I were walking along the bay front. A new high-rise was being thrown up in record time, and we watched the construction workers in their orange hard hats stepping across the open girders. I'd just been offered a full scholarship to Princeton and I suppose we were celebrating that fact. I hadn't even talked to Jane in seven, eight weeks. Somehow I'd learned to live without her in my life.

"Are you sure you're okay?" she said out of nowhere.

"Well, that's a non sequitur."

"I'm serious. Are you sure you're okay?"

"Of course I'm okay. I've never been better in my life."

A green-eyed man with black hair jogged by us. He looked me up and down, grinned, then trotted ahead.

"Did you see that?" Jane said warmly. "Did you see the way he looked at you?"

"Faggot," I muttered, and walked ahead of her.

"Hey!" Something wet bounced and spread across my back. "That doesn't sound like you. He was exactly your type. What's with you?"

She annoyed me terribly. First her judgment, then her rancor. I watched the people walking by us. I watched their simpering, self-satisfied faces and threw a mental message to each one: *Fuck you.*

"You're changing," she said quietly.

She sat down on a slatted bench. "You used to be so much fun. You used to have such an amazing sense of humor."

"I was never funny."

"Yes you were. And we always talked when things got bad. We buoyed each other." She folded her arms over her chest, frowned. "Fucker," she mumbled.

"Fucker?"

"You heard what I said."

"Keep talking like that and I'm going to leave you right here."

"So leave."

It came as unexpectedly as a fish in a flooded street gutter. I glanced to my right and saw William sitting in his parked car, with newspaper and coffee cup. I didn't think he was looking at me. He was simply another office worker spending his break in his car. The intensity of my argument with Jane diminished. I wasn't scared or sick or excited. I'd known this moment would come, but I never thought it would be so dull. My vision went runny; my words sounded stupid in my mouth. I might have been sitting on the mucky bottom of the bay. I glanced again, the car was gone, and I was afraid.

Why the hell hadn't I said hello?

We didn't speak for the longest time. A long train of motorcycles paraded past us down the street. When I looked back at Jane, her eyes were fixed upon a dead patch of grass. "What's up?" I said finally.

"I don't know. I was thinking about Mr. Hovnanian." She tried to laugh a little, embarrassed. "Don't ask me why. Remember that stuff about the eclipse?"

"Sure."

It wasn't so long ago: our tenth-grade class sitting before the TV, watching the total eclipse sweeping across North America. It was terribly, horribly beautiful, the quality of that darkness—birds falling silent, streetlights trembling on. Liquidy fires jetted around the rim. Then, just when the sky went dark and the corona shivered, Mr. Hovnanian switched off the set. "What makes you think that wasn't a hoax? How did you know that that wasn't a computer image, fabricated to drum up ratings?"

For weeks Jane seemed to take it personally, ineffably sad about the whole matter.

I said, "Is something wrong? You don't seem like yourself."

"Why am I thinking of tenth grade, for God's sake? What's gotten into me?"

We stared at a fallen tangelo while the heat crept into our scalps.

◇ ◇ ◇

I couldn't sleep. I felt something simmering in my body, a slow cooking, spreading up through the stem of my torso, then prickling, exploding in my throat like salad oil. I wanted to molt, I wanted to cut away the baggage of my skin. I kicked the wet covers off the bed, threw on some clothes, and left the house. I was going to walk it off. I was walking through developments, through people's backyards in the dark, over culverts, canals, retention basins. Hours had passed. I passed airport runways with their raucous blue lights, sanitation plants vast as cities, signs fizzing and sparking, arrows pointing in all directions. Two towns over, the boat factory was working overtime, and the junky hot smell of plastic lingered in the atmosphere. A storm threatened from the Everglades, then receded, pushing the humidity even higher. I took off my shirt and roped it around my waist. I decided to walk and walk, possibly to the Keys, possibly to the Card Sound Bridge, until I finally got rid of this feeling.

Hours later I was standing in William's front yard. I expected the lawn to be overgrown, ruined, bits of scale and dollarweed eating at the turf. But no. It looked even better than before. Moist, lush. I knew it: William had found another Lawnboy. I had lost him for good. I fumbled for some broken shells and started tossing them, one after another, at the glass of the window: *ping ping ping ping.*

Was I ready to give myself over to desire?

I knew myself too well: hyped up, charged, I'd lose everything. I saw myself fretting, always looking for something other, something better, something outside myself. I saw myself utterly alone in the world, a gleaming wasp inside a bright orange hive, alone with my anguish and raging hot need, and who'd be there to still me?

Was there anyone else at that moment who knew the pressure and potential of changing everything? I raised my hand and linked myself up with him, the longing, imaginary one, then pressed forward, my fingertip upon the doorbell, standing on William's front porch, waiting.

Chapter 4

My childhood suitcase was a rude, bulky thing, its surface marred by chipping decals—Kennedy Space Center, South of the Border, Sunken Gardens—which recalled family travels too heartbreaking to ponder. The packing proved harder than I'd imagined: what to take, what to leave behind. Forever? Was that the way it was going to be? My stomach simmered and groaned. I wanted to get it over with before they knew I was leaving.

Down the hall my mother was cooking pot roast. I thought about the signifying implications of pot roast: convention, structure, clean right living.

"Get ready for dinner," my father said.

He'd been standing at my door the entire time. I looked to the open window, thinking to toss the suitcase onto the hedge. *Don't let him get to you.* I turned my back to him, pitching in some socks and shirts. He still had the power to scare me sometimes, and he knew it; it incensed him. Was he going to hit me again?

"Beautiful night," he said, stepping into the room. He

picked up a tiny statue of Grover Cleveland from my Hall of Presidents—something he'd given me for my tenth birthday. He'd stared at its bloated gaze as if he'd never seen it before.

"You're right," I replied.

"Front's sweeping down from the Plains tomorrow."

"Oh yeah?"

"Highs in the eighties with a light north breeze."

Tears burned in my eyes. Outside a Good Humor truck careened down the street. *Don't you understand what's happening?* I wanted to yell.

A complex expression drifted across his face: defiance, jealousy, regret, fatigue. He left for the kitchen. Seconds later liquid plashed inside a glass. "On the rocks," I said, toasting my wall.

An ice cube popped, cracked. I waited until they were safely ensconced in their meal before I left through the mud room. *Bye, Mom,* I whispered. *Bye, Dad. I loved you once.* I hurried back to my room and shoved Grover Cleveland deep inside my pocket.

◇ ◇ ◇

Traffic roared past me on the street. Palms thrashed in the wind. I felt criminal and delicious, imagining a stocking cap pulled down over my face. I half expected the police to pull up, to ask me questions, to search through my belongings before taking me back home. Dogs barked as I passed. Lights flipped on in the windows. I pictured myself through someone else's eyes: a hushed, hungry boy, feet flying in the dark, switching his leaden suitcase from hand to hand.

I knocked twice on William's door. I watched him through the sidelight, his gestures frantic and distorted through the gold bubbled glass. He hurried from table to table, glancing under papers, feeling behind furniture. To my right, a white wicker chair rotted behind the bushes.

"Can I help you?" A lady in a paisley dressing gown hosed off a lavender Mercedes beneath the floodlights next door. She stepped toward me. Somewhere a bird—parakeet?—shrieked.

"No, I'm just—"

"Run along now," she gestured. "He hates solicitors."

William's door flew open, almost knocking me off balance. "Evan," he said.

"I'm taking you up on your offer."

He glanced down at my suitcase, a swab of shaving cream beneath his left ear. *What offer?* he might have said. He stood there in a pink polo shirt and tight, tight 501s. A splash too much cologne.

"I know this seems hasty," I laughed.

"Yes, but—"

"Didn't you say I always had a place?"

"I wish you'd called," he said, his eyes vaguely stricken.

My scalp felt tight. I kissed him. Awkwardly, I missed his mouth, pecking his warm whiskered neck. I tried again, inhaling his shirt this time: crushed plants, limes, beer foam. I turned my cheek against his chest.

"Listen," he said. "I have to find my keys. I've been looking for a half hour."

We stepped through the front door. "You'll find them," I murmured. I glanced down at a pulled loop in the aqua rug. An emptiness, wide as a body, opened inside me. I saw myself falling inside the body, reeling, tumbling, swallowed up by it.

"Welcome," he said, lips on my mouth. That was it, that was all I needed. Heat saturated my face, trickling down my spine to my groin, toes. I felt larger, warmer. Heaven. My leg muscles glowed.

"Jesus," I mumbled.

"Are you okay?" he said suddenly.

"Mmmm, hallelujah."

"You look a little crazed." His forehead creased. He tested the weight of my suitcase. "God, what's in here?"

I tried to recover myself. "Stuff."

"Stuff?"

"You know, books, clothes—" I shrugged. "Scary, huh?"

"Sorry. If only I could find those keys."

We stared at each other until he couldn't hold my gaze.

"Let's see what you think of this," he said finally.

I followed him down the hall. Claws scratched behind a wooden door, and William opened it to let the Dobermans—Pedro and Mrs. Fox—lick wet tracks on my shirt. He gestured to the utility room, a converted laundry, with smelly green carpeting and water-stained magazines along the walls. I glanced at the titles: *Bee Culture, Modern Liturgy, Physique Pictorial, Tom of Finland's Loggers.* Beside the futon an uncapped pipe jutted through the floor. I stared at him. "Not here," I said.

His eyes brightened, then dimmed. He rubbed at his forearm, as if warming himself.

I reached out for his shoulder. "But I wanted to sleep with *you.*"

He wagged his head. "Listen, we'll talk about it later. I have to leave for a few hours. There's a zoning-board meeting at seven."

"You're leaving now?"

"Have to. I don't want to see those condos approved. Once that starts the whole neighborhood goes."

"But what about your keys?"

He glanced at his watch. "I'll walk. *Jog,*" he said. "There's pancake mix in the fridge, sausages on the stove. Be back by ten." And then he pressed a fist into my rib cage.

I sat on the futon with my head in my hands. The dogs drooled clear strings upon my sneakers. "No biscuit," I said. "No biscuit."

◇ ◇ ◇

I hurried about the kitchen, opening cabinets, drawers. As my cooking repertoire consisted of sandwiches, spaghetti, and instant chilled puddings, I was in trouble. Still, I gathered what I could find—blue mesquite chips, party dip, cut vegetables—and arranged them on the coffee table. I clipped some ginger lilies from the garden and put on an old-fashioned party hat, a silver cone with an elastic string. It wasn't Joe's Stone Crab, but at least it was something. I sat with my feet up on the coffee table, waiting.

By ten o'clock my eyes felt the weight of their lids. By ten-forty-five they felt scratchy, hot in their sockets. My week had been wearing, and I stretched myself out on the couch, too rattled for sleep. The next thing I knew the front doorknob was shaking. Burglars? I bolted upright on the couch, panting. 12:45 a.m.

"What's this?" he said.

I looked up at him, rubbing the silt from my eyes. The silver cone lay by my side, dented.

He gave an appreciative smile. "A little shindig, a little wingding."

"What took you so long?"

"*Ugh,*" he said. He undid his pink polo shirt and flopped into the sofa beside me. "Relentless. This woman, some ex-colonel from the military, actually insisted that condos were going to upgrade the neighborhood. She monopolized the floor for twenty minutes. Imagine—cheap townhouses trucked in from Indiana. Forget about mangroves. Forget about roseate spoonbills. 'You can't stop progress,'" he mimicked.

"Payoff," I mumbled.

He regarded the clenched skin around my eyes. He glanced away, then looked back at me. "I'm sorry," he said, gripping my left knee. "Look at all this. How nice of you. You went to so much trouble." He stood up suddenly, thrust his hands in his pockets. His head pivoted toward the kitchen. "So everything's okay with you?"

My heart picked up pace. I felt its beating inside my cheeks, teeth, the thickness of my tongue. I tried it again. "I thought we'd sleep together tonight."

"Not tonight," he said, yawning good-naturedly. "I have to be up at five-thirty tomorrow. Taping."

My face flushed upward from my neck. "I'm not talking about sex."

"The mattress's broken. I thought I'd sleep out here tonight," he said, and gestured at the sofa.

What more could I ask for? I stood in the living room while he retrieved a pillow and sheets from the linen closet. My thoughts fractured, as if I'd taken one too many cold tablets in a row. I studied the narrow width of the sofa: no way could we fit together in that space.

"Nighty night," he said, and kissed me.

"Do you mind if I sleep on the floor?" I pointed to the carpet alongside the sofa.

He looked concerned now, his tanned forehead shining. "Of course not. Are you sure you're going to be comfortable down there?"

I started stripping down to my jockey shorts. "No problem."

"Want a pillow?" he said, offering me his own.

"No thanks."

Soon William was snoring in the dark room. A heaviness settled deep inside my marrow. *Aloneness,* I said to myself. *Aloneness.* I reached up and rested my palm against the warm ridges of his stomach, fingers just touching his waistband for energy, some sign of life. *My hope, my ring of fire.* The earth stood still, frozen. *My torch, my song of gladness.* I took my hand away, sighed. Headlights flashed on the Toulouse-Lautrecs on the wall.

◇ ◇ ◇

Weeks passed. It was summer. Now that I'd graduated, I had some time on my hands. While William went to work, I immersed myself in various projects, the largest of which involved chopping down the singed Australian pines. I wanted to fix things up. Luckily, William didn't force me to look for work, or to write to any of those colleges that had offered me scholarships, but I was grateful for the absence of pressure, for I needed some time to figure out what I wanted from my life. Doctor, architect, horticulturalist, weatherman, Django Reinhardt scholar—I still could be anything.

Years in the future, I'd look back on this time as our happiest.

How strange, though, to be entirely dependent on someone. Strange to feel absolutely no power next to him. Sometimes I'd be whacked across the brow with the uncanny realization

30

Paul Lisicky

that I had but $425.69 in my savings account. It was nothing, barely enough to cover an apartment's security deposit. All he needed to do was to kick me out, and I'd be out on my ass on the streets. Hustling, shoplifting, shooting up drugs. But I couldn't give everything over to him. I couldn't let myself believe that I was smaller than he was, a petty moon orbiting some planet, even though he was footing the bills. I had the right to make some decisions. It was just as much my house as it was his.

But I wanted to feel more enthusiasm for my new life. My happiness and sadness seemed to live side by side, like roots intertwined, feeding and depleting each other. What had I lost? Whatever happened to that purer emotion, that purer joy: a hot yellow beam knocking me off my feet? It had departed now, for good it seemed. I walked to the window one day and saw three high school boys in huge, sloppy pants roving down the street, laughing and rebellious, throwing a hockey puck, smoking stolen Marlboros. They appeared to be so much younger than I was, with so much possibility ahead, and I wanted to walk with them, wanted them to like me, to call me by my name, if only for an hour.

One afternoon, I sat inside the moldy den. I was flipping through an overdue library book—Sir Isaac Newton's *Opticks*—when I heard a timid gurgling from the floor. I looked at the pipe. I stood, then peered down inside it. A sheen of greased water. All the houses on Avenida Bayamo had the same pipe inside—a washing-machine hookup. My father had removed ours years ago when Peter had moved into the room, putting up some turquoise beaded curtains. Still, I often dreamt of our pipe. At four, I dropped my favorite trinket, a plastic blood-red fingernail, inside it. Once I wore it over the tip of my finger, extending my hand as if elegant, admiring it before my father and brother. They laughed at me, a drunken puppet, encouraging me to show off for them, before they stopped, uncomfortable.

"Stop being a sissy," my father said.

◇ ◇ ◇

We drove down the street, silent. It was a glorious wet night, masses of hot and cold air bumping up against each other. Our tires flung arcs of water onto the grass, the sidewalk. Toward the north, the clouds were underlit with a soft, baby-pink light.

Just outside Publix stood a group of people waiting for the rain to stop. One old lady in a transparent raincoat kept looking at us, not with judgment or curiosity, but with the oddest benevolence. I dislodged a shopping cart from the train and kissed William, just once, on the cheek, in celebration. The world seemed dangerous and hopeful all at once.

He stiffened. His body language changed, its dark energies curling inward. The clouds had shifted, the rain stopped, and a bronze moon—tropical, haloed—hovered above the palms.

I said, "Are you okay?"

His back straightened. He walked through the automatic doors, eyes fixed on the shining banks of limes. He picked one up and rotated his thumb across its green, pocked surface. It might have been a beautiful grenade in his palm.

"Is something wrong?"

He glanced at me as if I'd hurled a glassful of water at him.

He inched the cart forward and picked up a box of pineapple gelatin, pretending to study its contents. His Adam's apple was hot, gleaming. He held up his hand: he didn't want to talk to me.

"William?"

"There's a time and a place."

"I don't understand. Nobody saw us."

He was frowning now. "*Somebody* saw," he said.

"But—"

"Listen—"

"Is this our first fight?" I asked, more baffled than I'd intended. Was it coming this soon—only weeks into our living together?

He stopped the cart halfway down the aisle. "Evan," he said. "Now listen to me." His voice was kinder now, a whisper. "You never know what these people'll do. They might look friendly enough, but all it takes is one false move."

I considered his statement. Only a few days ago I'd read about two men in Dallas who'd been scorched with blowtorches after they'd been loitering in a park. Certainly these things happened in the world, but they were rare. Or were they?

"But she *liked* us." I nodded toward the old lady, who'd somehow wandered back into the store. She, too, was picking up limes. "She wasn't upset."

"No, she wasn't," he agreed. "But maybe her husband would be, or maybe her son. Her grandson, for instance, might be a skinhead. I'm just telling you, you can't be too careful."

I sighed. I sensed she was listening to us. Her eyelids grew heavy as if she were beginning to feel depressed.

"Anyway," he said, his voice softening. "We aren't the average couple. Especially in these parts."

"What do you mean?"

"We're not your average sissy interior-decorator couple. I mean think about it—an older man, a younger man. We're a threat. We push their buttons. We have to watch ourselves every step of the way."

I didn't want to watch myself every step of the way. I wanted to be deeper inside my life. I walked ahead, wandering about the freezers, as he straggled by the olive jars, the sardine tins. His anger seethed, completely out of proportion to the matter at hand. What was his deal? I'd only kissed him, for God's sake. If he wanted to be upset, I could pull down his zipper with my teeth, and take him deep inside my mouth, right here, right now, in front of everyone in the store. Then what would he do?

My throat pulsed. What was I doing with him, anyway? Could I be making a mistake? For all I knew there were already warrants out for his arrest. I walked ahead, my rage heating up my face to the burning point. Would I catch on fire? A cold drop of sweat rolled down my temple. I thought about his wizened shoulders. I thought about his bald spot glistening beneath the glare of hooded lights. *William, William,* I whispered. *How I want to punch a spoon deep into the valley of your back.*

"There you are," he said brightly.

He nudged me with the shopping cart, and I flinched, startled by the intrusion on my thoughts. "Where were you?"

"Look." Inside the cart were three pints of strawberries, taco shells, a half-dozen chocolate bars—my favorite foods.

"Thank you."

A mute smiling panic took hold of his face. "I bought these for you."

"I know, I know."

Outside in the car, we waited for the light to turn green. A man in the Camaro beside us banged on his dashboard like a conga drum, eyes gleaming as if he were high. He was singing now. Salsa music cascaded from his speakers. William turned to me then and kissed me hard, a bright dense charge coursing through my nerves. The other cars shot forward. The roads steamed beneath the streetlights. How quickly things could change, the world sparkling, full of rollicking possibility.

◇◇◇

The storms continued through the night. An electric smell hovered in the air, smoke rising from the trees. I rolled onto my side and pressed my lips into the warmth of his back. His skin smelled of rainwater, ferns. I thought: *Everything has been leading here. All those nights spent alone, all those nights listening to my parents' silence—all were in payment for this. I'll never be happier.*

34

Paul Lisicky

Chapter 5

When I was finally adjusting to my new life, when I'd started sleeping eight hours straight without waking at 4:00 a.m. to the burning pit of my stomach, I saw her. The night was hot, sodden. We'd just watched *The Bride of Frankenstein,* and William was in the bathroom, flossing, then rinsing with water and two droplets of grapefruit-seed extract. I sat in the living room, my hands folded on my lap, feeling at peace, feeling entirely and utterly at peace, when I heard the familiar scuff of shoes on the pavement outside.

The curtains shivered in the breeze. I thought of Dr. Frankenstein's creation, lonesome and yearning, lured to the blind man's cottage by the plaintive call of his violin. Something scrabbled at my stomach. I had the distinct feeling I was being watched, so I stepped toward the window, closed the curtain.

I might have been dreaming. Ursula was standing on the sidewalk, hands in her pockets, waiting for me. Drizzle streaked her orange windbreaker. I stopped dead, then switched off the light.

"Evan?" she called.

I froze, hoping she couldn't see me. My pulse thudded in my head. Was she really calling my name, or had I just imagined it?

Then I got it: they were waiting for us—my mother, my father, the police. I looked for the squad cars, their engines running, headlights off beneath the trees. They'd shoot him, I knew it. A clean white wound, a pucker, right through the center of his forehead, as I stood off to the sidelines, doubled over in shock.

Then I looked closer. No cars, no police. My mother.

"Evan? I want to talk to you."

Her voice was sweet, unbearable. I wanted her to come inside. I wanted her to walk away. Her presence brought back everything I'd driven out of my head—that I'd given up a past and a future; that I'd gravely disappointed somebody close to me; that I'd been truly, genuinely missed. I felt it in my gut, an icy deadening ache. Who was she to tell about her sadness? Who was she to talk with about Peter, who hadn't come home for so many Christmases?

"Why's it dark in here?" said William, walking into the room.

I looked at his domed forehead, dumbstruck.

"Somebody out there?" He edged toward the window before I could stop him. He gazed across the glittering lawn, the empty floodlit street. His eyes registered nothing, and he turned to me. "Let's go to sleep, kiddo."

I stayed before the window while William shooed the dogs to their respective beds. My heart was breaking in two. And then I saw her again, this time her head low, her hair unbraided on her shoulders as she walked down the street to the house of my childhood.

◇ ◇ ◇

I lay on the floor beside the sofa, curled on my side, listening to William falling asleep. I often took refuge in that sound as I let myself go, synchronizing our breathing. Tonight, though, it distracted me. I lay with my eyes open, dwelling upon the singing tires from the distant turnpike. I tried to fix upon the sound of an individual tractor trailer. What was it carrying, where on earth could it be headed at this hour? I pictured starfruit to Atlanta, contact lenses to Key Largo, walking catfish to Montreal.

Was it Peter's leaving that had changed her? He'd always been her favorite. Not that she'd admitted it, but I knew how she felt: her eyes glistened whenever she talked about him. He was the first, born after two miscarriages—a terrible labor that almost killed her. She named him after an old boyfriend, an amateur gardener and lineman who'd died on the job. For years afterward she'd stumbled from one thing to the next—secretary, bookkeeper, restaurant hostess. She was even a lounge singer for a time. Still, as much as she'd worked to cheer herself up, she couldn't get Peter out of her mind. How he'd fallen against the transmission tower. Hanging, lifeless in his safety belt. Turning like the hands of a clock. An aerialist, a four-pointed star.

She'd never loved my father as much as she wanted to. She'd never felt that "gut-level charge," though when she first saw him, in a shiny red jacket, surrounded by the prettiest girls at the party, she'd convinced herself that he was the one. "I want him," she'd said to her friend Marilyn. "I want him to notice me." She was tired, after all, of so much loss, the deaths of Peter and her clinging mother. My father had just been hired in the university's chemistry department, and all she'd wanted was to rest.

Her beauty faded after the wedding. You could see it happening in their pictures, when she traded in her makeup for jeans and workshirts, as if she'd told herself that this was it—the end of possibility. "Where's the girl I married?" Sid teased, hugging her from behind. "Where's the beautiful girl I was so proud of?" He couldn't get to her, though. After all, she'd gotten what she'd wanted. And now the only thing left to do was to have a baby.

She thrived once Peter was born. He was long, gangly, with

tufts of dark hair, overly large ears, and a curious bump on his temple where the forceps had clamped. Eight pounds, seven ounces. Handsome, she knew he was going to be handsome. And it felt good to say that name again, Peter, as if her boyfriend had inhabited her baby to keep her company once again, to bring her back to life.

For five years he was the most important thing to her. She took him to the supermarket, to her gynecological appointments, to lunch at the Silver Wheel with her friend, Astrid Muth. She wouldn't even consider a babysitter, wouldn't let Peter for one minute out of her sight, convinced that mishap was lurking just around the corner. Peter grew anxious, cranky when she wasn't around. On his first day of kindergarten, after promising he'd never cross the street without the assistance of the safety guard, he strayed far behind the others, fearful, shy, only to find that the fifth-grader in charge was already off duty. He trudged up the wrong side of Avenida Bayamo. He sat down on the curb across from the house and waited—ten, twenty minutes—before Mrs. Feldman, hanging up violet socks on her clothes tree, spotted him.

"What's the matter, Pete?"

He was sobbing now. "The safety went away. I can't cross the street."

Mrs. Feldman glanced in both directions and crossed over to him. There wasn't a single car in sight.

"Do you want me to help you cross the street?"

Peter gazed up at Mrs. Feldman. Her body was huge, luminous, the size of a planet. He swiped at his nose and nodded.

"Okay, honey. Look both ways. And take my hand."

He took her hand. Once on our yard he skittered across the grass to the back door, forgetting to thank Mrs. Feldman.

"You tell your mother to watch you," she called.

"Okay," Peter said. "Bye bye."

And years later I was born, and things changed once again.

◇ ◇ ◇

We'd passed the critical point. It seemed that we'd crossed some mine-strewn landscape, that if we weren't meant to be together we'd have found out by now. I wanted to take William out to dinner, to give him a card, to buy him a pair of boxer shorts patterned with pink cocktail glasses and swizzle sticks, but I stopped myself, as if doing so would only have called attention to the possibility of conflict. Remarkably, there was no conflict between us. We were learning to live together, falling into our respective routines as all companions do. What was the point of deeming that an accomplishment?

And yet there was the issue of the bed. Were we becoming too comfortable with the situation? Were we too afraid to wrest ourselves out of the familiar, with William on the couch, and me on the floor with my blankets, sheets, and pillows? We certainly had sex—good, ravenous sex, though it was less than I'd expected. Once a week? Once every two? Was something wrong? One evening I'd even convinced myself I preferred sleeping this way to having his warm body curled around mine, grasping me, taking me with him as he turned from side to side. After all, for most of my life I'd slept alone, liking it, imagining it the only possibility for a good night's sleep.

And yet?

It was time to do what I'd been putting off. One afternoon, while William was away at work and I was home alone, I walked into the master bedroom to check out the mattress. Couldn't I fix it myself? I sat on the edge of the bed, bouncing slightly, staring at the framed photos of Lorna and Poppy. They covered every square inch of the dresser—images of his former life, which unsettled me sometimes. Where were the pictures of me? I looked at Lorna. It was hard to imagine he'd ever been married to her, with her expensively treated hair and plucked brows. Even more unsettling was Poppy, whom I'd never met, and never cared to. Though we were close in age, we'd probably never get along. I studied her tilted, heart-shaped face, the precise, calculated sweep of hair across her

39

Laundboy

forehead, knowing she would have all but ignored me in high school because I wasn't interesting or fabulous enough.

Or maybe I wasn't giving her a chance.

I bounced again on the bed and decided to check out the underside. I crawled upon my hands and knees, left eye close to the floor. Dust, nickels, chewing-gum wrappers, used rubbers— it was enough to make me lug the vacuum from the closet. In about ten seconds I discovered the culprit: a dislodged support board. I hefted up the mattress with one arm, slipped in the board with the other, and that was that. I laughed. I started laughing so hard that I couldn't stop. It was strange to think that we'd exiled ourselves to the living room for this.

I lay on the restored bed, basking in the light of my accomplishment. The palms outside the window threw golden shadows on the wall, weaving. I felt so good that I unwittingly pulled down my pants to my ankles, palming the head of my dick, not intending to come, of course, but consoled by the ministrations of my hand. I realized how much I'd missed jerking off, how I'd always thought it an essential activity, a primary component in the development of one's imaginative life.

Glancing up, I saw William standing in the doorway.

I had no idea how long he'd been watching me.

Immediately I wriggled up my pants and sat up, my face hot with shame. I was too unnerved to laugh at myself.

"What are you doing home?" It was only four o'clock; lately he hadn't been coming in the door until nine.

He looked harried, uncomfortable. He walked over to the window and pulled open the drapes, flooding the room with a yellow light.

"I fixed the mattress," I declared. My voice sounded starved, panicked, as if I were trying too hard to please. What was the matter with me? He wasn't my father.

He flopped deliberately on the bed.

We were silent together. I sat down beside him, diminished and disabled, entertaining the possibility of him spanking me across his lap. I'd pull in my breath, eyes squeezed tight, jerking at the sting of his slaps. The heat swarming in my butt.

Afterwards, he'd hold me in his lap, wipe away my tears, tell me he'd be kinder to me from now on, a better person. I took a photograph of us in my mind, a tableau.

"So you're home," I said, venturing an observation.

"Yeah," he said. He leaned back and crossed his arms behind his head. He pulled in his lips. "We had a bomb scare at the station."

"A bomb scare?"

"A bomb scare. Terrorists. They sent everyone home until further notice. Station's off the air. Turn on the TV."

I reached for the remote. The picture was snowy, the audio a harsh scratch. I shuddered. "God," I said, picking at my lip. Why hadn't I recognized that my lip was chapped?

William closed his eyes. I rested beside him on the bed, wanting to recapture the uncharged emptiness of everyday life. How could I calm down? How would I interpret this moment, years in the future: masturbation, spanking fantasy, terrorism, bomb threat? And yet a part of me liked the unsettling rush: I wanted to have sex. I wanted to climb on top of William's prone body and fuck him, savagely, with gritted teeth, like an animal, though I didn't think I'd get away with it.

"I worked hard all day," I said suddenly. "I vacuumed the living room, I scoured the rust stains from the kitchen sink, I did three loads of laundry, I walked the dogs in the storm—" The blood was beating in my ears. Was I more upset than I knew? "And that was all today. Would you like me to show you what I did?"

Cautiously he opened his left eye. "I know you work hard," he said, "I'm sorry," and offered me a sad, depleted smile.

Inside of me a door creaked open. I felt vindicated—yet exposed and repentant. We stood. We walked into the kitchen where we fixed ourselves an ample, pleasant dinner: rice wine, peanut sauce, stir-fry. That night we still slept in our usual settings, the repaired bed glittering in my mind like some remote island.

Chapter 6

Sometimes I worried that I wasn't a complete person, that I couldn't label myself. What if I was just a composite of everyone who'd passed through my life—strangers, family, friends—all of whom had inhabited me, taking over my thoughts and gestures before departing, leaving me defenseless? Looking back, I saw how I moved not in a straightahead line, but in lopsided, parabolic circles. I pushed myself out, I reigned myself in. I craved sex, I didn't crave sex. I wanted to transgress, I wanted to conform. I wanted to be brilliant, I wanted to be a mindless fool.

Was I becoming myself? Or was I stalled, trapped before some rust-clenched gate while everyone else was getting somewhere?

◇ ◇ ◇

The night before William's trip to Key West, we finally ended up together in the master bedroom. I didn't know quite how it happened, but that seemed to be beside the point. I lay beside him, my chest flooding with gratitude and energy. I held him closely under the hot tent of the covers. His body felt foreign, huge to me. *Hold me back,* I thought. *Hold me so tight that it hurts. Keep close now. Stay, stay, stay.*

The next morning we waited at the front window, watching for Lilo Patrick, the reporter with whom he was working on the assignment, to pull up in her yellow Toyota. He stood beside me, jittery, shifting his weight from foot to foot. He'd been anxious about the project—something about the recent decline of Key West—the incursion of national chains, the dearth of affordable housing, the dead-end alcoholic culture—none of which, William believed, established a single point of view. My pulse quickened in the core of my chest. He was to be gone for the entire week. I didn't want him to leave, especially now that we'd finally become so comfortable with each other.

At two past eleven—the designated time—Lilo pulled up front, her car engine purring, finely tuned as a sewing machine. I motioned to walk through the front door, until he stopped me, asked me to stay put.

"But why?" And then I remembered that he didn't want Lilo or anyone at the station to know about me, so much so that I was not to answer the phone, but to let the machine take the message. "It's a high-powered job," he'd once explained. "I mean, I don't think I'd get fired, but you never know. I don't want to chance it."

I looked downward. A vault of emptiness opened inside me. "You better go," I said miserably.

He kissed me, before opening the door. The dogs stepped backward in the foyer, already lonesome, already resigned. Soon enough they'd start longing for him, cocking their heads at any sound of footsteps outside. "You'll take good care of the dogs?" he asked. "You'll give them walks?"

"I'll take good care of the dogs," I singsonged. "I'll give them walks."

He looked at me curiously. "You'll behave yourself?"

I tried to connect with his gaze, but couldn't. His words seemed laced with all sorts of innuendo and danger. Did he expect me to spend the entire week locked inside with cartoons and a full refrigerator?

"I'll miss you," he said dully.

"I'll miss you, too."

"Call you tonight," he said. "Take good care of yourself."

"You too."

He shrugged. "I'm off."

I lay on the couch, both comforted and alarmed. The house seemed oddly centered: all the various pieces of furniture in their proper place, the two Dobermans lying like sleeping Sphinxes beside me. It occurred to me, when I thought about all I'd been through, the collisions with my parents, my separation from Peter, that I was lucky. Once again I reminded myself that I could have ended up on the streets, strung out, penniless, hacked to death.

Then, for whatever reason, I remembered something else about last night.

"I'm not going to see you for seven days," I'd whispered.

We were lying in bed, in the still seconds after the lamp had been switched off. Across the street an animal—dog? raccoon?—was rooting through somebody's trash cans.

"Eight days," he corrected.

I thought about eight whole days by myself. I reached over for him, pressed my palm upon his taut stomach. I waited. Nothing. Then I waited longer.

"I thought we could make love or something," I said.

My voice sounded tentative, vulnerable. I couldn't stand the sound of it. I couldn't stand the way I had to ask for it, begging, as if it cost him. Already, in memory, I could taste him, like blood, like steel, and now that I'd had him, it wasn't enough. I needed more, even though I knew my wanting was going to do me in someday.

He heaved a tired sigh. I already knew his answer.

I turned away, moving to the farthest edge of the bed until my face pressed up against the wall.

◇ ◇ ◇

I plodded through the arcade in my workboots. I kept my expression remote and aloof as if to indicate that I wasn't new at this. But I was dying inside. I wasn't ugly. I wasn't desperate, hopeless, dumb. Adult book stores: weren't they meant for those who led secret lives, who hated themselves? Who else would put up with nasty attendants, filth, that fruity metallic smell? But I'd walked the entire seven miles, not even bothered by the sand in my sneakers, the blisters on my feet.

I kept threading down the halls, if only because I couldn't stand still. I didn't want anyone to greet me, or touch me, or pay me the slightest bit of attention. But I liked being in the thick of it, little dramas of pursuit and rejection crackling around me like fires. Gathering my nerve, I glanced at the faces of the—customers? There was an old man—tall, slouchy, wedding band tight on his finger—who might have been on his way home from choir practice. There was a coke dealer, I presumed, with vibrant blue eyes and sunwrecked hair. There was a businessman, sleeves still crisp from the cleaners; a dark-skinned guy with tiny red rings in his ear. All told there were nearly a dozen—fat, skinny, old, young, rich, poor—none with anything in common, but for a melancholy expression, which clearly masked what I felt too: a longing for escape, otherness, transgression, connection.

I calmed down soon enough, fed my coins to the soda machine: a lighted box with a smeared, eye-shaped logo. The soda tasted delicious, an abrasive splash against the back of my throat. Actually, most of these fellows seemed to be having a decent enough time. Doors kept banging shut, then opening, admitting and releasing the hungry. One trucker-type practically danced a jig down the hall. Another strolled past with a look of dumb wonder on his face. "Oh, what the hell," I said to the graffitied walls. It was time to stop thinking so much.

Still, I imagined William staring down at me through a hole in the ceiling, cataloging my gestures. I imagined his footsteps clomping across the parking lot, his husky brusque voice taking over the sound system. The music faded to static. "What are you doing here?" he said, grabbing me by the collar. "I can't believe you'd punish me like this."

Foolish thoughts. Foolish.

I found an empty booth and bolted the door. I panted slightly, dazed. Was I going to be sick? It still held the scents of its last inhabitant—perspiration, Right Guard, spilled semen, body heat. I rested my head on my knees. I glanced upward. Al Parker floated across the flickering screen, legs shining like the flanks of some heavenly animal. My vision blackened for a moment. I loved Al Parker. I concentrated on his exuberant brown beard, his hard vascular chest, his rakish Semitic nose. I concentrated on his dick, an enormous fleshy thing that wagged when he walked, with a jaunty personality all its own. But there was more to him than that. It wasn't just his body, or his personal warmth, or his casual, fluent masculinity. It was his very persona, which told us that sex was fun, that there was a wide, wide world out there, more complicated and various than we'd ever assumed. He'd never call anybody else a faggot because he himself was a faggot, and he felt just fine about that, thank you. Unfortunately, he wasn't here anymore: another soul, lost, like half the world, to AIDS. At least his image still quivered with life. I looked at the screen, then down at myself. There was Al, there was me.

I closed my eyes. When I opened them, Al was fucking a tall, rangy kid with a gap between his teeth. Together they gyrated over a workbench. The camera panned the kid, surveying every square inch of his skin, grazing past a deep violet mark on his wrist. A burn, a bruise, or what I feared it was? His hair—parted down the middle, shaggy over the ears— seemed right out of 1979, just before protected sex had become an issue. I hated to think the kid had done this while sick, all for the sake of making a few fast bucks. But who would have known then? Who would have thought the world was on the brink of such threat?

I went soft in my palm. I wanted to be home. I wanted its banality, its routines, the anonymous sanctuary of its dull gray rooms. Already I thought of the dogs barking as I worked the key into the lock. I thought of their tails whipping my legs, the weight of their snouts in my palms. And their eyes—how they closed them in gratitude whenever I stroked their heads. Time to get out of here. I pulled up my pants, my right leg prickly with sleep. Home: odd to think of it that way, but that's what it was now, for better or for worse.

I opened the door. Before me stood the most beautiful man I'd ever seen.

We looked at each other, quizzical. An awful thrill went through my stomach. Had we known each other once? "Evan," he might have said.

He stood there longer than was exactly comfortable, as if he, too, felt paralyzed. Though he was altogether perfect, it was his eyes that drew me to him, large brown eyes that revealed a soulfulness, an abundance of spirit, with just enough wryness thrown in for good measure. There wasn't a wall between him and the world. Everything, I imagined—praise, insult, injury—registered on his psychic screen. I glanced about the booth as he walked down the hall. What should I do? The wadded tissues on the floor, the twisting bodies of the videos seemed otherworldly, radiant now, imbued with the richest amber light. I imagined taking him in my arms, nipping him, tugging the skin of his neck between my teeth. Then reaching downward for his belt buckle, rubbing circles on his stomach with my fist. A shard of paper dropped through the chicken wire overhead, and a note? Was that what this was? *I want you right now. Meet me in #2.*

My face blazed. I strolled down the hall toward the indicated door and entered the booth, reaching out into the darkness. My breaths quickened. His chest was warm, softer than I'd imagined, yielding. He smelled of orange rind, fresh laundry. He exhaled in a slow, satisfied half-whistle.

Only when my eyes adjusted did my presumptuousness become clear to me.

"You're here," whispered an odd, balding man.

"But—"

"What took you so long?"

He pressed a soft palm against my cheek. He gazed at me with such tenderness and awe that I couldn't say no to him. He wasn't attractive. His forehead sloped, speckled and vulnerable like the underside of a fish. I'd like to say that I treated him with warmth and compassion, some modicum of fellow feeling. Instead, I guided him to the floor, jerked down my zipper, and gave him exactly what he wanted.

"Suck it," I mumbled.

"Mmmm." He gazed up at me with glistening eyes, so grateful, relieved.

"Don't say a word, faggot."

I crossed my arms over my chest in a complete affectation of boredom. I thought: *You can be whoever you want. Your name's not Evan, and your longing isn't killing you.* I gazed down at my cock slipping in and out of his mouth, numbing every sensation from it, refusing to admit that we were even engaged in the same fundamental work. I didn't touch him or urge him onward. Loneliness, I thought. This was isolation, and this was loneliness. I saw my bones turning at once to powder, particles of me flying up through the air filters. A broken bell chimed in a distant tree. Was it even sex that I wanted, or something more elusive, more rigorous than that? Had I wanted William to change my life? Had I wanted him to solace my pain, to exchange my former home for a better, more protected one? Had I wanted him to embrace every last facet of me—my speech, gestures, flaws, potential? And in expecting these things, was I pushing him away?

Or, simply, did I want a fraction back of what I was giving to him?

I thought of Al Parker's bearded face. I pulled back from the stranger while there was still time.

"That was terrific," he said, smiling.

"Thank you," I said nervously, giving his shoulder a squeeze.

"No. Thank *you*." His face glowed with a freshly pink sheen. "I've never seen you here before. What's your name?"

"Kevin."

"I'm Irwin," he said, offering his hand to shake.

"Are you okay?"

"Of course I'm okay," he laughed. "Couldn't be better. You're a very hot boy, Kevin."

"Thanks," I said shyly, bowing a bit, and left.

I stood upon the hot surface of the parking lot. It was twilight now. Cars rushed by on Route 1, careening past the tank farms, the container complex, the clumps of palmetto in which someone could get lost. The air smelled of napthalene, forest fires. I glanced once up at the sky, the harsh bowl of it, thinking about its indifferent blue, knowing its eye had already focused on the next brutality. What was one more tiny crime? I held up the stranger's note and released it, watching it blowing out into the traffic. The warm-eyed boy was gone now, gone forever. Whoever told me I didn't deserve to be loved?

◇ ◇ ◇

When I was eleven, I thought a lot about a boy named Douglass Freeman. I was fascinated by his house. There was nothing else like it: its Colonial-paned windows, its cupola, its gardens with the plywood comic-strip characters (Nancy, Sluggo, Aunt Fritzi). And beside it all, gleaming in the driveway, a new Winnebago like the showcase prize from *The Price is Right*. For most of that year I wanted more than anything to live there.

He was in every appearance an average eleven-year-old with freckled skin, tetracycline-stained teeth, and a stunted brushy plume on the crown of his head. It wasn't until the end of the school year when every sixth-grader from Gus Grissom was bused off to camp that we learned something else about him. The rumors had been flying even before Mr. Albertson sat us down in the cabin.

"Tonight most of you boys'll be taking a shower."

We nodded. We gathered around a citronella candle in the dark. His voice was hushed, grave, as if he were trying to scare us.

"These showers are what we call communal. Have any of you showered with other boys before?"

My upper arms itched. I'd never heard of such a thing. I couldn't help but think the idea was a little outlandish, even obscene.

"I want you to know that Douglass Freeman doesn't have a penis."

Eric Woodworth fisted the air. *"Yes!"*

"Quiet!" Mr. Albertson cried. The entire campground stilled, crickets and tree frogs falling mute. "Once more and I call your parents."

Woodworth trembled, pretending to quash the triumph from his eyes. I was mortified. All this time I'd thought that Douglass's newest nickname—Dickless—had been nothing more than a harmless, ongoing prank. Hadn't we all called him that?

"I want you to put yourselves in his shoes," Mr. Albertson said. His eyes shone with great intensity and warmth. "I want you to imagine what he lives with every day of his life. Do you understand?"

We nodded, humbled and ashamed.

"He's all boy. That's all I want to say."

We nodded again.

"Good. Very good." Then Mr. Albertson started a story. "There was a boy, there was a girl, and there was a ghost . . ."

But I couldn't follow his words. If I'd only known that Douglass's condition resulted from a birth defect or cancer, I'd have felt better. I imagined my own penis, a thing I'd learned to like, crumbling off in my hand as I cleaned myself with a washcloth. The truth was I'd been touching myself a lot, probably more than I was supposed to. I pulled my legs closer to my chest. Around me boys were laughing, utterly immersed in the tale. Mr. Albertson crouched and tiptoed about the cabin, illustrating his drama with little props: a pin light, a tennis ball, a handkerchief resembling a lady ghost. What was wrong with me? Was I the only one who felt like this?

Mr. Albertson left for the showers, Dobb kit in hand, white towel slung over his shoulder. "Keep an eye on the ship," he said, his eyes meeting mine.

"Five bucks," Woodworth mumbled. "Five fucking bucks."

Steve Strandberg gazed out at the empty, starlit paths. "I wouldn't go to the showers now," he said in a lonely voice.

I said, "Why?"

"That's when Dickless's there," said Steve. "He won't go till everyone's finished. Sometimes it's midnight, sometimes it's three in the morning. The school board had to approve it."

I pictured Dickless standing outside in the middle of the night, his chest peppered with goose pimples, scrubbing himself with a soap-on-a-rope (a gift from his mother?) while he looked repeatedly, anxiously over his shoulder. It pissed me off to think that only a few weeks ago these boys had played kickball with Douglass, calling him by his correct name, treating him like the quiet, unremarkable boy he was.

But who was I to talk? I'd already made my decision not to shower until I got home.

The week was relentless. Our days were crammed tight with activities—math classes, crafts seminars, athletics—as if our teachers were fearful of leaving us unoccupied. I missed the girls, their precise, intricate outfits, their kindness, their expansive senses of humor. I missed Jane. Without girls, the boys grew wilder, more aggressive, as if shot up with hormones. Gregg Novak, for one, a skinny thing with twig-like arms, lifted me up, spinning me around and around in full sight of seven boys—my legs flailing all the while—if only to show them he could do it.

This wouldn't have happened back home.

The week creaked onward. I ticked off each day on my calendar, striking it out with a wax pencil, pretending I was doing time at Sing Sing. Soon enough it became clear to my cabin mates—Eric Woodworth in particular—that I hadn't taken a shower since my arrival. By this time, they'd all showered together and had gotten used to it, barely mentioning Dickless's name as if he were already old news.

"You haven't taken a shower," said Woodworth one night.

"Yes, I did," I answered. "Two nights ago. You weren't paying attention."

He knew I was lying. I stared at his slight chubbiness, knowing that at twenty he'd be ugly, fat, and unlovable. I didn't know why this comforted me. He glanced over at the top bunk. "Hey, Strandberg, has Sarshik taken a shower yet?"

Steve stared down at his dirty pink feet, utterly silent.

"Your hair's greasy," Woodworth said to me. "What's the matter? You don't have a dick either?"

"Shut up," I cried.

I might have downed a glassful of paint. Was I a coward? I couldn't bear to be talked to like this. It was the moment I'd been afraid of. All at once I leapt up and rummaged through my backpack for my shower supplies.

I hurried to the outdoor shower stalls, leaves rasping beneath my feet. You had to do these things, win the races, catch the fly balls hit to your corner, even if it killed you. If you didn't do it, you got them mad, and they made you an outsider— someone who was pounced on, spit out like week-old food— and there was nothing worse than that.

But none of these thoughts steadied my pulse.

When I arrived at the stalls I heard a shower running full force, a drain sucking water. I stopped at once. Was it Dickless?

My steps were timid. To my relief Mr. Albertson stood underneath the showerhead, hair flattened to his scalp. I couldn't take my eyes off him.

"Hi, Evan," he said affably. "Beautiful night."

My throat was too tight to respond. I nodded, then crept inside the changing room. I stared down at the pocked floor, breathing, yanking off my shirt and pants, dropping them in little balls upon the exposed wooden slats. I was going to do this. Once and for all, I was going to get this over with.

Mr. Albertson smiled at my reentrance. I stepped toward the showerhead beside him and turned on the faucet, testing the temperature. I'd never felt more naked in my entire life, my arms like insect feelers, my chest like the cheapest concave trinket—something to be bought at Woolworth's. Mr. Albertson rubbed the shampoo from his hair. He dug his fists into his tightly closed eyes. I couldn't stop staring at his hard furry butt, his balls, his dick—alarmingly big, its head the color of a plum. I'd never seen anything like it before. *And you call this a dick?* I thought, speaking to my own parts in disappointment.

"Who won the softball game?" he asked.

I swallowed. Had he known I was looking at him?

"Huh?"

"Greens," I said finally. "Greet hit a fly ball over the fence."

He nodded. He turned off the faucet, reached for a towel on the hook. "Don't use up all that hot water," he kidded. He stepped past me, mere inches away. His dick swung gently as he walked. I shuddered. If his towel had been bigger, he might have snapped it against my butt.

I stood under the showerhead for another five minutes. The water felt hot, consoling upon my shoulders. Why had I waited so long? I shampooed my hair over and over, waiting for someone to step around the corner. But when no one did, I turned off the faucet, and stepped into my clothes, letting my hair drip so all my cabin mates would know that I was just like them.

Two nights later, we all sat around the campfire, singing "The Circle Game"—an old Joni Mitchell song that Miss Mastrangelo strummed on a busted guitar while everyone squinted at their song sheets. We were due to leave Saturday morning, and I was already feeling nostalgic. It wasn't that I didn't want to go home. I still hated it here, there was no doubt about that. It was that looking into the flame-lit faces of my classmates around the campfire, I thought, *Time is already sweeping us forward. Our bodies are changing. We smell like our parents. Soon enough we're going to separate and move away, and some of us will die sooner than we think, and as a group we'll never be together again.* Was this a pop song? I was shocked by my corniness. But maybe it was only because we'd all fallen into our respective routines, learning new skills, growing more relaxed with one another. And unfortunately, there was that other thing: Mr. Albertson had announced earlier that evening that Douglass Freeman was leaving camp two days early. He'd had a hard adjustment and had come down with a sore throat. And there was the sticky issue of contagion. "It would be best for everyone," Mr. Albertson assured us, "if he left us." He was right, for the announcement of his departure made an immediate difference. Everyone relaxed, became themselves, as if the world were returned to its proper order.

It was dusk. I was walking down a path through the woods. I wasn't supposed to walk alone, not without another camper, but it felt good to be lost in my thoughts, listening to the cheers and yelps of my classmates in the distance. I stepped up on a riverbank. I looked at the sawgrass weaving in the water, the impossibly vivid sky, thinking about how nice it would be to go back home again, to sleep in my own bed, to take a hot bath while my mother sat on the closed toilet seat listening, pretending she was interested in my stories. I wouldn't even let my parents' fighting bother me.

I stepped closer to the fallen log beside the shore.

And all it once it moved toward me.

My whole body clenched. I didn't yell. I'd seen alligators in our very neighborhood, where on winter mornings they'd crawl up out of the canals, sunning themselves in the backyards, looking for handouts of marshmallows. They seemed almost benign, *bovine* in that context—dumb, leaden beasts too stupid to fend for themselves—and yet they were known to have swallowed a neighbor's Boston Terrier in one gulp, a veritable raisin. But this was the wild. It came to me that alligators had the capacity to run up to 60 miles-an-hour in short distances. The peach fuzz bristled on my neck. I started running, feet pounding the sand, all the way back to the dining hall.

On the way I ran into Dickless standing in the path. I'd actually seen his face only three times all week.

My chest heaved. "Alligator—" I said, winded.

Dickless smiled in utter calm. "Oh really?"

I swung my head back and forth. "Big. thirteen feet or more. Tell the teachers. Dangerous."

"Fuck the teachers," he replied.

I stared at him, blinking. I caught my breath. He'd never

talked like this before. These simple words unsettled and mocked me, more than I could say.

"I'd like to see it," he stated.

"Get out."

"I'm serious."

I slapped at a mosquito on my wrist. "You sure?"

He followed me down the path. By the time we got to the shore, the alligator was gone, leaving no wake in the river, no imprints on the sand.

"Liar," he smiled.

"I'm telling you. I saw it *right here*." But for some reason I found myself smiling along with him. Had I been imagining things?

We sat upon the shoreline, watching the pelicans gliding inches above the brackish river. An air boat whined faintly in the distance, diminishing. The sky darkened a notch. Above a hammock of palms, a lone planet sparkled. The first star.

"I thought you were leaving," I said.

"Tomorrow," he said, leaning forward. "My dad's coming. Sometime after breakfast."

"Your throat still hurts?"

He laughed through his nostrils. "My throat feels fine. It's never been better. I just needed to get out of here."

I laughed. I was going to tell him about the time when I, too, wrangled my way out of a school obligation, mimicking a sprained ankle after a basketball game, when I noticed the stricken, unsettled look on his face.

"Do you hate it here?" he whispered.

I glanced at his muddy shoes. I thought of all the things that had been said about him, things I knew he'd heard, how his time back at school would never be the same. The inside of my lip tasted like a penny. I couldn't say anything but yes to him.

"I thought so. You don't seem like you belong with them."

"I don't?"

He rested his sneaker atop mine. For a few seconds I tried to ignore it, but the gesture was intentional, a game of sorts.

He wanted me to play. I didn't like such games, thought them childish and beneath me, so I slipped my shoe out from under his and dug my heel into his toes so that he winced, tears springing to his eyes.

I looked in his face. He was laughing now. I had an uncomfortable feeling, an odd buzz of shame, excitement, sadness. Then something else took hold of me, something comfortable and friendly that told me I could be what I was with him. Why wasn't I afraid anymore?

"Hold still," he murmured.

It happened too smoothly for me to stop. I pulled in a breath. He fumbled for my fly and—to my discomfort—reached into my pants, pulled out my dick, holding it, watching it harden in his grasp. It would be years before it would even reach its adult size. Still, he looked at it like he'd never seen anything like it before. I thought of Mr. Albertson standing under the showerhead, confident, at peace with his body. "Amazing," Douglass whispered, moving his small brown head.

I leaned backward on my elbows. He began stroking me, dutiful and tender, the leaves turning silver, vermilion above us, making me forget that anyone else could even travel up the path, though, thankfully, they didn't dare.

Chapter 7

William came back from Key West on schedule, tanned and fit, more energetic and relaxed than he'd been in weeks. He knelt down to embrace the Dobermans, and they rushed to him, licking his face, nuzzling, nearly knocking him over until he shielded his head with his arms.

"How are my children?" he asked them. His voice was sweet, in the manner of Mr. Peabody. "How are my pretty, good-for-nothing, well-behaved children?"

They rolled on their backs, scuffing their hindquarters against the rug.

He looked up at me, smiled. His eyes were nearly bloodshot. "And how are you?" he said merrily.

"Good," I said, and squatted down beside him.

We kissed. I was relieved to see him back, though a small part of me already missed the longing, the empty space I'd contemplated in his absence. The week had been odd. Once I stopped resisting my aloneness, I gave myself over to it, relaxing, even cultivating this new privacy. There were certainly worse places to be. I felt confident, capable. I took a greater interest in the house without anticipating the repercussions of my gestures. I threw out the stained bathroom rugs. I threw out a malfunctioning lamp—a hurricane lamp, a divorce present from Lorna to William, which William had actually liked. I taped a picture of some sexy young daddy to the refrigerator, his smile, his black furry chest on display for the whole household. And all the while I read, staying up half the night, immersing myself in projects I'd been putting off for months: Blake's *Marriage of Heaven and Hell, The Collected Works of Flannery O'Connor,* the Osteology and Lymphatics sections from *Gray's Anatomy.*

William undid his tie. He flopped into the sofa, loafers up on the coffee table, telling me about his adventures of the week, how Lilo Patrick had been arrested outside Sloppy Joe's, drunk, sobbing, after taking a poke at a female tourist who'd made fun of her purse. The station was doing everything in its power to hush-hush the incident. He seemed overly excited, manic, as he relayed this tale to me. Spittle dried in the corners of his mouth. A bleak thought crept into my head: this is the person I missed so much?

"And how was your week?" He looked at me directly. Had he recognized anything foreign, the stranger's hands upon my body?

"Stayed at home. Cooked, cleaned, walked the dogs, read."

Before we could get too settled we put on our jackets and left for Arigato, our favorite restaurant. I loved Arigato—the koi pond at the front door, its cool, tinkling music of koto and gong, its overly solicitous waitstaff, clad in their blacks and whites, smiling just a tad, never talking louder than a whisper. I followed William past the cash register; the inner legs of his 501s made loud rubbing sounds. I thought, since when did your ass get so big?

Our waiter—middle-aged, unfamiliar, Caucasian—seated us in an alcove near the front, not where we usually sat. William regarded the gas grill in the center of the table, stricken. This wasn't good. He didn't take well to change.

"What's the matter?" I asked.

He looked up. "Waiter," he called out across the restaurant. The man walked to the table. "Yes, sir?"

"What's this?" he said, gesturing at the gas grill.

"A grill, sir. Does that bother you?"

I knew what was going on. I got the "sir" thing, the slight sarcasm of it, the waiter's recognition that we might be a handful at the end of a long day. But I didn't get the look on William's face, a look which said, I don't like you, though he'd barely given the waiter a chance.

"Where's Hatsuko?" William said. Hatsuko, a pretty long-haired woman from Nagasaki. Our usual waitress.

"She's off for the night, sir."

"She'd never seat us here. You can tell your manager that, he knows us. We come here all the time."

The waiter looked to me then, flummoxed, his face softening as if he felt some concern for me. He clearly didn't know what was motivating William's anger, and nor did I, for he'd seemed buoyant and cheery only a few short minutes ago. Or had I misread him? A hot, waxy bubble swelled inside my chest. The waiter left us now, shifting to another station.

"What's the matter?" I said, frowning now.

"Oh, that *guy*." His eyes drifted over the menu listings. "It's weird. He reminds me of my brother."

"Your brother?" This was even more of a surprise.

"Yeah, Henry. You know, the one who never paid my parents back, who wouldn't talk to me after I left Lorna."

His family was off limits. I knew better than to open up that subject. "That's no reason to hate the waiter."

"I don't hate him," he declared.

I heaved a sigh. What were we talking about? "Forget it," I mumbled, propping up my head with my hand.

A tense quiet stood between us. Across the room an older couple broke open their fortune cookies, scrutinizing the printed messages with great interest and pleasure. They laughed, then chewed the broken pieces with calm, measured satisfaction. It was clear that they were happy together.

"So I've disappointed you," he said suddenly. "All right?"

I looked down, attempting to dazzle myself with the renderings on the placemat: yellowtail, sea urchin, salmon roe, sunomono. But I wasn't hungry anymore. Too bad, I'd been looking forward to our first night together again.

◇ ◇ ◇

The funny thing was I'd been thinking about my own brother. Not in the usual sense, in which I couldn't forgive him for leaving my parents, but in a stranger, more complicated manner. Many years ago, I spotted him in the powder room one day. He lingered before the mirror, examining the recent changes of his body—the weight of his genitals, the dense tangle of pubic hair—proud, excited, frightened at once. I was five, he thirteen. Odd, I thought. What we choose to remember.

◇ ◇ ◇

Standing in the bathroom one morning I saw a bump—a tough, painless eruption on the base of my penis. I shrugged it off. I went back to my projects for the day. I transplanted the bottlebrush to the backyard; I opened up the circles of the royal palm beds. Two days later, though, when I saw it again—its margins still hard and not at all diminished—I literally moaned out loud.

"Are you okay in there?" William said.

He was working on the opposite side of the door. It was Friday, his day off. He'd gotten it in him to paint the hall ceiling the palest yellow, and I pictured it misting down on him from the roller, a cool citrusy rain stippling his forehead. The smell of fresh latex leaked beneath the door.

"I'm fine. It's just a backache."

"A backache? Since when do you get backaches?"

"Always."

My secretiveness got the best of me. I should have opened the door, pointed, and shown him what the problem was.

"Don't worry," I said, and stood behind him. I scraped some paint off his forehead with a fingernail.

"Are you sure you're all right?"

"Absolutely I'm all right," I said, a little peeved now, and wandered outside.

I lay down on the backyard lawn in the sun, panting, the blades of Floratam scratching into my back like quills. I'd all but banished the arcade incident from my mind, but here it was back to haunt me, as if my life were some great morality tale from the Middle fucking Ages. We hadn't been having sex much—a whole other issue that completely eluded me—but what we'd done was enough to transmit it to him. He wouldn't take it well. Not only had I done something completely behind his back—a spite fuck—but I'd done something worse: I'd shown him, in the most trenchant terms, how completely inadequate he was to me.

My relationship, as I knew it, was about to end.

I had to tell him. There was no other way. I pictured sitting down with him one evening, placing a hand on his shoulder. "You have an STD," I'd say simply, in absolute calm, with authority.

A puzzled look would capture his face. "What do you mean? How could that be?"

"You have an STD. There's absolutely nothing to be afraid of."

He'd frown. "That doesn't make sense. I haven't had sex with anyone but you."

I'd nod, waiting for him to piece it together. He'd look at me in a kind of vacant, childish wonderment. Then his face would crumble and he'd bury his forehead in his palms.

I stayed up the entire night, trying to calm down, convincing myself that the announcement wouldn't be as bad as I feared. He wouldn't raise his voice or beat me; he wouldn't kick me out of the house. He was a rational, reasonable man. After all, we'd never declared monogamy, and though it hadn't come up as an issue, he wouldn't have been completely surprised, given the state of our sex life. Right? And yet I wasn't convinced he'd take to it lightly.

Was it possible to live with an untreated venereal infection? What about Flaubert, Maupassant, Jules de Goncourt? George Washington, for God's sake? I went to the library and read through every medical reference text, pored through every online database, until my eyes were scratchy and sore. According to the facts, it was indeed possible to live with the disease for years; if untreated, sufficient defenses would develop to produce a resistance to reinfection, even though these very defenses would fail to eradicate the existing infection, leading to lesions involving bones, skin, and viscera; heart disease; a variety of ocular syndromes; and the weakening of the central nervous system. In worst-case scenarios: tissue destruction. I pictured us sitting together at the dinner table, chewing on the softest foods, watching our incisors wobbling out, then coughing once, spitting them discreetly into our napkins.

If only I'd had a two-week supply of penicillin.

I checked myself daily. To my amazement the blemish wouldn't go away.

I buckled down finally. I went to a local specialist, Dr. Maltman, who informed me in no uncertain terms that I was fine, that I had a pimple. It was hard not to feel foolish, cheated. But he'd given me back my life, and the story of our daily unraveling.

Chapter 8

It was on a hot, swampy morning, after dropping William off at Channel 7 Studios, that I saw my mother shopping at the Town and Country Publix. My initial impulse was to leave the store or hide. What was she doing so far from home in an emporium that catered primarily to wealthy retirees? Once I got a hold of myself, I took to following her through the crowded aisles. How lonely, ponderous, and insignificant she looked as she tilted her head upward to examine the scribbled shopping list, which undoubtedly contained the same staple items we'd consumed for the past twenty years: chow mein, frozen peas, watermelon. Etcetera.

I realized at once that I loved her more than anyone.

"Hello, Mom."

"Evan?"

She tilted her head, her eyes fiery and alarmed, their slight almond shape enhanced with liner. Gone were the sweatshirts and the oversized glasses of the past, replaced with contacts and a deep blue Merino wool skirt. She looked healthier, actually, prettier and in better shape. Had her makeover been triggered by my absence from the house?

"You look beautiful," I said, releasing her from my hug.

"I do?"

"Yeah. I never remember you looking so good."

"That's nice." She sipped from a Styrofoam cup of coffee, a vile, watery concoction provided by the supermarket to pep up the customers. She grimaced down at the lipstick mark on the rim. "I'd come to the point in my life where I realized I had two choices. I could either shoot myself in the temple or reinvent myself. Needless to say, I went with the latter option."

My mouth fell open. "You were going to shoot yourself?"

She winced. "For Christ's sake, no. Don't be so literal."

She told me about what she'd been up to. She'd been working on the garden, uprooting the liriope to replace them with spreading junipers. She'd been attending a flamenco dance class at Miami-Dade Community College, where she startled the others with her quiet proficiency. She was even writing, she'd said, a good six pages a day.

I asked her what on earth she was writing.

"Journal stuff. Stuff about my life. It wouldn't be of interest to anyone."

Her words stung, though I know she didn't intend it. She kept talking and talking, mindless things that had nothing to do with us. I saw the apprehension on her face. And then the veil went up: I almost watched it: a thin, filigreed thing through which she wouldn't let me in. I heard the thoughts working behind her starched, fiery eyes: *I am not going to let him hurt me again. I cannot bear any more loss. I can go on without him.*

We might have been two longtime friends who'd had a falling out, still shaken, resentful, not knowing what was to become of us. She spoke with the slightest edge. But I believed it was possible to renew. I thought of all the times I'd had reunions with Jane. It was always tentative at first, as if we were both dreading and expecting the first signs of conflict. And then the path would clear, opening up, and we'd relax, remembering what we'd once been for each other.

"So what have you been up to?" she said in an overly cheery voice.

I walked with her side by side, up and down the crowded store aisles. I knew better than to talk about William: this was not what she'd wanted to hear. I might have been eight years old, helping her fetch Mrs. Paul's fish sticks—once my favorite childhood food—from the steaming caves of the freezer. I might have been basking in the drab, comforting days when Peter was away at school, before anything complicated like puberty and desire had gotten hold of me.

But once I erased William from the picture, I had nothing to say for myself. For some reason I thought of the mole on his left wrist, the moist pink skin of his hot fleshy neck.

"Mom," I said, surprising myself. "Would it be okay if I stayed with you and Daddy for a few days?"

She inhaled, pretending to examine the ingredients on the back of a cake mix.

"Mom?"

Her head pivoted back to me. "Sweetheart," she said with a wounded smile.

"I don't understand." I'd only wanted to get away; if only I could talk to her about William.

"Your father—"

"Yes?"

She glanced to the floor, sniffed, and cleared her throat.

"You mean to tell me that he doesn't want me at home?"

Her eyes filmed. "Of course not. He's not like that. Don't talk about your father like that."

I shook my head back and forth. I decided to let her have it. "So you're saying he's abandoned me, then?"

Her face hardened. Deep lines bracketed her mouth. "You're the last one to—"

"What?"

"Who's abandoned whom?"

I felt myself getting smaller, a pinpoint, a particle, an atom. I fixed all my attentions on the teenager in the big jeans, the big sneakers, on his tiptoes, helping his grandmother—

great-grandmother?—pick out a bagful of orange lentils. He placed them in the child seat of the cart, and she smiled dimly at him through her warped glasses, welcoming his presence.

"Listen," she said, more gently now. She touched my arm. "Let's save this for another time."

I glanced down at her fingers resting on my arm, the wedding band, the abrasion beneath the knuckle. It might have been the hand of somebody foreign.

She exhaled once, noisily. "I'd love to have you back. I'd love to have you home more than anything. It's just—"

"What?"

"If you promise never to see him again . . ."

"Fine," I mumbled, though I was prone to say, *Fuck it. I don't need your kindness. I don't need your mercy.*

"Keep in touch," she said. "We want to know how you are."

"You do?" I said.

She nodded and walked ahead. "Be good now."

I watched her threading down the aisle, maneuvering the cart in and out through the stalled shoppers. It was hard to keep from walking after her, from prolonging the discussion, from saying, "I'm sorry. I love you. Don't you know how much I love you?" Anything to keep her from leaving the store.

"Wait," I said at once.

She turned just slightly to her left, as if she were hiding her face from me.

"How's Peter? Have you heard from him?"

She shook her head, looking with some urgency toward the checkout.

"What's he up to?"

"Naples," she said, and shrugged her left shoulder. Once again her shoulders slumped.

And then I watched her leave. This was rupture. The longer we were apart the more damage we created. Was it ever possible to move back and forth across that bridge, that bridge between the two fenced-in countries?

◇ ◇ ◇

Younger, I could have watched them forever. My mother with her peat-rimmed cuticles, trimming the flame vine beneath the rain spout. My father with his flasks and his beakers, mixing up some fizzing compound. My own puzzles and toys often bored me in five seconds, but the study of my parents within the laboratory of their household afforded me the richest pleasure. Nestled between them in the secluded valley of their king-sized bed, I knew that life was never meant to be so sweet.

School made a difference. I trudged to the bus stop through rough games of tag, coins aimed at the bulb of my skull. Immediately I felt indifferent toward anyone my own age. I wanted to be with my parents. I wanted to be encompassed by their routines and manners, their dignified, high-minded chatter. School might have been a zoo. I might have been caged up with monkeys, their golden shit still fresh between their teeth. All day long I gazed at the droning clock, lonesome and yearning, pretending to be immersed in the swirls of my finger paintings, counting down the hours when I could be safe with my parents again.

It wasn't that they were flawless. Even before they started drifting apart, they had had their tensions, which they occasionally took out on us. A bitter word, a slap out of nowhere. But these were the occasion rather than the rule. The money was racking up in the bank; Sid was still ascending the mighty ladder of the chemistry department, and there was the sense of dizzy optimism about it all, the belief that they could still redeem every disappointment in their respective pasts.

So it wasn't without sense that I felt an enormous loss when I thought of them now, that the combination of their absence and proximity—their house within (I'd counted it) 1,260 feet of William's—unearthed me as it did. For years, I'd lived with the naive assumption that nothing would rattle their deep links to me. I could rob a bank, could pass nuclear secrets, and still they'd love me. Had I been wrong? My eighteenth birthday, July 12th, passed without a note. My card congratulating my father on his promotion to full professor—something

I'd heard from Wendy Park, his former student—remained un-answered. They knew where I lived. It was as if they'd moved. I imagined sometimes that they'd fulfilled their lifelong am-bition to buy a sailboat and negotiate it through the locks of the Panama Canal. Sometimes in the middle of the night I'd sneak out through William's garage and wheel my bike past the water tower, taking the jogger's path behind Country Club Plaza. I'd spot the house, then taste it, the flavor of fear, a rubbery dank taste like sucking on an inner tube. Something would have been different: a new set of gray trash cans, a sap-ling Norfolk Island pine, and I'd think, Goddamn it, god-damn them, they've gone somewhere without me. But then I'd see some touches that could only be theirs: the copper wind chimes, the old weather vane glinting on the roof, my broken ten-speed leaning against the fence. Relief.

They'd never do something as terrible as that.

Wasn't it time I stopped thinking about them so much?

I didn't expect kindness or wisdom or solidarity overnight. And yet they weren't making the slightest of efforts on my part. Did they actually believe that every decision and ges-ture I executed was simply to spite them? Some people wanted to be boneheads, some people didn't want to feel good about their circumstances. The truth was that my parents, Mr. and Mrs. Sid Sarshik, wanted to think that they'd failed somehow in their raising of me.

Well, fuck that.

◇ ◇ ◇

Nights later, lying in bed, with William at my side and the Dobermans at my feet, I was still thinking about my parents. Was my mother so fearful of aggravating my father that she'd do anything to avoid a conflict in which she'd eventually side against him? Did she feel so awful about her compliance, her lack of nerve, that she couldn't stand the sight of herself, the sound of her own voice? Or did she, on the deepest level, share my father's point of view?

My feet were freezing. "I can't sleep," I said out loud, if only to myself.

William turned on his side. He punched softly at the pillow behind him, then offered a low moaning sound. Seconds later, he turned on the lamp beside the bed. "What's wrong?"

"I ran into my mother in the store a few nights ago."

He sounded dehydrated. All week he'd been working on an expose about the nuclear plants of South Florida, a project which involved hours of overtime. His face said: *Do you know how hard I've been working?*

"And how was that?"

"Strange. I asked her if I could stay at their place for a couple of days. She more or less said no."

"Mmmmm." He stared upward at a fissure in the ceiling.

I felt emboldened and exposed at once. "What are you thinking?" I asked him.

"You're not happy here?" he said, curious. His eyes worked to seem bright, anything but startled and hurt. Up to that point I hadn't indicated that things had been anything but cheery between us.

"No, it has nothing to do with us. Don't you ever miss Poppy?"

He looked at the trim on the blanket, withholding his response. It happened that Lorna had forbidden him from seeing Poppy in the wake of their divorce, even though the agreement was far from legal. To make up for his silence, William wired 500-dollar deposits into Poppy's Winter Park checking account 4 times a year.

"She doesn't mean what you think," he said, but his voice faltered.

"How would you know? You've never had a real conversation with them."

"I've seen them outside your house. I've seen your father fixing your bicycle for you—watching you pedal away, making sure the chain didn't fall off." He looked at me. "They love you."

I blew my nose. "If only as a concept. If they love me it's

only because I'm their mutual creation. I represent a certain lost thing between them. But they haven't been behaving toward me with anything approaching affection."

He was silent for a time, breathing. "Aren't we erudite?" he said finally.

"Don't make fun of me."

"Too many thoughts," he said. "You're thinking too many thoughts. Calm down now, turn off your mind."

I rolled my eyes. "I'm hardly a child."

"Get over here," he insisted. *"Now."*

Slowly, methodically, he began rubbing my head. I tried to relax, concentrating on his weighted palms working the contours of my skull, its bumps, gullies, and planes. He got me then. He knew me this well: nothing anyone did could center me like this, could demarcate my borders with such easy precision.

"Feel better?"

I nodded. I glanced over at him through one eye. *What was I doing with him?* So what if I decided to say it?

"Why haven't you been having sex with me?"

His eyes blinked rapidly. I might have asked him if I could taste his blood.

"We have sex," he said softly.

"When was the last time? Tell me. Has it been a month, two? You don't even remember."

His brow clenched. He seemed truly, deeply flustered, so much so that it was hard not to back down and forget it. "I've been busy as hell with my job," he rasped.

And yet I could answer: two months, eleven days. My eyes watered. *"See?"*

He propped himself up, held up a hand like a crossing guard. "Hey, that's not fair. Just let me off the hook, okay?"

"No one's putting you on the hook."

"I don't need to be accused of something at"—he picked up the alarm clock, held it mere inches from his face—"at three in the morning."

"That's not what I'm doing."

"I don't believe it," he said, yanking once at the covers. He turned away from me.

"Are you impotent?" I said quietly.

"No."

"Are you pushing me away?"

No answer.

"Hel-*lo*—"

"No, I'm not pushing you away."

"Do you have another boyfriend?"

"No. Now stop it. I'm not subjecting myself to your interrogation. Just go to sleep."

I settled back in the bed. "If you gave me an explanation, I'd understand. I could be patient, okay? I want to help. All I need is a little explanation."

He seemed enwrapped in some tendril of thought. He glanced away. Quietly, he said, "Did it ever occur to you that you're just too damn horny?"

I laughed out loud. The idea was preposterous. Wasn't everyone horny? "You've got to be kidding."

"No, let's shift the light to you. Do you know what it's like to feel that you're disappointing somebody every minute of your life?"

My face heated. "What?"

"I'm talking about your neediness. You're putting too much pressure on me."

I glanced at the picture of Lorna on the bureau. "Oh, it's my fault, I get it. Christ." I shook my head, hard. "You're a gay man, for God's sake." And then I leapt out of bed, walked down the hall, and curled up on the kitchen chair.

I sat there, palming the loose change he'd left on the counter. I loaded it in my pocket—forty-five cents, no big deal, but it was the gesture that shocked me. In the entire realm of his life I meant about as much to him as a chauffeur or a pet. He liked the *idea* of having somebody around, but when it came down to the day-to-day obligations of living with someone, the duty to affection, he came up unbearably short.

No wonder Lorna wanted him to have nothing to do with Poppy.

I walked outside, crept into the garden. The sounds of the night: a plane overhead, blinking, vanishing, then nothing. Shifting circuits on a sprinkler system. I edged closer to the property line. A rustling beside the pool cage. I knew it: red stripe, yellow stripe. Black snout. Coral snake.

But it was only our neighbor. She was sitting in a lawn chair in her backyard, pressing a cup of coffee to her chin. She gazed out at the trees with such intensity that it was hard to watch her. In the one and only time we'd ever talked, she spooned bloodmeal around the roots of her begonias, her personal trick for keeping their colors so vibrant. Now, for whatever reason, I lost my usual sense of shyness and caution. I decided to walk over to her.

"I hope I didn't startle you."

She kept staring at her garden wall, and shook her head. "I heard you coming," she whispered.

A silence between us. Dew dripping from the staghorn ferns. "You couldn't sleep, either?" I said finally.

She nodded, sniffed. She wiped at her nose with a balled Kleenex in her fist.

"Your begonias look beautiful," I said.

She glanced over to them. "They are," she said quietly, satisfied. "Aren't they? Thank you. Thank you for noticing."

She turned to me then for the first time. Her chin glistened in the dark. I wanted to step back, embarrassed. "Are you okay?"

She started crying again. I stood beside her, looking down at the sparkling grass.

"I'm sorry," she said through a low sob.

"How's your husband?" I asked, glancing over at the single light in the window.

"Drunk," she said. "A basket case."

The dew felt icy on my forehead. A warm breeze rattled the coconut palms. "If you ever need help," I said, "with your garden . . ."

"You would?" she said, her eyes brightening slightly.

"I'll water your begonias," I offered. "I'd love to feed them."

"I'd appreciate that. What a nice gesture. Thank you—"

"Evan," I said, and extended my hand.

"Mrs. Stendhal," she said. "Virginia Stendhal. Thank you very much."

"Have a good night now."

I walked back into the house, down the hall to our room. The door was half closed; I stopped. Already I heard the snoring of Pedro, the Doberman, a full sawing throttle that could make us laugh when our moods were right. I didn't expect that now. I pushed open the door, reluctant. Had I harmed him beyond imagining, underestimating my own capacity to hurt?

He sprawled on the bed, motioning me toward him. His eyes, though sad, glimmered in invitation.

"What?"

"Be quiet," he said with tenderness.

My gratitude was boundless, large as a country. Why was I crying? He took hold of my arm, pinned me to the bed, and to my bafflement and surprise began to make love to me.

Chapter 9

I had to know things. I had to take apart everything I saw, even as a kid: lamps, toys, hairdryers, toasters. The world was a flurry of blues, oranges, and golds, unbearable in their vibrancy. Sid and Ursula tried their best to calm me down, but I skated away from their grasp, agitated, voracious. I had to ask, where is this going, how is this put together, why are we so shy, so brittle? There was Beau Roberts's mouse. I wriggled it in my cupped palm, on its back, eyes red, astonished. I fumbled for the toy knife, gently nicking its fur, wanting more than anything to peel back that white, exposing the pulsing wet bead inside, before Beau's mother caught me in the act. Our phone rang later that evening. I tried to tell my parents I only loved the mouse, but my words fractured in my mouth. They sat across the kitchen table, fingers latched, gazing at me with their wet, dazzled eyes.

◇ ◇ ◇

The morning air was sluggish and sweet, yellowing the surfaces with pollen. We lounged inside the pool cage, reading through the *Herald* and eating carambola. On such mornings it was easy to convince myself that there was indeed something between us, that, together, we were actually immersed in the moment. We felt a pleasure in our silence, a camaraderie and a comfort, a mutual respect for the distance between us.

The week had been a good one. On Tuesday, William had surprised me by taking me to the Channel 7 Studios (at last breaking his pact to keep me hidden from his coworkers), where he introduced me to Dinah Strang, aka Dusty Cartwright, host of *Casper's Corners,* my favorite childhood TV show. She'd been out of work, in hiding for years, after the FCC crackdown on the endorsement of products by the hosts of such programs—in this case Dinah's own Dusty Cartwright Dairy Bar. A host of rumors had swirled around her disappearance—one, that she'd lost her leg to gangrene; another, that she was living on the streets of Newcastle, Delaware, a sometime prostitute, after draining her bank accounts and turning over the funds to the SPCA. It was hard to believe any of it now, as she stood before the flying-fish sculptures outside the studio, preparing for her local comeback program, which already gave off the queasy scent of failure. I wasn't giving up on her, though. She held me close—a big blowsy grandma in a fringed white cowboy suit—as William snapped the picture. "A big smoocheroony for your Aunt Dusty," she cried, and I kissed her then, unfazed by her pancake makeup, her whiskied breath. She looked at me, confused, stricken, as if I were some demanding child.

William flapped the newspaper once on his lap. In Virginia's trees next door: a riot of orchids. "Did you know a Todd Bemus?" he said offhandedly.

I moved to the edge of the patio chair and leaned toward him. "Yeah, I went to school with him."

He raised his brows. The headline of his page read OBITUARIES.

"He died?"

He handed the paper to me. I pulled in a breath and held it. Over his name I saw Todd's yearbook photo, his white hair—"bleach out," we called it—his pink, dangerous lips. Already he looked like he knew so much more than the others, his eyes bitter, yet willful. He might have been someplace far ahead in the future. I passed over the announcement: *Todd Bemus of Coral Gables, Florida, died Thursday of complications due to AIDS in San Francisco, California. He was 20 years old and is survived by his mother, Cherry, his sisters, Heather, of Port St. Lucie, and Tabitha, of Nags Head, North Carolina.*

"He was a friend?" William asked.

I kept shaking my head. "We were in gym together for two years."

"Twenty," William said. *"Shit."*

I clenched my right hand tightly, rubbing a knuckle with my thumb. My throat filled quickly with tears. Still, it didn't seem quite real to me, not only because I'd been out of touch with Todd for two years, but because the event seemed like something he'd have staged, watching it take place from afar, then obnoxiously showing up at his own funeral—*"ta da"*— laughing at everybody, then apologizing for all the grief he'd caused. Dead. How could Todd, of all people, be dead?

William rested his arm on my shoulder. I must have looked sadder than I knew.

"Wasn't he too young?" I said. "I mean, I thought it took ten years to come down with symptoms."

He raised his eyebrows again. "Not always. Sometimes—" His voice trailed off.

We sat still, reading about the impending water shortage and the proliferation of hi-tech firms in Boca Raton, pretending that it was just another humid South Florida morning, that something of consequence hadn't split open the day. A sluggishness settled in my arms, the tips of my fingers. I wasn't used to seeing my friends die. There was June Pulte, of course, whose car had sledded off a storm-slick road into a cypress stand after leaving Disney World, and Mark McNitt, who'd OD'd on a lethal cocktail of speed, Valium, butane, and vodka, but neither of these had been close friends of mine, and these incidents were mere accidents, quick dealings of fate that hadn't mucked with the deepest part of their identities. It was happening all around us, I knew it, though it was sometimes hard to believe. William, for one, had lost nearly all of his friends: Thomas and Mark, David and Larry, Tony and Richard. But it was something that happened to older men, men in their thirties and forties, not to people like me.

William took the Dobermans for a walk, and I squatted beside the pool, testing the water chemistry with the little kit, waiting for the PH to go pink. I strained out some leaves from the surface. Poor Todd. I thought about how he'd tried to get closer to me, how he'd called me one day out of the blue to watch videos with him. He'd gotten a hold of the whole Pam Grier "ouevre," he called it—*Coffy* and *Foxy Brown* among them—and he'd wanted to watch them with me because he thought only *I* would appreciate them, and then I promised to get back to him. I knew what a big deal it was for him to call, how he'd probably worried about it all day, and yet I completely and totally blew him off.

Secretly, I believed he had a crush on me. True or not, this was the real reason I kept my distance from him. I preferred to spend time with him in public, at Dadeland, at Haulover Park—any place where he couldn't jump me, for every time I was alone with him I felt a tremendous pressure, even if it was only communicated through the weight of his gaze and the way he sat so close to me. It was too bad that I didn't feel the slightest bit of attraction to him.

Still, I believed he was the funniest guy in the world. He could make me fall down the stairs in stitches, mimicking friends or second-rate celebrities like Joan Van Ark or Tori Spelling, though he also embarrassed me with his airy-thin voice, his occasional cackle, his broad, overreaching gestures. More than once I'd slipped into an empty classroom when I saw him walking toward me down the hall, clutching to his chest his three-ring binder—decoupaged with sunflowers, smiley faces, Day-Glo peace signs—as if he were shielding his breasts.

Once he'd worn makeup to school. Some of the boys had finally had enough, and he'd probably called one a name, and he was going to get throttled. I could hear him now: *Hey straight*

boy, hey pencildick. Want to get fucked? Straight boy loves to get fucked.
He was too much for them. His very presence mocked, and
they couldn't stand it, couldn't stand it at all. Eric Woodworth
went first. He tugged Todd's earring, and snagged it once, rip-
ping it right through his lobe. A dark drop of blood pearled on
Todd's ear. "You'll get AIDS," Convey cried, looking at the red
on Woodworth's palm. "Drop it, you fool. You'll get AIDS!"
Still, Todd walked ahead, a determined look on his face as if he
were telling himself that nothing could harm him.

Then Woodworth turned and noticed me. He knew that
Todd and I were gym buddies, banding together during softball class, deliberately, flamboyantly missing the fly balls that
dropped in our direction.

"Hey, Sarshik," he said. "Here's your friend, he's bleeding.
Why don't you come over here and take care of your friend?"

I looked at him as if to say *What friend?* then left Todd to his
own devices as I hurtled down the steps to the locker room.

Two mornings later I went to Todd's funeral mass. I dropped
William off at work, then drove around Coral Gables looking
for the church. I found it after a few minutes, a large Catholic
church with ocher brick walls and a round rosette window—
St. Michael the Archangel. I sat in the back row, near the bap-
tismal font, in my single white shirt and ill-fitting suit (an old
thing I'd borrowed from William's closet), and stared down
at the initials etched into the soft wood of the pew. Ten rows
ahead were his cousins, dozens of them, all bused in from
Allentown, Pennsylvania; his former neighbors; his most recent friends, two of whom appeared to be models or porn stars;
and his parents, Francis and Dot, who seemed alternately
composed and quietly devastated. It was hard to imagine that
they'd ever been cruel to Todd, but they'd been awful, literally
locking him out of the house upon learning he'd had sex with
Lloyd Scarborough, the marching-band director. Still, they'd
welcomed him back home when he'd come down with his first

78

<>

Paul
Lisicky

symptom, a case of CMV retinitis, realizing that he had no other choice but to stay put, that he wasn't going to run away, or frighten or surprise them anymore.

But it was foolish to expect anything but surprise from Todd. Even in death, he still managed to unsettle. Before mass, standing outside with his cousin Ricky (who'd allowed me to bum a cigarette, something I did from time to time), I'd learned that before moving to San Francisco, where he'd butched himself up and started sleeping with porn stars, Todd had been an accomplished composer of liturgical music, something he'd hidden from almost everybody, including his parents. He'd taken it quite seriously, taking pride in his designation as the youngest composer ever in the catalog of UIA Library, his publisher. Now the choir was performing some of Todd's music for the service. The cantor intoned his setting of my favorite psalm, one of those I still knew by heart, Psalm 42—*Like a deer that longs for running streams*—and then we all repeated it, its antiphon rising, lifting us up, moving and unnerving everyone in the congregation.

Outside the church, Todd's other cousins, three of whom had been linebackers for Penn State, hefted the shining casket down the steps. The sun went in. People milled about, jabbering. It was hard not to feel cheated somehow, though it was a nice mass, a nice sermon. There were only veiled, uncomfortable references to AIDS, the priest assuring us that God, in his infinite mercy and wisdom, was blessing Todd, seating him at his right hand. I tried not to be miffed. The palm fronds glistened in the heat. Karen Kenley, a mutual friend of Todd's and mine, spotted me in the throng. To my dread, she made her way toward me.

"What have you been up to?" she asked.

I visored my eyes. Already she'd aged. She might have been five or ten years older than I was with her brittle blonde perm, her pitted skin. She waited for me to answer.

I hadn't anticipated the question. Since I'd been with William I'd more or less isolated myself from everyone I'd known. I couldn't possibly tell her the truth, that I'd been staying at home, immersed in a relationship that I worried about more and more with each passing day.

"I took some time off from school," I said. "But I'm going back someday."

Her face betrayed surprise and relief. "I thought you'd have been in grad school by now. You seemed so brilliant. You were always throwing off the curve on tests."

Her words barbed and shamed, though I doubted she'd wanted to hurt me. One thing you could say about Karen was that she was kind. She might not have been smart or attractive or ambitious, but she was kind, and no one would take that away from her. I turned the question around. "So what about you?"

She was hostessing at a Perkins Pancake House in Naranja, on the seedy deadbeat strip to the Keys—most of which had been torn open by Hurricane Andrew. Already she'd divorced and married a second time, but the current marriage—to a guy twenty years her senior, a former real estate salesman for General Development—wasn't working. She was thinking of moving back in with her mother, if only to put some money in the bank. She was twenty years old. I couldn't have imagined a life so different from my own.

"And I have a baby!" she cried.

She reached into her wallet and passed me a cellophane-wrapped picture of a baby, a little girl with blonde hair, blue eyes, and white shirt patterned with golden pachyderms.

"Her name's Lola. Seventeen months old. Don't you think that's the coolest name?"

"Wow." I wanted to feel what I was supposed to feel. She so much wanted my approval, even though I could barely muster it, with Todd on my mind. What was she doing with a baby when she could barely take care of herself?

"Let's get together sometime," she said. Awkwardly, as if on impulse, she hugged me.

"We should," I answered. I felt her gripping me closer, her tears hot on the cloth of my shirt.

She laughed, sniffed, pretended she wasn't crying. "Remember when the three of us went to the drive-in, and the tire blew out, and we had to walk six miles to the Texaco?"

I nodded. I'd had such a horrendous time that night, bickering with Todd, walking with him in a pair of thrift-store shoes that were one size too small, that I'd all but suppressed it. But maybe I'd had a bad attitude. Was my recollection any truer than hers?

"So give me a call, please? How's Jane, by the way?"

I shrugged. "I don't know. I haven't seen her."

"You haven't? That surprises me. You two used to be like this." And she crossed two fingers together, holding them up for me to see.

"People drift apart."

She nodded. "I never liked her," she said, admitting to something I'd always suspected. She rubbed her arm as if chilly. "She always made me feel fat, stupid. Maybe I'm jealous of her."

I grabbed her tightly by the hand and shook it, in full measure of my support. "That's Jane. Well, we won't ask her along this time. How's that?"

"Good," she said, laughing now.

I walked away from her. The cars, headlights on, inched down the road toward the cemetery. Driving home, I knew that we'd never get together. I was in another life. I'd never see her again.

Three weeks after Todd's funeral, on a night marked by the arrival of a cold front, with violent bursts of lightning, and eerie passages of calm, I locked myself in the bathroom and pressed a damp washcloth to my face. My stomach lining popped and burned. There was no question: I knew that I was infected, and that it was only a matter of time before I came down with it—the night sweats and fevers, the rashes and gum disease, the odd tingling and numbness that would prevent me from walking.

I crawled back into bed and sidled up to William, deliberately waking him.

"Do you ever worry?" I asked him.

He opened one eye. "What now."

"Don't you ever worry about AIDS?"

He breathed deeply, patiently through his nostrils. "We've been safe," he said blandly. "What's there to worry about?"

But we hadn't been safe, even though we tried to be. There had been that time or two when just before he'd rolled on the rubber, he'd pressed his dick inside me, just an inch or two deep, just for the thrill of it, just to test something. Wasn't that a part of it, the thrill, the daring? Wasn't that the thing that drove people to let down their guard, to stare down death in the face, or to finally stop fighting, because it took all of your resources to keep it at bay? I thought of the first time we were together, the hot afternoon on which I'd fucked him, the smell of cut grass in the air, only to find a rusty, bloody bloom on the top sheet after he'd left for the bathroom. I looked at the spot, thinking, we're never going back from here, we're linked together now—William and Evan, blood brothers—brutalized and comforted at once.

"We never talk about it," I said. "Don't you think we should at least talk about it sometime?"

"What's there to talk about?" A grimace passed over his face. He twisted his hands together, once, not even knowing he was doing it.

I sat up. I tried my best to sound rational, nonchalant. "Maybe we should both get tested."

He shook his head from side to side, emphatic. "No way. I'm over that idea."

"Why not? We'll just get it over with and we won't have this dreadful thing looming over us."

His face looked empty, bleak. "It's always looming over us."

He stood. I followed him into the bathroom, watching him pour baking soda into a juice glass. Carefully, he filled it with tap water, stirred it with his finger, then sipped it as if it were champagne.

I sat on the closed toilet seat. If I were sick, if my time were really limited, I wanted to be doing things. I wanted to be living like Todd did, having experiences, fucking, becoming somebody new, changing my name, somewhere on the opposite side of the country.

"Do you think you're positive?" I asked.

He swallowed, testing the condition of his throat. "I feel fine, if that means anything." His face looked brighter, calmer all of a sudden. "How about you?"

"I'm fine."

"That's good. That's all we need to know."

I followed him back to the bedroom. Outside, the sky lightened notch by notch. I expected him to be resentful, silent. Instead, he turned to me and held me tight, breathing slowly, at regular intervals, until he was fast asleep, as if he'd convinced himself the world was nothing but a restful, safe place.

Chapter 10

I found it in our mailbox, without postage, in a used, brown envelope once addressed to my parents. A ghastly photograph of Ed McMahon peered down from the upper left corner. As it had been deposited after 2:30, the last time I'd checked the box, I assumed that my mother had delivered it herself.

Dear Evan,

I'm writing this in the kitchen. I want you to know that this is the first letter I've written in thirteen years. I know I told you that I've been writing about my life every day, but this is different. It takes a special kind of attention that I don't know I'm capable of these days. In any case, the house is quiet without you, and I miss your spirit in these empty gray rooms.

It was terrific to see you at the Publix. You looked better than I'd imagined—though there was something about your eyes. (Are you taking zinc? Dr. Oglethorpe says that there's nothing better than a good dose of zinc for the eyes. One or two tablets a day—I forget which dosage.)

You asked about Peter. Luck has it that he called not long after I saw you. He's bought a bankrupt motel somewhere near Naples. We don't know how on earth he came up with the money—he doesn't tell us anything. Anyway, if you don't waste too much time, you can probably reach him at King Cole Resort, Tamiami Trail and Boca Palms Parkway, Naples, Florida. I told him that you'd like to talk to him and that you'd be getting in touch with him soon.

The fish are doing just fine, and we've gotten a new wall hanging for over the sofa—you'd probably hate it, but there. Speaking of your father, he's driving me nuts, as usual. He's on his way to Austin, Texas, for some academic to-do, and it's a relief to have some time to myself. FYI: on the subject of your staying with us, he came to the conclusion that it would be too much right now. Let's face facts, dear—you like the IDEA of staying with us, but once you moved back in, you'd be miserable. The thing is, you can't be two things at once. These things are hard for me to write, and that's one of the reasons it's taken me this long. Forgive me. I want you to know that I love you, and miss you terribly, but, damn it, it's hard. When I think of you living just down the street, the way you've chosen to turn your back on us, it's hard not to feel hurt. And a little rage. You'll see things sooner than you think, perhaps when you have children of your own. We're waiting for you, Evan. Please make up your mind. We love you more than you'll ever know.

Mom

I read the letter twice more before I tore it in half, then pieced it back together with strapping tape. *Goddamn,* I thought. They were locking me out. I really had no place to go.

◇ ◇ ◇

William's solution to my seething rage was to take me out to a party. He received the invitation from Cleve Stern, a sound engineer from Channel 7, one of the few employees he was officially "out" to, so I assumed there'd be people like us there. William wouldn't tell me anything specific about the party, except that it would be taking place in a loft in an industrial area of Little Havana, and that I shouldn't worry too much about what I was going to wear.

"What kind of party? Who's going to be there?"

"You'll see," he said, nudging me onward. "Hurry up, get moving. It starts in forty-five minutes."

I felt a dread coupled with a low-key anticipation. We hadn't had much of a social life. All these months it had been just him and me, and I'd been feeling the pressure of that, the sense that we needed to open ourselves out. It made me wonder why he'd waited until now to do this, when we were practically crawling around on our hands and knees. But any change was potentially refreshing, especially from someone who was so dependent upon routine.

It took us a good fifteen minutes to find a parking space. The neighborhood wasn't great. I looked up to the sky above the warehouses and high-tension wires, lines of pink and red light creeping across its map. I thought, this is the Florida that no one sees in postcards, the Florida that's always there behind the palms, the bronzed bodies, the swept, glittering surfaces.

Inside, the loft we were met by a line of men in a graffiti-scarred hall. The music was loud beyond imagining. I recognized the song, a remix of "Rude Thing," by some alternative band that Todd had introduced me to.

> You can kiss me, you can torch me
> You can touch me, you can scorch me
> Cause you just mean nothing
> You just mean nothing to me

It certainly didn't seem like William's kind of party.

The line inched forward. We stood at a table where two men sat in nothing but their jockey shorts beneath a hand-printed sign: SUGGESTED DONATION: $10.

I turned back to William. "You mean we have to *pay?*"

"Quiet," he said, passing a ten-dollar bill into my hand.

"And who's this?" said one of the men to William. He was talking about me. He smiled. In different circumstances I'd have liked his chiseled chest, his lacquered Caesar haircut, shorn on the sides, but now, for whatever reason, he reminded me of Frankenstein's monster.

"Where do we go?" William said, unnerved.

"Around the corner, to the right. You can check your clothes in there."

I blinked repeatedly, not yet processing these instructions. I followed William down the hall, and, to my left, I saw it: a great room, perhaps forty feet long, its concrete floor covered with a plastic tarp, on which a hundred men of all ages, races, and levels of attractiveness, were clumped in threes and fours, standing in their perfect underwear and Doc Martens, leaning into each other, jerking off.

I stood there for a minute, intrigued and repelled at once. The participants were suffused with a crimson otherworldly light. A vision of terror and beauty. A J-O party, of course. What, then, were William and I doing here?

"Are you okay with this?" he asked. He seemed more than a little bewildered.

My brow tightened. I didn't know how I felt. "Why didn't you tell me?"

"I thought it would be a surprise. I thought you'd get a kick out of the surprise."

I shook my head, a numbing sensation between my brows. My head itched. I followed him down the hall. We took off our clothes, shoved them inside numbered Winn-Dixie bags, and handed them over to the clothes check, a sweet geeky fellow who might have spent his days as a programmer. I imagined the flashing beeper on his belt, summoning him to fix the bug on some trust-accounting system so the dividends could get posted by day's end.

We walked back to the big room and observed, like an audience at some Roman bacchanalia. It wasn't what you'd think, though. A lot of it was just plain dull. I got the feeling that most of the guys liked the *notion* of the spectacle more than anything else, longing for intensity and pleasure, hoping to confront, then push past the boundaries of shame. Did they leave feeling empty, unsatisfied, going home by themselves, more solitary than ever before?

Around us "Rude Thing" spun out from the speakers, the longest dance track in history.

"There's Cleve," William said.

I watched Cleve, a randy, bespectacled thing with an amazing physique for someone of his age, fooling around with a kid twenty years his junior. At one point he glanced toward us, and—to our discomfort—waved. At once the cracks in his armor asserted themselves. I saw how Cleve had grown up thinking he was unattractive, knowing that his opportunities for sex were limited by his essential homeliness. I saw how his first visits to the gym at thirty had literally changed his life, how with the simple repetition of a few free-weight exercises four times a week, he could transform himself into the man he'd always wanted. I saw how his fooling around with the young muscled boy in these circumstances was all meant for display, not fun, how it was ultimately about declaring his status: *Hey, boys, look what I got. I'm not worthless anymore.*

I wanted to relax into the situation, but I couldn't stop stepping out of it, couldn't put to sleep the critical apparatus—a necessary condition if I were to have a decent time. But already I saw myself fifty years in the future, telling younger people about what was transpiring before me: This is what we did to amuse each other, to kept ourselves from going crazy in the age of AIDS.

Not ten seconds later, a middle-aged man—a leather-daddy type—walked up to me with a posed, stern expression on his face. I felt a twinge of erotic feeling, a pleasant discomfort, though I couldn't get beyond the fact that William was standing beside me, territorial, possessive. I couldn't get into this. I held up my right hand.

The guy nodded, walked away, moving on to someone more willing.

"Creepy," William said, his eyes fixed to the guy's thin white waist.

I shrugged. "He wasn't so bad."

"You're kidding."

I dulled the expression on my face. On some profound level, I'd wanted to provoke something akin to jealousy, though I couldn't say why. The air vibrated between us. I looked over at William, his grim, hopeless face, his pale, pockmarked back, and imagined him tasting flavorless in my mouth. Above our heads, a poster: Five Easy Steps to Safer Sex. I still didn't know what we were doing here.

"Now that's cute," William said, pointing to a kid across the room.

William kept staring at him with an intensity that seemed forced, inappropriate. I didn't see what was so great about him, but I kept quiet, trying to make sense of his interest. Maybe it was only because he looked like me, and I liked men who were older, butcher, who'd been around the block a bit. I'd have taken the leather daddy over the kid any day, but again, I kept my mouth shut. Soon enough, William's stare had drawn the kid toward us—a calf to a block of salt.

"Howdy," he said, quizzical.

I smiled, in welcome. Something hooked into my stomach. He stepped closer to the kid, then, to my confusion, stepped backward, disengaging himself. He nodded toward me, as if in collusion. What was going on here?

The kid leaned into me, kissed me ripely with his full red lips. His tongue was scratchy and sweet as he reached up, rubbing the knots from my shoulders. It felt good, unbearably good, but I couldn't get into it—at least not with William standing there. The hook snagged deeper into my stomach lining. Was I going to be sick? I realized then that William didn't want to participate, that he only wanted to watch, and that was the sole purpose for bringing me here.

"I can't get into this," I said, and pulled back from the kid. "I'm sorry."

Both William and the kid looked at each other. The kid's eyes seemed hurt and alarmed.

"I'm getting dressed," I said, and hurried toward the clothes check.

"I thought you'd be happy," he called out after me. His footsteps were brisk down the hall. "I did it for you."

"Well, thanks," I muttered to myself.

"Huh?"

"Fucking clueless."

"Fucking what?"

"Fucking *me.*"

We sat in the front seat of the car without speaking. My back teeth ached to their roots. I felt something deeper than rage, a blank, zeroed-out place, a null set. I couldn't find my foothold, for everything was rocking now, spinning too fast.

I went straight to bed. For whatever reason, I pulled out the obituary of Todd, which I'd kept inside the night table, and started reading it to myself. William stepped into the room, glowering, wounded.

"Are you still reading that?" he whispered.

They were the first words we'd exchanged in close to an hour.

"Yes, I'm still reading that. What's it matter to you?"

He shook out a pillowcase he'd unfolded. He wagged his head. "This isn't healthy. This feels inflated."

"He was twenty years old!" I yelled.

"What does that have to do with anything?"

"Everything," I said.

He worked the case over the pillow. *"Fine.* Just don't expect me to participate." Then he crawled into bed, switched off the lamp, casting the room in darkness.

The burning crept higher in my stomach. My mind started wandering. I thought about the fact that he hadn't encouraged me to work, hadn't encouraged me to contact all those schools that had once accepted me. Or to make friends, for that matter. My thoughts were all over the place, scattered, as if hammered around the edges. What was I doing here?

"What am I doing here?" I said, repeating my thought aloud.

"Immature," he muttered, staring at the ceiling. "Don't be so fucking immature."

"What?"

"You heard what I said."

He'd hit bottom—a declaration that insisted only upon his age, his power over me. Something against which I couldn't stand up. "At least I'm not shut down," I said after a few minutes. "At least I've given myself permission to be affected by things."

"La tee da," he said.

Fine, I thought. Take the last word. You don't know how to fight anyway. Or I don't. Our gestures said it all: this wasn't working out. I decided that minute: it was over, kaput. Fine.

◇ ◇ ◇

I waited three days. I picked a morning on which the sun wasn't too hot and the wind was calm, a light southeast breeze pushing the fried leaves across the lawn. The weather was good. We might have been someplace ghastly, beautiful like Barbados, Antigua—islands to which I'd never been, but had imagined as real. I drove William to work, taking the long route on the bay front, past the mirrored towers and the marinas, actually feeling comfortable in his company. How civil we were, how amiable—no allusions to what had been happening in the last few weeks. Any bystander would have thought that there was nothing lethal between us. We were perfect for each other, no? I'd given him not one inkling of what I'd worked out, which buzzed me and prodded, slapped me high about the head as if I were stealing something expensive—a watch or a jewel.

I cleaned the house from top to bottom. I cleaned the sinks and the showers, the oven and the baseboards, the tile grout, the exhaust fan, the medicine chest. Then I went to work on the garage. I could have been Astrid Muth, my mother's fanatical, desperate friend, who cared for her yard with such scrutiny that she literally probed through her flower beds in order to stop the weeds before they'd sprouted. I got it now. I was something like Astrid. After an entire afternoon, only two hours before I was to pick William up at the station, I set to work on my backpack. As I wanted to travel light, I didn't pack much. Some T-shirts, a pair of jeans, shorts, underwear, jacket, sweater, flashlight. The rest of it? The truth was I didn't need anything more than that.

I walked into the den, the room in which I'd been scheduled to sleep on the day of my arrival. What had I been thinking? I stared at the rusted pipe on the floor. The water murmured. And all at once a scorpion pulled itself out of the neck, nearly translucent, creeping over the rusted rim.

I paused once before the front door, patting the Dobermans twice, three times upon the head. "You be good to Daddy, now. Will you miss me?" I spoke aloud to the empty white walls. The house was still, unbearably still, yet starting to turn. "You really weren't a bad guy," I said. "Son of a bitch." And then I left.

Part Two

Chapter 11

They huddled beneath a lone palm in their bright yellow jackets. I walked faster. Something twinged my shoulder blade. I had to tell myself that the simple fact of my appearance was not the prime reason for their gathering, that they didn't exist to taunt, to yell *faggot* to any lone boy who happened to walk through the field. Clearly, I said to myself. See clearly. They were simply conferring, talking about tonight's football game. Nothing wrong with that. Paranoia. Residue, it seemed, from an earlier time.

I walked along the treeline. My sneakers caked with marl. It took all of three hours for me to start asking myself why I left. He wasn't the worst of partners. He wasn't condescending or surly; he wasn't unctuous, lunkheaded, dishonest, or cheap. His breath was fresh, pleasant; he smelled good—lavender and sea salt, a surprising mix. Each Wednesday night, as part of his weekly caretaking ritual, he tweezed the hairs from his earlobes, back, and shoulder blades, leaving behind a trail of fibers, like carpet threads, all over the bathroom tile.

It occurred to me that I had hurt someone.

Sometimes in passing moments I still wonder what he might have thought when he finally returned that night from work, having taken a cab home from the station, only to see the car lolling in the driveway. Was my absence in the house instantly palpable? Or had he dropped into his favorite chair, switched on the lamp, called out *Evan*—only to realize minutes later that I had really gone? Was he angry or wounded, searching urgently for a note, an explanation that would never surface? Or did he feel a certain satisfaction, a smugness about it all? Could he have said to himself: *He will be back?*

He really wasn't a bad guy.

I found the pipe at the end of the path. The scrub had thickened since I'd last been out here, denser since the brushfire, but I appreciated that, knowing I'd be sheltered, safe. Vapor trails stitched across the sky. I eased down into the pipe feet first, pulling myself across its floor, its cylinder surprisingly warm, dry, cocooning. I fumbled for my shirt and balled it behind my head. I had no good reason to feel this good. It was hard to believe that so few people had ever known the humble pleasures of sleeping outside.

The sky went dark. In the distance I heard the boys, more ominous now, their war cries coiling up into the trees. They were starting a fire. Laugh it off, I told myself. Means shit. And then I fell asleep, not waking up until a full night later, when I sat up, feeling a seepage of water on my shirt.

◇ ◇ ◇

I started walking. I stored my backpack up inside a rotted palm—"Old Merv," I called it—freeing me up to go anywhere. Coral Gables, Westwood Lakes, Medley, Aladdin City, Cutler Ridge, Coconut Grove—I walked through half the towns of the county, over dams and drainage ditches, past service stations trembling with orange strips of neon, jogging, then running, then jogging again. A chevron of sweat dripped through my shirt. A white ecstatic granule vibrated inside my head, and I wanted to aim myself into that place, to break through its crust and explode it, to *be* that—that calmness and void, that place without movement.

I walked down a street on which most of the houses had been totaled by the hurricane. Roofs pulled from their joists, stucco stripped, fancy furniture still floating in the pools. There was something incongruous about the wreckage, for the worst damage had been centered ten miles south, in Homestead, Naranja. This region had escaped the fiercest sustained winds, but thunderstorms had spawned tornadoes here, imploding the houses as if they were toys, only to leave the next block unscathed.

Up ahead, something called to me. Soon enough, I was walking toward the house of Douglass Freeman. Dickless, who'd moved to California years ago.

No matter how many others had lived here after his departure, it was still his house to me. In some inexplicable way its walls contained his very spirit, his bafflement, despair, and slanted curiosity. I stared upward at the roof beams, sheared from their trusses by the winds. The house was hopeless. The most recent owners, gone for good now, had spray painted the garage door with harsh jagged letters: ANDREW, GO HOME. Then beneath that: ALLSTATE DOESN'T DELIVER and their policy number.

I stepped up the driveway. The street was empty now, a ghost town of ruptured houses. No one was watching. The front door opened as if its former occupants had been expecting me.

It was worse than I'd imagined. Insulation sagged; walls buckled under the displaced roof. Mildewy curtains flapped on a rod above the open back wall. Beyond that, the pool cage. It lay twisted in a particularly crude fashion. I studied the family portrait above the mantel in which a father, a mother, and two little boys—all with bottle-thick glasses—were trying desperately to enjoy themselves, to show the photographer—a dense, falsely enthusiastic teenager, I decided—they were a well-adjusted family. They'd left everything here, throwing up their hands. I rifled through a desk to find something with their names. I found a short stack of wet envelopes—tithing envelopes for St. Michael's Parish. Mr. and Mrs. Joseph Carson.

I sat upon a ruined pit sofa. A dome light lay perilously on its side. For a few seconds I imagined the Carsons in the contented period before the storm, milling about the rooms, carrying presents to each other at Christmas, the particular smell of this family together—fabric softener, reheated turkey, tube socks, carpet freshener—still wafting through the house. But overlaid were my thoughts of Douglass Freeman. I pictured him sitting in one of the chairs in the dining room, his arms folded over his chest, shoulders hunched, trying not to contort his face as he told his parents he wouldn't ever, ever go back to Gus Grissom.

"We'll see what we can do," Mrs. Freeman said, glancing over at her husband. He sat opposite from them, an older version of his son, slouching forward, thinking.

I walked the halls. I chose the back bedroom, a tiny cubicle in which a Spirograph box with faded, soft corners lay on the bureau. There was no question, I felt him here. And soon enough my premonitions were confirmed. I saw his name, and beneath that a date—7/9/73—etched above the light switch in red pencil.

I lay on Douglass's bed, closing my eyes, drifting. He was out there somewhere, but I was falling asleep, and the world outside was shifting, slipping away, too fast for me to hold onto it.

◇ ◇ ◇

I was down to zero, zilch. No job, no car, not even a credit card for emergency's sake. I used to think that I was safe from bad fortune, that personal catastrophe was ultimately self-willed, that we all have the power to make our own luck. But that's bullshit.

I plodded up Dixie Highway beside the buzzing transformers. I might have been Peter years before. Peter, who'd landed the greatest *drop dead* on my parents' threshold by leaving the house without warning one day. Ever since, he'd been only two things to me: a torn postcard from Beach Haven, New Jersey—

I'm happy, but you're not—and a vague standard of disaffection and disillusionment against which I measured myself.

Now he was where I was going.

I'd finally allowed myself to call him. "So, could I stay with you for a while?" I'd said.

My tongue tasted hot, grassy in my mouth. The tip of a palm frond squeaked against the phone booth. I'd just watched an older man—formal, crisply dressed—holding out a cupped, tentative hand to passersby at the Coconut Grove Metrorail. He looked like he'd never fallen this low, all his dignity coming down around him like rags.

"How long?" Peter said after a silence.

My throat went dry. "If it's a problem, I understand."

"No, no. I'm just surprised."

"Well, I've been thinking about you."

"You have?"

"A lot, actually."

A siren wailed somewhere in the distance. Wind rattled the seagrapes, foam cups blowing across the street. "Did Mom put you up to this?" he said warily.

"Are you kidding?"

"Well—"

"Daddy doesn't even want me at home anymore."

His voice thawed, relaxed, as if we'd gone crabbing together that morning. I tried to block out my last picture of him: crying, high, after my father had discovered the bag of bright pink pills in his room. The ground might have heaved beneath my feet. His voice went on and on. And all at once I heard him say yes.

"So I'll pick you up in Fort Myers?" he said. "You'll take the bus?"

"Right," I answered. "I'll call tomorrow."

I walked up Jane's sidewalk now, pressing on the bell. The doleful notes of an oboe drifted out over the roofs of the neighborhood. The door opened, and she stood there in lycra shorts and black T-shirt, cradling her instrument in her hands. Her hair was brighter, the color of cranberries.

She troubled her chin with her fingertips. "You look awful."

"Thanks a lot."

"You were in a fight?"

"No."

"Why is your hair such a mess?"

"I walked out on William."

"You *what?*"

I nodded once, twice. "You'd look like this, too, if you'd spent your last two nights outside."

"You what? Oh God. Come in here. Come in here and sit down."

We sat upon her parents' couch beneath the harlequin pictures. I talked for a good half hour. I told her about the breakup of the relationship, filling her in on the grittiest details as she listened attentively with the gravest expression. She fidgeted with her bracelets on her wrists.

"That's awful," she said.

"I know."

"I had a feeling something was up."

My head hurt. I leaned over, massaging my eyebrows, making circular motions with my thumbs. For some reason, I couldn't say another word. "And what about you?"

It turned out that she'd started oboe lessons again. She'd found a stern, demanding teacher, a retired player from the St. Louis Symphony, who was pushing her, excited about her potential. Even though she'd put off college for the year, she felt ready now. In only a few short weeks, she was auditioning for Juilliard, Eastman, and New England Conservatory.

Then, to our mutual discomfort, she'd run out of things to say. Inside the kitchen, Mrs. Ettengoff was tossing avocados inside a food processor.

"I just came to say good-bye," I said after a silence.

"What do you mean?"

"I might not see you for a long time," I explained.

"Like I'm not going to see you again," she said with a throaty, abrasive laugh. Had she been smoking again? "Naples is only two hours away, for God's sake."

"I'm not kidding, Jane," I said quietly.

She saw the seriousness on my face. She turned toward the kitchen and left for a moment without excusing herself. The dense smell of yeast hovered about the rooms. Over the whir of the food processor she and her mother carried on a conversation.

"Do you have enough money?" she said upon her return.

"Of course." I nodded twice, though she knew me well enough. My forehead felt tight, sunburnt. I hadn't been drinking enough water.

"My mom says you're welcome for dinner."

I shook my head from side to side. "I have to go."

"You'll call if you're in trouble?"

"Of course I will."

"Take care."

"*You* take care," I said, laughing now. "And good luck with those auditions."

We stood, holding onto each other by the front door. Her right hand wandered down my back. I tensed slightly, resisting the warmth of her touch as she slipped something—two fifties and a ten, I found out later—into my pants pocket.

◇ ◇ ◇

Before I left for Peter's, I needed to do something.

I waited until I knew he was at work. More than anything I didn't want to see him. I knew he'd be livid; I imagined the thick cords of his fingers tightening around my throat. It was one thing that I'd departed without a note or good-bye when I was still living with my parents. It was quite another that I'd done it after living in his house for months, when I theoretically knew better. Perhaps I was too hard on myself. I didn't owe him my future if he wasn't willing to work for it. But I at least owed him an explanation, some acknowledgment of the fact that something important had transpired between us. I wasn't a kid anymore. My decisions mattered, had consequences, and I carried within me the lulling, intoxicating power to hurt another human being.

But right now I was thinking about my notebook. It was

the one physical thing that I needed in the world. It was the repository of so much—addresses, quotes, phone numbers, clippings, lists, equations, names of books, fractured diary entries, even doodlings—things so important to me that I felt unwhole without it. Leaving it behind had been nothing more than an indication of my fissured mental state. Not a page of it was blank, but I still managed to scrawl things inside, as if I inherently believed in its possibility to always yield some space to me. In its details one could piece together the narrative of my life, and I couldn't leave it with him no matter how many times I'd said: *Just let it go.*

His car was gone. I stepped over the driveway's expansion joints, glancing over the anise hedge to see if Virginia, the neighbor with the beautiful begonias, was watching. She wasn't. I made it to the mud-room door, fumbling over the door frame for the key, but what was this? No key. The spare, the ever-reliable duplicate, wasn't here. My eyelids burned. I read it as nothing more than a statement to me: *You're not welcome here. You've disappointed me. Fuck you. Keep out of my house.*

I might have broken the windows, each and every one of them. Instead, I sat on the slab and pressed the heels of my palms into my eyes. *Calm, calm,* I said. *Calm yourself down.* After a few minutes I remembered the loose window over the bathtub, and before long I was crawling inside, headfirst, my ass hanging over the sill for all of Avenida Manati to see.

I walked swiftly through the cool rooms, my bare feet *shushing* the white terrazzo. Absolutely nothing had changed. The rattan lamp, the stacks of newspapers, the framed Toulouse-Lautrecs—every one of them assumed the same coordinates they always had. Even the dogs, Pedro and Mrs. Fox, hadn't barked upon my intrusion, only glancing at me in utter ennui before retreating to their respective beds as if I were still the resident boy.

Given what he'd put me through, I decided it was my right to enjoy some air-conditioned comfort and a good hot shower before conducting my business. I still had two hours. At that moment he was most likely seated behind the camera, squinting into the lens with his astigmatic eye while the technicians cued up the theme music for the Florida Noon Report with Sally Reedy. First, though, I needed to eat.

I breathed in the chill of the open refrigerator. Sun-dried tomatoes, yogurt, pears, and raspberries—I had it in me to eat them all with my fingers, swallowing without benefit of spoon or fork before opting for the civilized. I hadn't realized how hungry I was. And I hadn't realized how fortunate I'd been. The life I'd once taken for granted now seemed decadent and lush, a golden treasure inside a chest. But should I have stayed here? I already knew the answer to that.

I sat on the Chesterfield. Without thinking I aimed the remote at the TV, only to discover that the Channel 7 News was already in full swing, seventeen minutes into the broadcast. I couldn't not watch, if only to satisfy some morbid curiosity.

Sally Reedy blathered on about the development of a tropical storm sixty miles southwest of Great Abaco. Sally's face betrayed a curious combination of motherly concern, wry sex, and grace. The idea was to convince the viewer that the set was a purely jovial exercise, that the staff was comprised of good pals who met five days a week for the sheer fun of it. Off camera Sally could be distant to the point of downright cold, though rumor had it that she was suffering terribly, that her gynecologist husband was about to be arraigned for the alleged rape of four of his patients, that once this broke on her own broadcast, Sally's celebrity (and credibility) would forever be dimmed.

It was perplexing to think that such gossip was no longer a part of my life. I prepared myself to switch off the TV when an auxiliary camera panned the behind-the-scenes staffers, and in an utter affectation of highjinks, they mugged in feigned horror at the prospect of the developing tropical system.

William's face flashed briefly before the screen.

He looked fit, trim, the hair on the sides of his head just a little too long.

He sickened me. It was strange to have spent so much time with somebody, only to find that with each passing week I knew him less and less, instead of what one would have expected. It certainly hadn't started like this. After I'd first moved in with him, we were still careful to wear our best faces, to grant tolerance and respect for each other's tics and idiosyncrasies. Occasionally I saw that darker knowledge passing over William's eyes: *Who are you? What are you doing in my life? I didn't ask for you. I only want to be myself in the world.* I'd walk into the woods behind the house, picking up stones, bottles, Coke cans, throwing them as high as I could into the dull blue of the sky until my wrist snapped, until my joints ached. How could you have done this? I loved you, you jerk. I've given up everything I had—my family, for God's sake—for you. You owe me much more than this. But I'd walk back to the house, tasting disappointment like weeds in my mouth, knowing I wasn't the easiest person to live with, that two people could still love each other and not be able to forge a life.

Why did this seem to be one of the most difficult things to learn?

I turned off the TV. I walked to the bedroom and found my notebook in the night-table drawer. I drank in a breath and looked once about the room. I concentrated on its details, its rugs and books, its curtains and bedspread, taking a mental photograph. Then just as I was leaving, I spotted William's flannel shirt, with its intricate plaids of tan, yellow, and forest green. I raised it to my face and breathed, naming in detail what I smelled: its resinous cotton, its suggestion of sweat once his Right Guard gave out, its piquant smoky odor, like pine, or roasted cypress chips.

I pushed my arms into its sleeves, vaguely comforted by its possibilities. The shirt would come to good use. I was going on a trip. It was chilly at night on the other side of the state, with temperatures expected to dip into the upper fifties.

Chapter 12

Immediately I picked out my brother from the small crowd at the bus station. My heart shuddered. My toes curled inside my sneakers. His oblong forehead, his benign dolphiny smile, those long-lashed, yet lusterless eyes—all these features suggested that he was a younger, better-looking version of Sid, with more hair and less baggage in the stomach region.

We hugged each other at the curbside. He was bigger than I remembered, his body softer, wider, warmer. He smelled of deodorant, chewing gum. There were little creases around his mouth. We started laughing. He took my bag from me, then led me to a van parked beneath some nutrient-starved palms. He dressed exactly as I'd expected: khakis, chambray shirt, wire-rimmed aviators—practically the same uniform he'd always worn.

We stood at the back of the van. On its pitted bumper were two stickers: a radio station's call letters in the shape of a guitar, and a purple sticker with chipped edges: PRACTICE RANDOM ACTS OF KINDNESS AND SENSELESS BEAUTY.

He grinned at me. "I can't believe you're here."

"It's kind of weird."

He blinked rapidly for a second, then calmed himself. He really did look a lot like our father.

"I mean, a good weird. Who'd've imagined this a few days ago?"

"I know," he said, clapping me on the shoulder. "I didn't think I'd ever see you again."

We slouched in the bucket seats. I stared through the fly specks on the windshield. I pressed the back of my scalp into the headrest, my bare legs sticking to the cool, damp leather. My head felt blasted. Throughout the bus ride, I'd churned with worry. I sat for hours and hours, staring at the truck farms and phosphate mines, digging for opening lines, most of which were of a highly adult nature, engineered to generate conversation. Meanwhile, the driver shouted out the names of each stop: Moore Haven, Port LaBelle, Lehigh Acres. Well, maybe we didn't have anything to say to each other, but that seemed to be all right. He wasn't making an issue of it.

The landscape shimmered and prismed in the sunlight. All around us vast stands of slash pine and swampland were knocked down and filled for new construction. Billboards everywhere announced splashy white houses on cul-de-sacs— The Pinnacle, The Brightness, Indigo Lakes, Pineapple Lakes— all of which ruptured the virgin terrain. Businesses serving the dwindling rural population foundered on the roadsides, their days already numbered: Beverage Barn, The Shellpile. A Christian campground: Don and Veda Shea's Hallelujahland. It might have been the Gold Coast thirty years before. Florida, place of our birth, chewed up its marshes, sucked its aquifers dry until there was nothing left but a parched bed of limestone. Already it was a busted balloon, a bloated appendage at the end of the United States, a veritable Toledo, Ohio, with palms. A vessel of people's myths, its image had nothing to do with its essential character—the turpentine state. Once that realization was assimilated on a wider level, the cities themselves would wither and burn, and the people would forsake them, moving on to ruin someplace else.

Still, I loved it more than any other place. Florida, oh Florida. Embodiment of wrecked dreams.

I couldn't believe I was sitting next to my brother.

We sped down the Tamiami Trail in silence. He slowed. We passed a fence, a row of broken gaslights, turned right, signal ticking, at a stucco wall with missing letters. KIN CO E. The place looked deadened, vacant. Peter parked in a back alley. He stopped, got out of the car. He led me up a flight of open stairs before walking me down several long, long halls. I couldn't take it all in. My sinuses filled, pounded, a stuffed duffel bag in the center of my head.

The place needed some work. The hall carpets, a dull turquoise, carried a complex union of scents: smoke, mildew, spilled fluids. Cracks spidered the length of the pink stucco walls as if the building were gently insisting upon the presence of the former mangrove swamp beneath it.

Peter worked a key into a lock, then flipped on a switch. The room was about as big as the old space William had offered me in his den. A skyscraper collapsed inside me. I forced a look of gratitude in my eyes.

"Well, what do you think?"

"Great," I said too loudly.

He lifted his brows, then clenched them. "Do you want to take a shower? Would you like some towels?"

I slapped my back pocket for the whereabouts of my wallet, a paranoid gesture for which I was famous. Once I felt it, I dropped down upon the bed. "No, thank you. Do you mind if I just sit here for a while? I need to be still."

"You're hungry, I guess."

I wasn't. I bit into my lip, harder than I thought, until my eyetooth pierced the skin. I winced. He sat down upon the armchair across from me, then tilted his head. His eyes glowed behind his glasses. I ran my tongue back and forth across the puncture, my mouth tasting of zinc.

"Are you sure this is all right?"

"You're so nice to do this." I looked carefully at the room for the very first time, its wood floors, its perfect rows of laminated

Lawnboy

shelves. I leaned backward, propping my weight with my elbows. I pulled up my feet on the bed. "You did all this work yourself?"

He nodded, then told me how he'd gone about remodeling the room, an intricate, laborious process. About two minutes into the tale, I began picking out random words, phrases. I breathed deeply through my mouth, holding it, telling myself *deep, deep, deep, deep,* until my heart slowed, until my nostrils opened up, my face relaxing. I could smile again. My cheeks felt hot. For all he knew, nothing was happening inside my head.

Silence. Then footsteps down the hall. I drew my arms tighter to my ribs. "Who's that?" I said.

A man in a white T-shirt, cutoffs, and combat boots appeared in the doorway. "Well, look who it is," he said with a sly, gritty whisper.

Abruptly, my brother stood, almost losing his balance.

The man offered me a dark, veined hand with oddly thick fingers. "Hector Ybarra."

"I'm Evan," I faltered.

A pinch in my back, a chill. We held each other's gaze longer than was exactly comfortable. There was something about his voice: arrogance, authority. A certain "fuck-you" quality. Yet his eyes hazed with a funny, self-deprecating glint. I stared at the exquisite curve of his deep pink lips, their fullness, his dark, nearly black skin. Was my brother watching? My throat tightened, then burned. *Shit.*

His T-shirt was imprinted with the logo STAR BOY IN FLAMES.

"Hector's my assistant," Peter said. "You'll be working with him, so you better get used to his jokes."

I couldn't lift my head. "Oh really?"

"Yes, really," Hector mimicked.

"Are you done for the day?" Peter asked, creasing his forehead.

"More or less," mumbled Hector.

Peter turned to me. "You have no idea how much we need you right now. Things're a mess."

"How come?" I said.

"All our staff just quit."

"Oh boy," I said. And all at once I knew we were sunk.

"Well, the RoadStar lured them all away. People who'd been here for five years. Bigger money, day care, benefits . . . I mean, I wouldn't say no if I were in their shoes."

I tried to look at Hector but couldn't. Why was he staring at me like that? His gaze felt fraught, heavy on my head like a hand.

"And of course the worst situation happens when we're least equipped to deal with it. A bus full of senior citizens, get this, thirty widows, breaks down by the bridge and they're all tearful and shrill. We're filled up, but it's not good. They want extra towels and hot coffee, and before we know it, they've broken both ice machines and practically blown out the switchboard by calling home to Bountiful so many times. By the time they left we actually put a NO VACANCY sign in the office window and slept for two days straight. I didn't even get up to drink or pee."

My brother's eyes went glassy. He clearly enjoyed talking about the struggle as it were a soccer game. He was more like my father than he knew.

"So is this what I'm supposed to expect?" I said.

"Not all the time. But I just wanted to let you know. You never know what could happen." He grinned again, revealing a darkened eyetooth. Root canal.

"Welcome to Planet Hell," said Hector.

"Hey—" said Peter.

"God's Little Acre, God's Little Asshole—"

"Now *stop*," Peter chortled. Forced, I thought. Nervous.

Hector shrugged his left shoulder. He blew out some air through his lips. "It's good to meet you," he said with a smile. He squinted a bit, raising his chin, showing off the squarish nugget of his Adam's apple. "Welcome, my friend. You're in for a big adventure."

He left. Some residue was suspended in the air, an explosion of sorts, a storm of fine particles. Ten seconds later, I still felt his presence in the room.

Peter stood. "So if you need anything, don't be afraid to let me know. I'll be just down the hall."

"Sure." I reached down to unlace my hightops. "Peter?"

"Yeah?"

"I really appreciate this. Thank you for being my brother."

"I'm glad you're here," he answered. "We're going to get a lot accomplished."

Accomplished, I thought. I lay down on the floor as Peter left the room. My pulse started racing, but the worst part was over. Anything might have happened. He could have mouthed off about me. I could have mouthed off about him. It was all so civil and pleasant and sweet. Listening to them knocking about the floor below me, I had a very distinct impression that it was going to be all right, and even if this weren't true, there was Hector, whose very presence reminded me that I wasn't alone.

◇ ◇ ◇

Once, I couldn't stop looking at him. I loved nothing more than the bristles on his face, the depth of his voice. I crouched in the upstairs hallway where I knew he couldn't see me, peering through a crack in the door. He stepped out of the shower stall, his wet hair splayed across his scalp. A pang in my gut. A smell—stale ice? iron?—wafted through the room. In truth, he was the first boy I'd ever fallen in love with. (His dusky eyes, his shoulders.) I think he must have known this on some level, for soon he was pulling back from me, detaching himself from the family, entrenched in his daydreams and silences.

I'd wanted to be him. I'd wanted to be him more than my-self, though I didn't admit it. I kept my hair the same scrappy length, combing it across the cowlick whether it stuck there or not. I wore the same painter's cap, the same chambray shirts, the same wire-rimmed glasses, though my eyes were near perfect. I copied the arcs and slants of his penmanship; I imitated the hard supple bounce of his stride. Once I even practiced talking like him, opening up my vowels, digging my teeth into the consonants as if I'd been the progeny of some speech therapist and not the second son of Sid and Ursula Sarshik, born July 12th, 1973, on the burnt fairway of an abandoned golf course, somewhere south of Coral Gables.

A stormy August morning. Peter exits the downstairs bedroom and I plant myself before the mirror, holding his damp towel to my face, breathing in his rich, fluvial smell. I reach for his shaving cream, then lather my jaw, imagining it hatched with stubble. I stop, thunderstruck. I start spraying my nose, brows, forehead, ears. Warpaint, a mask. And—*boom*—it happens: my legs grow lush with hair, my muscles rumble, my penis thickens like a chain. I can knock down buildings with my voice, I can soar past rockets in the firmament. I close my eyes and take myself deeper. I am wise, responsible, brilliant, and funny. I can make you laugh. I can speak long fluid thoughts before television cameras, in the pool of burning light, without stuttering or unease. I know things. I tell you the square root of 1,738, all 8 names of Saturn's moons, the total air mileage between Jakarta and Buenos Aires and Las Vegas. Even when I trip or fuck up or do something patently wrong, you smile and think I am charming.

When I opened my eyes I was only myself again.

Then I became him: our roles shifted. I started doing well in school. I loved hunkering down in my quiet corner of the library, devoting my attention to my work while things fell apart at home. If I was good enough, smart enough, I could bring my parents—the whole lot of us—back together. They were talking again. A start, at least. Science-fair ribbons, perfect report cards.

"Evan," Ursula said one day. "All A's. This is amazing, terrific."

I stood before her in the kitchen, satisfaction beating in my face. Peter walked past us, winded, in his green nylon shorts.

"Did you see this?" Ursula said to him.

"Who ate the Oreos?" He hunted through the pantry shelves.

"Peter. Your brother just came home with all A's. Aren't you excited for him?"

"Great," he said dully, then lurched out of the room.

Something changed after that. A quiet tension hummed between us. Once, pretending I was asleep, I heard him come into my sunshot room. Midday, the hour after lunch. Our parents were at the store. He stood beside my bed, twirling the mobile above my head with his fingertips. He spun it so fast that I was afraid it would fall down, crashing on my forehead. Would he kill me? Cooling shadows swept across my face. I loved the fact that he wouldn't leave, spinning the thing until he expected me to give in to him. Still, I refused to open my eyes.

I chalked up good grade after good grade. I was the only one Sid and Ursula ever talked about. I felt fat with their pride, unbearably rich, as if I'd consumed an entire loaf of pound cake. They made no secrets of their love or their favor. But there was my older brother, who was cutting classes now, stumbling around the house with the harsh glare of speed in his eyes.

We started swimming. We swam every day, in the moments before twilight, at the house of his friend Javier Rodriguez, whose parents had the largest pool on Avenida Bayamo. Each of us had our respective routines, but our last five minutes together always culminated in a race that involved swimming ten laps. It goes without saying that he always lurched ahead of me at the finish. I didn't care. He was the natural athlete between us—the older, the stronger. But this day, when the air smelled curiously of clematis, datura, and burning charcoal, when it seemed all but apparent that I'd be the victor, Peter hefted himself out of the water mere seconds before my forehead slapped the tile.

"Winner!" I cried, gulping air.

He sat on the edge of the pool. In his boredom, he inspected a cut on the ball of his foot.

"What are you doing?"

"I hurt my foot." He dangled his leg in the water, watching the trails of broken blood turning rusty in the chlorine.

"You mean you couldn't wait five seconds?"

He stood, then dropped his Speedo to the concrete. I tightened inside. I looked away. He routinely did such things in my presence, trying to provoke me. "I'm taking a shower."

"You did that on purpose," I said, and slapped at the water.

"What?"

"You did that on purpose. You didn't want to finish because you knew I'd win. I scare you."

"You scare me all right." He hobbled to the outdoor shower enclosure. His blood left stains on the bleached concrete like drops of rosehip tea. "You have a complex."

I didn't have a complex. All I know was that we stopped swimming together from that day forth.

Chapter 13

The following morning, after I'd unpacked and settled in, I got the tour of the 55-acre King Cole property. Peter's manner was formal, almost distant, as he led me around. Had he gotten enough sleep? His voice was hoarse and whispery as if he'd stayed up all night.

It was hard to stay cheerful. My face felt tired from smiling too much. The place was a pit. Not only was it a good thirty miles from Naples, but it was situated in a battered glade with such a high water table that it needed a sump pump to keep the parking lot dry. Still, the place practically shimmered with its history. Here's the story: in 1964, Clem Thornton, the big Florida developer, platted a city called Boca Palms on the surrounding land. Two years into the project, the whole thing was halted, after several of the buyers—senior citizens from Massachusetts, laborers from Detroit—learned that their lots were under six inches of water. But who could have blamed them for buying? They got a free trip out of it, after all. Flown to Miami, they were bused across the Everglades by a cheery driver who called them by their first names. Upon arrival,

though, things heated up. The pitch took place in the conference room, a spiel laced with threat, guilt, and the possibility of wealth. Salesmen (undercover, of course) cried out for
the lots, creating the illusion of demand. It goes without saying that 75 percent of the detainees bought property out of
fear and confusion, not even balking when they were told they
couldn't tour the place beyond the fenced-in resort.

We walked farther. Peter's face was drawn, a little chapped,
fixed upon the ground, as he pointed out the various wings of
the building—Solar, Nurmi, Seven Isles, Bontona—all named
after the fanciest lagoon streets in Fort Lauderdale, where
Clem Thornton had spent his halcyon years before landing in
jail. Peter kept chatting up the property, promising improve-
ments, but I couldn't help noticing its inadequacies: the cracked
parking lot, the sudsy pool with its algae-coated walls. Past
the deserted golf course and the landlocked marina were a set
of burnt-out buildings. They hulked there with their charred
walls and broken windows, separated from the nicer part with
a makeshift wall.

Fortunately, none of this was visible from the highway. On
balmy winter nights, it still looked nice enough to lure that
certain kind of guest, retirees on their way to the Gold Coast,
charmed by the jungly landscaping, the golden gas lanterns,
the curved driveway leading to the on-site mineral spring—all
the symbols of a more innocent, unfettered era. I couldn't help
but feel both affection and pity for it.

After the tour I was put directly to work. Immediately I was
shown the correct way to answer the phone, a veritable mouth-
ful: "Good Morning, King Cole. It's 82 degrees and sunny.
This is Evan speaking. How may I help you?" I was told how
to log reservations in the black book, how to run applications
and utilities on the computer, how to process traveler's checks,
how to swipe a credit card through the ZON. I was told how to
smile. I was told to look all prospective guests directly in the
eye—"not intrusively, but gently. They're friends, after all."
Once I passed Desk Duty with flying colors, I moved on to
Housekeeping 101, a post I was assigned to for the remaining

three days of the week. I was shown how to make beds, how to fold bath towels, how to tuck in the sheets to make crisp hospital corners. I was shown how to Windex mirrors and windows. I was shown how to wrap glasses, how to apply the sanitary paper strip to the toilet seat. I was shown how to run the mighty washers of the laundry room, how much bleach, Sta-Puff, and soap to use, with severe instructions not to over-burden the delicate, malfunctioning septic system.

It all seemed a bit much, especially since I'd never had a real job, unless you could count the two traumatic days I spent working at Dairy Queen when I was sixteen. Not to mention the fact that nothing was said about any days off. But the truth was that none of these tasks took a Ph.D. I imagined complet-ing my duties early every afternoon, spending the rest of the day reading, swimming, or landscaping, my raw hands work-ing the loam.

That night the three of us ate in the northwest corner of the banquet hall, the huge 60 × 20 ft. room in which the Boca Palms sales staff had unloaded thousands upon thousands of underwater lots 25 years before. Our voices echoed off the walls. Beyond the closed curtains was the golf course, its waist-high weeds shrouding its once-molded fairways.

My favorite childhood foods had been lovingly prepared by Peter: corn on the cob, hamburgers, sliced tomatoes, water-melon. I pointed my fork to the chain of leaping blue marlins on the outer wall.

"What was this about?" I asked. "The Clem Thornton fish-ing tournament? All-expense-paid trip to the Riviera?"

I hadn't even noticed that Peter had stepped out of the room. I glanced up at Hector, his sleeveless T-shirt, the vaccination print on his upper arm. I jiggled my foot, slumping my shoul-ders until my chest caved in. Did he enjoy my shyness, my fool-ishness? I had the unsettling sense that he knew what I was thinking, that all my thoughts were broadcasting from some golden transmitter planted inside my brain.

"You have the same speech patterns," he said blankly.

"What?"

"You and Peter. You both have the same speech patterns.

It's funny, I've never heard it in anybody else. The way you cluster your words."

"Really?" I said.

He nodded.

I nodded back, but I didn't quite agree with him, and for the first time, I noted an odd, lilting turn, an accent of sorts, in his own speech.

◇ ◇ ◇

Could fifteen years have passed since I almost did myself in for him?

Peter and I slipped past a security guard, scampering out onto the roof of Miami Beach's Shelborne Hotel. Sid and Ursula were dressed to the nines, oblivious of our whereabouts, still smoking Lucky Strikes in the restaurant twenty-some floors beneath us. We laughed at their ignorance. The sun beat the strength from our backs. I walked to the side, poised myself on the ledge, breathing, vertiginous. We gazed out over Miami, its deep aqua water, the patterned beach umbrellas like hard Venetian candies.

Peter stepped beside me. "Would you jump for me?" he whispered in my ear.

He stood to my left, his hand firmly weighted on the small of my back.

"Would you? Would you jump?"

I sat down on the ledge. I began easing my butt over the side, watching my legs, as if they were someone else's legs, flailing in the air. Already I pictured the people watching on the street. I saw the rescue-squad truck, heard the megaphone, saw the young mother covering her mouth with her palms. I would put on a show for them, but I would flourish, thrive.

"Don't. I didn't mean that. We better go."

I didn't say anything back to him. But he had his answer, and his face reflected that, though it was shadowed and unassuming.

◇ ◇ ◇

Something soon became clear to me. Our guests were so few and far between that working the front desk became downright tedious after a few hours, and once I finished my book (*The Life and Trials of Angie Dickinson,* a paperback that I'd retrieved from the library), I found myself staring at the phone, willing it to ring. I talked for a while to a lady from Scotch Plains, New Jersey, who wanted to know what particular measures we took to keep the local mosquito population under control. Once she seemed dissatisfied with my fabrication, I hung up on her, then gazed at the brass arms of the starburst clock. Ten-forty-five. I stepped to the front window, hands pushing deep in my pockets, staring out at that hot mossy swamp of a pool, where a girl in an orange life jacket snorkeled within sight of her father. My breath fogged an oval on the glass. I transmitted a mental message to the girl: *Don't put your head under that water. You might as well be swimming in liquefied lead.*

I had to set some projects for myself or I'd go nuts.

After Peter dismissed me from my duties, I wandered through the halls for a while, admiring of and appalled by the vastness of the place, its tributes to ball-breaking work, its misguided faith in a corrupt future. There was something especially deathly, yet beautiful, about this kind of silence in the middle of the day, when it seemed all but natural that everything should be revving in highest gear. At the RoadStar Inn ten miles down the Trail, I imagined just the opposite—soda machines knocking, ice machines humming, teenagers gossiping by the pool, people driving back from the Gulf beaches, the sand still hot inside their sneakers.

There was no way Peter wasn't losing tens of thousands of dollars per week.

I returned to the confines of my little room. I couldn't have been lying on my bed more than ten seconds when someone started rapping on the door. I sat up at once.

Hector said, "Are you busy?"

I rubbed some grit from my eye. "No, I was just taking a rest."

"I have to drive to Cape Coral, bank stuff. Want to come?"

"I don't know. Maybe I'll just stay here. I'm kind of tired actually."

"Oh come on. It'll do you good to get out."

His face was lively, yet glum, as if he'd wanted to be any-place else in the world. He was again wearing cutoffs and 18-hole workboots, a look which, though essentially ludicrous, es-pecially worked for him, calling attention to a pair of the most alarming and voluptuous calves I'd ever seen. I saturated myself with the most deadening facts imaginable: the latest NASDAQ average, the current price of gold, the winners of the American League pennant. Anything to distract myself. I wouldn't look at him. Too long, at least. It would be a mark of my growing up: I didn't have to see every attractive man as a potential sex slave.

"You sure you want to do this?" he said, stopping midway down the hall. He grinned demonically.

"Why not," I said, and shrugged.

Outside, Peter stood with a big-bellied workman, choosing sites for a well out near the old golf course. Complaints about the water quality had risen. Only recently the guests had caught onto something as if it were part of some national trend, blam-ing the water for a whole host of ills, from stomach flu to night sweats to yellowed dentures. One woman had even insisted upon showing us the crystallized salt upon her liver-spotted wrists, as if it were an emblem of our inherent disregard and in-competency. "What if somebody sues you?" she'd said merrily. Peter glanced up at us and sighed, then waved us on, as if he were sorry he couldn't join us.

We were speeding through the glossy subdivisions on Rattle-snake Hammock Road, a former country lane converted to a four-lane parkway. Blue tile roofs sparkled behind walled yards. Stopped at a traffic light, Hector turned to me and said, "So tell me all about William."

"What?"

"Your old boyfriend, William."

"You're kidding."

He wagged his head. "Word has it that you've been around the block once or twice."

My chest tightened. I might have been pushed facedown into cement. "Who told you about William?"

The left half of his face smiled. He shrugged smugly as if to indicate he wasn't telling me.

The blood hummed between my shoulder blades. I felt a peculiar combination of vulnerable, betrayed, destabilized, and pissed off. I didn't think he was at all funny. Was it that the mere mention of William's name still managed to trigger a whole host of feelings when I wasn't prepared for it? Or was it that I thought my privacy had been walked on, disregarded? It was one thing that Peter knew about William; it was quite another if his business partner knew the details of my personal life. I thought about packing my bags, handing over my money to the ticket clerk, taking the last bus back to Miami.

"God, are you burning up. I didn't mean to upset you."

"No," I mumbled, as if talking to myself. "I'm sure you didn't."

"What?"

I turned to face him with a mocking, fabricated smile. "Do you always like to make fun of people you don't even know?"

His eyes widened a bit. "I said I didn't mean anything."

"Just forget it," I said testily.

He mumbled, "Drama queen."

It would have been too easy to dismiss him at that point, for I had every right to. But he wasn't worth it. Instead, I made a pact with myself: I wouldn't trust him. I could learn to work with him, I imagined, even like him to some degree, but I'd never fully trust him. He was too much about himself. I thought of a ten-year-old splashing around in a puddle, throwing cinders, doing anything to get a rise out of passersby. I should have listened to my gut. It would have been better had I not gone alone with him.

And what about my brother's role in all this?

A silence took over the van. I loaded a tape into the stereo, and Laura Nyro's "Timer" made its first fumblings toward coherence.

"Frankly, I'm over him, if you want to know the truth," I

said after the song had finished. "I don't even think about him all that much anymore."

"Well, you still seem pretty upset."

"Well, you seem to have pretty bad instincts. Everything's fine, okay? I'm not the least bit upset."

We kept driving. Something clattered and buzzed inside my head. He seemed to be one of those people who respected you more once you flexed your grip and stood up for yourself. It didn't make it any easier, though. Was I already fucking things up for myself? We passed a two-story green dinosaur outside a mechanic's garage, which prompted me to glance over at him. I expected to see that arrogance again taking hold of his face, but there was something more complicated there, a look that told me that he knew it too—an emptiness, the loss of something nameless yet profound. I thought about my earlier assertion that it was unreasonable to have sex with every single person whom I thought was attractive. And then I reconsidered it. His arms were chiseled and bronze. His head was shaved. His eyes shimmered with an irradiated, wilting light. And then I changed my mind again.

It turned out that Ursula, mistaking Hector for Peter, had many months ago called the King Cole desk in a minor fit to inform him that a neighbor, a Mrs. Diane Petrancouri of Avenida Bayamo, had spotted me standing naked with William in the window. Too immersed in the story not to reveal his true identity, Hector listened to my mother's words with a keen interest, her fear that the neighbors were talking, her realization only minutes before that I was actually involved in a "full-fledged imbroglio." She was beside herself with frenzy and grief. It wasn't until a full three minutes had passed that she'd realized she wasn't talking to my brother, but to someone with a Cuban accent, whereupon she promptly hung up the phone.

"God, she was a trip," he said.

My face burned hot with shame. Still, I was compelled to know more. "Is that all?"

"Well, it was too much to take in all at once, though she said something about—yeah, this was my favorite"—he began mimicking my mother with disturbing accuracy—"This kid was accepted to *Princeton* for Christ's sake."

He started shaking his head. "And I thought *my* mother was a lunatic."

"Oh God." My stomach was a nervous pit. I laughed hysterically, exaggeratedly, somewhere between dread and relief.

As if to make up for his earlier misstep, Hector started telling me about himself, an activity with which he seemed well acquainted. Apparently before he'd moved back to Florida—he'd grown up off Hialeah's Red Road, within earshot of the racetrack—he'd lived in the East Village for ten years, where he'd waited tables at various restaurants, sold clear plastic clubwear at Patricia Field's, and tended bar at the Tunnel. He'd immersed himself in as many crowds as he could. He knew—"only casually," he insisted—the Lady Bunny, Misstress Formika, Sherry Vine, Tabboo!, and Girlina—the fiercest drag queens in New York. He faithfully attended Monday-night ACT UP meetings, participating in the Labor Day march on Kennebunkport when George Bush was still president. He appeared in several films—"bit parts"—among them *Paris Is Burning,* a Super 8 short for a Jack Pierson installation, and a homo horror movie called *Boys on a Meathook.* He had a boyfriend of six years, a Welsh guy named Simon. He spent four summers in Provincetown where he danced nights at the Crown and Anchor and was a go-go boy (nickname: Lanolin) in Ryan Landry's House of Superstars. He was photographed by Nan Goldin for the *Ballad of Sexual Dependency.* He lived in the same railroad flat for ten years, until one day, after waking up to frozen pipes the fourth time that month, he decided he'd finally had enough and packed up a suitcase and moved back to Florida, whereupon he immediately took a job at Disney World, of all places, selling mementos of Mickey Mouse and Dumbo to children from the Midwest.

It was terribly interesting to me, probably more so than it should have been. Something became clear. It seemed to me that young suburban homos had one of two options: either you could do what Hector and Todd had done, move to the city and turn your back on your past, giving yourself a new name, or you could stay where you were, attempting to hide yourself, becoming nothing but paltry, constricted, cowardly, and dull. It worried me that I was veering closer and closer to the latter category.

"How come you didn't stay?" I asked finally.

"Tedious, tedious. Homo High School," he said, shrugging it off. "A big old charm school. After a while it's time to pick up your certificate."

"But didn't you have fun?"

"Of course, I had fun. But," he sighed, "it's like this: I was thirty-two years old. I wasn't a kid anymore. I was tired of seeing all my friends die."

"Your friends died?" I said dumbly.

"This was New York, honey. I'd buried four of my closest friends in four months. Five guys I'd been a buddy for: Leo, Rex, Israel, Duncan, Thomas. Only months before Simon died."

"I'm sorry," I said.

He shrugged again. "There's nothing to be sorry about. It's like, I didn't give a damn anymore. I'd been to so many memorial services that they didn't mean anything anymore."

His fingers tightened slightly on the wheel.

"And it just seemed like everyone I knew was positive. I'd hear about someone else getting sick, riding out the first symptoms, and it didn't touch me. It didn't make me sad. I'd perfected this reaction, this absence of reaction, as if this whole mess were perfectly par for the course, the way it's supposed to be."

"So what about your friends?"

He fiddled with the sun visor, then flipped it up again. "That was terrible, it was the worst. You know, it's bad enough watching an old person die, but"—he started shaking his head—"these were my lovers and friends. I didn't want to remember them lying on the floor with shit staining their pants."

I eased down into my seat, holding my arms over my chest.

"It wasn't good for me after a while. It was too easy to be detached and hard about things, and I hated that about myself. It killed all my enthusiasm, though I didn't know it at the time. I needed to get the fuck away."

"So you went to Florida."

"So I went to Florida," he said. "Some decision. Go south in hopes that all your troubles'll melt away."

"And you met my brother."

"And I met your brother." He turned to me with a weary, troubled grin. He blinked as if flummoxed. "Do I sound like an asshole? Does any of this babble make sense to you?"

"No," I said, then, "yes," though I couldn't be completely sure of either answer. I looked at the parkway ahead. Above it, the sun loomed heavy and white, boring a hole through the clouds.

◇ ◇ ◇

The van skated down Cape Coral's Diplomat Parkway, a four-lane highway bisecting a lunar landscape, a *tabula rasa* of sorts, on which kids in convertibles threw cans, pulled down their pants, and hurled the occasional racial epithet. I imagined this place from the air, a vast, chilling land mass the size of Phoenix or Detroit, with its 100,000 lots, all of which had been initially sold, like the failed Boca Palms, through high-pressure vacation packages 30 years before. It was slowly but surely cocooning itself into a kind of hell. I thought of news reports I'd watched in the last week, footage of throats slashed in West Palm, home invasions on friendly streets, race riots, huge chimneys jetting flame, layoffs at Digital Equipment, clouds of chlorine gas wafting over a Little League game. I thought of these stories, and of myself in them, and what kind of part we'd all played in their creation.

The bank stood in an especially desolate socket, bordering a lily-choked canal with clots of scrub on the banks. The earth was the color of pulverized soap. It shouldn't have surprised me that my brother chose to do his banking here, a good forty miles from the King Cole, all for the sake of saving a few bucks. It was just like Sid, whose savings multiplied in a series of dubious Dallas banks, all of which paid back the highest dividends, yet offered minimal protection from risk.

"Look around," Hector said, parking the van. "Isn't it thrilling?"

"You're serious?"

"Of course, I'm serious. It's so awful it's beautiful. It's like that scene in *The Snake Pit* where that woman's singing "Going Home" and before you know it, the whole mental hospital's joining in with her, and it's awful, corny, and moving all at once."

I nodded. I understood what he was getting at. I thought of Wolfie Cohen's Rascal House, Piccadilly cafeterias, all notions of a similar point of view, but they were all about wreckage, fading emblems of a sweeter era. This place seemed like something darker.

"Watch these kids," he said, pointing to the Circle K next door. They circled about ominously on their little bikes, like fevered mosquitoes. "I bet they're going to call me a fag. Just watch."

"Careful," I said.

He was already heading toward the bank. He deliberately flounced up the sidewalk, in full view of the teenagers, in boots, tiny shorts, and a Hooters Boca Raton T-shirt. He might have been Todd Bemus, the tougher, more streamlined version, the city boy, the one I'd never known. Sure enough, behind his back, I heard talk of pussies and fags, uttered just loud enough for me to hear.

It occurred to me that I was no longer annoyed with him.

"So what happened?" he said when he returned to the van. "Anything happen? Did they call me a fag?"

I shrugged. "More or less," I said. "Yes. I guess they did."

"Great," he said, not the least bit ruffled. A satisfied smile spread across his face. "Just what I told you. *Yo, pencildicks,*" he shouted to the astonished kids. "Greetings to Cape Coral." Then he threw the van into gear and we were off.

◇ ◇ ◇

Twilight was falling on the neighborhoods outside Naples. One by one the amber streetlights trembled on, saturating the houses with an orange phosphorescent haze. By the time we pulled into the King Cole driveway, the sky was nearly dark, the color of burnished ebony. Beside the chickee hut a young woman struck a match, then began lighting the torches beneath the baobobs. There was something so lonely and comforting about her attentions, her complete immersion in the task, that I couldn't take my eyes off her. She stepped backwards, holding her arms over her chest. For some reason, I felt oddly magnanimous. I loved the world.

"What's she doing here?" Hector said, not moving from behind the wheel.

"Who?" I said.

A disapproving noise came forth from his mouth. He nodded in the direction of the woman.

"Is she a guest?"

"Don't tell me she brought the kid here too. Tacky," he said, shaking his head. "Tacky. That's about as tacky as you can get."

I opened the van door and stood on the parking lot. I heard a single child splashing around in the pool. "Hey, Mom," he cried, "I'm making up swimming strokes. This one's the turbo. Look at me, you're not looking!"

"If she's not a guest," I said, "she shouldn't be here. I don't have any qualms about telling her to leave."

"Oh right," he mumbled.

"Who is she, then?"

He looked at me as if I were a lower form of life. "Peter's girlfriend," he said, frowning.

"Peter's girlfriend? Since when does Peter have a girlfriend?"

"He hasn't told you about Holly?"

I looked over at the woman standing by the pool. The fact was Peter hadn't told me anything. I hadn't known about his drinking: only recently had I figured out that he faithfully attended AA meetings two times a week. I hadn't known other things: how he put the money together to buy this place, or how he'd spent the many long years away from our family. But that was Peter, a wily, mysterious sort, always negotiating behind our backs, resisting at all costs any movement toward overt explanation.

"So she's a jerk?"

"No," he said, "Not really. She's actually a very nice, decent woman. I mean—I mean I could even imagine being friends with her in a different context."

"Then why are you so upset?"

He shook his head.

"Did she do something to Peter?"

He didn't answer. I stared at his face, that wry, exhausted gaze. My stomach pressed against the plate of my ribs. I needed some food. And then I got it: this was jealousy. Peter wasn't only involved with Holly. He was also fucking Hector.

◇ ◇ ◇

There was so much to talk about. I wanted, once and for all, to tell him about my time together with William, so he'd hear it from my side, not processed through Ursula or Hector. I wanted to tell him that whatever he did was fine with me, that he didn't have to worry about feeling self-conscious or judged or anything but comfortable. I wanted to tell him that I cared about him deeply, that I couldn't have been more grateful that he'd invited me to live with him, giving me the opportunity to offer my help during this chaotic time. It seemed that our situation couldn't have been more ideal, for who could understand each other better than two brothers, after all? I knew exactly how he felt. What better person to talk with? I imagined that we'd grow closer in the coming time, that I'd start living the kind of life I'd always longed for, a life without dissembling, or second-guessing myself.

Still, there was Holly. Was he primarily involved with her, with Hector as the occasional diversion, or was it the other way around, with Holly there for appearance's sake? Did he even know what he wanted? I thought about the time when, during one of his brief surprise visits home, I'd declared, without warning, at the dinner table, that I'd liked another boy in my class. "I can't believe you'd do that to Mom and Dad," he'd said with disgust, not three hours after my admission. "Anything to get attention. Anything to aim the lens back on yourself." Why hadn't he, as older brother, stepped in, telling them, "He isn't the only one"?

Step up, step right this way. Secrets, secrets: welcome to Sarshik's House of Secrets.

I believed that both Sid and Ursula still held more sway over us than we realized. It was hard not to imagine our lives in a shadowbox, the two of them still hovering over us, twisting our strings. How we wanted to please them, to bring them their happiness, as if their success actually depended upon *our* achievements. It wasn't like they'd actually prepared us for a life apart from them. Once in the dentist's office I read a magazine article about a certain kind of family—"The Self-Sufficient Family," as the author called it—so self-absorbed, suspicious, and dependent upon one another that it couldn't help but cave in on itself. It described us to a T, in such an eerie fashion that I couldn't help but throw the article down, convincing myself it was horseshit. It made me think about Holly and her presence in my brother's life. Could his relationship with a woman still primarily be about pleasing my parents, even though he'd kept her hidden from them?

I thought about the one time that Peter had brought a girl-friend home. I still remember her name, a beautiful name, DeeDee Middlebrook. She lived in a big house off Old Cutler Road in Kendall—the daughter of an obstetrician and a law-yer. Ursula talked about the dinner for days, planning the menu, pondering what dress to wear—all to the dismay of Peter, who didn't want to make a big deal of it. I didn't think he was all that interested, anyway. Upon meeting DeeDee, they made every effort to be nice to her, to welcome her, delib-erately restraining themselves from saying anything patently provocative. Still, beneath it all was the disturbing sense that Peter had to choose between the family and DeeDee, that a decision to spend a Saturday night with his girlfriend consti-tuted an implicit betrayal. Something was at stake here. I sat at the dinner table, listening to the jovial conversation around me, a dread settling into my marrow. Just one false word from Sid, and she'd find out we were freaks, that we weren't like other people. "I guess you'll be out having fun tonight," my mother had said glumly on more than one occasion. Though the evening went off without a hitch, Peter stopped seeing DeeDee not two weeks later.

◇ ◇ ◇

It was the quiet, laid-back hour before dinner. The guests were already in their rooms, taking their showers, rubbing sunburn cream on freckled shoulders. I walked farther into the woods than I ever had, past the burned-out buildings and the marina, across the single, unfinished bridge on the property. Here, before the state land commission had issued the sales moratorium on Boca Palms, Clem Thornton had actually started constructing a semblance of a city, all for the benefit of his prospective lot buyers, though not a single house had ever been completed. The roads now were crumbling at the edges, coarse weeds growing through the sun-bleached asphalt. On every corner stood a moldy concrete marker, its exotic name printed vertically—Miraflores, Isla Dorada, Tulipan, Costa Nera, Costa Brava—each derived from a street in Cocoplum, the gated section of Coral Gables, of all places, near where Peter and I had grown up.

I stepped into a partially built house on Pan American Boulevard. It was the only one of its kind, an unfinished model home with a faded sign hidden in the brush: THE BAL BAY. The exterior, though finished, was chipping, the window glass peppered with BB holes.

The inside was another matter. A mere shell, its floorboards were weathered to the point of rotten, and I stepped cautiously, testing their strength. The air smelled of dust. My eyes drifted through the cobwebs toward the corner. I jumped. Instantly, my stomach was in my mouth.

"You scared me," I said.

Peter sat on the floor, legs drawn up to his chest. He looked bemused. He shrugged once, a gesture toward apology.

"What are you up to?" I said finally.

"Thinking." He smiled more openly, then shrugged again.

I sidled up next to him, leaning back into the wall. My heart was still beating. I glanced at his bent legs, conscious of the space between us. I imagined that space itself vibrating, charged with a complexity of emotions I couldn't name. "What are you thinking about?"

He rubbed his whiskered face with his palms. "Bills, bills." He sighed once, loudly. "More bills. They'll be the death of me. And you?"

I made a steeple with my fingertips. "Just taking a walk."

The afternoon light was orange, thick, almost sticky on the floorboards. I was going to tell him what I assumed, ask if it were true. Then something told me not to: any inclination toward openness had always shut him down. It wouldn't be any different now. My secretive brother.

"You and Hector—" he started.

I looked at him. I tried not to register any expression on my face. "What about?"

"The two of you. You both seem to be getting along fairly well."

I nodded, pushed out my lips. "I guess so. Well enough, I guess."

"That's good," he said. "He's quite an interesting guy. I'm glad you two are getting along." He pushed himself up off the floor, glanced down at me.

"We are."

"Good, good. Just watch yourself."

His words burrowed in the pit of my stomach.

"I don't mean to sound corny, and I don't mean to exaggerate."

I laughed out of sheer nervousness. "Could you be clearer?"

"You'll know," he said, and offered me his hand. He made a face. "Now get up." And, in silence, I followed him through the door, down the wrecked road back to the complex.

Chapter 14

I slumped before the TV in the guests' lounge, sitting before a rerun of *Lost in Space*, barely processing the images. It was early afternoon, a little after two. I'd already done my assignments for the day: I'd retested the pool water twice. I'd rewired the noisy switches in my bedroom. I'd even fertilized some plants—the loquat, the pitch apple, the clematis, the breadfruit—an intricate, complicated procedure that involved the consultation of several guidebooks; I didn't want to burn anything. Now I sat here in stillness, too bored to read, too fidgety to immerse myself in anything but the fact of June Lockhart's appallingly tight spacesuit. My eyes drifted to the granulated spray ceiling. I pictured mold spores growing on those dusty clumps, mold spores turning to protozoa, then to more complex cells, then to flesh-eating bacteria, then to: *Where's my arm? Where's my arm?*

Hector walked in the room. I jerked awake, afraid it was Peter. What was the matter with me? He was hardly my father.

He collapsed into the vinyl chair beside me. He was shirtless, revealing a torso so sculpted and defined that I looked away—so much for my notion that I'd stop thinking about him in those terms. The night before, trying to cheer each other up, we found ourselves exchanging our most embarrassing personal stories, and before we knew it, we were laughing like old friends, a peculiar comfort and intimacy passing between us. I thought now about his date with Ted Gessler, a famous music producer, in a trendy, pretentious Upper West Side cafe. I thought about how he'd excused himself to go to bathroom, returning to the table only to see that a thirty-foot length of toilet paper was sticking to his shoe.

"What's so funny?" he said now, laughing along with some nervousness. "You're laughing at me, aren't you?"

"No," I said, pressing my palms to my face.

I looked up. He was staring back at me now with an expression I reserved for the best of my friends, something open, without judgment, as if he simply liked the experience of looking at me.

"You're making me crazy," I said after a while.

He squinted slightly, confused.

"Stop—"

"You know what I think?" he said, looking at the top of my head.

"What?"

He shook his head emphatically. "Forget it. It's none of my business. Forget it."

"Unh-uh," I said. "You can't get away with that."

"Okay," he said. "Okay. I don't like to tell other people what to do. It's one of my worst habits, I'm always getting crap for it, but—"

"What, *what?*"

"I really think you'd look good if you buzzed off your hair."

We made faces at each other. My laugh was sloppy, out of control.

"What's so funny?"

"No way," I said.

"What do you mean?"

"No way, Jose," I said, wagging my head three times.

It wasn't that I was so attached to it, that I was afraid of giving it up, like my poor aging brother with his bald spot, his bureau topped with Minoxidil bottles. It was that I knew I didn't have the head for a buzz cut. It was too long, too narrow, with hard angular features—in particular, a straight pointy nose with a high bridge—that needed to be softened. I knew myself too well: it just wouldn't work on me.

"Another time," I said, standing up. I turned off the TV. "Do you want something to eat?"

"Oh, change the subject, why don't you."

I stared back at him, annoyed. "You're really into this."

"Well, I think it'd look really hot. I'm not bullshitting you. Everyone else would think so, trust me."

I looked back at him, my face heating. He'd hit on something. He knew where I was confused, unsure, and took advantage of it. I might have pushed him over onto the floor. I glanced at the blank TV screen, waiting to see what he'd do next.

"You're bad news," I mumbled.

"Come on." He smiled, buoyant with newly won power. "Just give it a try. It'll grow back in two weeks."

Pulse pounding, I followed him up the stairs to his apartment. I'd never been inside before, but I was intrigued. What a place! Aside from the expected—unopened letters, Japanese comic books, precise stacks of porno magazines—there was an entire wall devoted to Laura Nyro artifacts: posters, autographs on napkins, bootleg album covers, as well as newsletters from her fan club, which operated out of a post office box in North Jersey.

"What's that about?"

"Greatest fucking singer/songwriter on the planet." He tapped out some pot into the bowl of a red pipe. "My soul mama."

"I don't know her very well."

"*Know* her," he demanded. And he handed me the pipe, lighting the bowl, before wandering off to put on a CD.

"Christmas and the Beads of Sweat," he said, closing his eyes.

I pulled the smoke deeply into my lungs, tasting its harsh

acrid scratch. I was curiously out of practice. It made me think
about that one and only time I'd gotten stoned alone with
Jane. The pot crept up on us, cunning, mysterious; we could
barely keep our hands off each other. I dragged warily, worrying about Peter finding out. What about those AA meetings?
What about that twelve-step sticker on the bumper of the van?
PRACTICE SENSELESS ACTS OF SELF-DESTRUCTION
or whatever the fuck it was.

"Now let's get to this hair," he said, wielding a clipper at me.

"Are you sure you're in good enough shape to do this?"

"I'm fine, for God's sake." His smile was trumped up, ma-
niacal. I couldn't tell whether he was playing with me or not.
"Now take off your shirt and shut up."

I sat. I did what he said. The minute "Brown Earth" kicked
into rhythm, he took his place behind me, pressing the contours of my head. I couldn't tell him how good that felt, that
the last time I'd gotten my hair washed at a salon, I'd literally
moaned aloud in ecstasy, unnerving the poor old guy. I apolo-
gized immediately, embarrassed by my outburst.

"You have a good head," he said, flipping on the clipper.
"You're going to look great."

I held perfectly still. The blade was cold against my neck;
my chin tucked into my chest. Hector hummed tunelessly to
the song about Freeport. On the tiled floor were the feathered
shreds of my hair. I thought of a sheep being shorn, tied up,
then trucked off to slaughter.

The clipper switched off.

"My God," he said, as if amazed.

"*What?*"

"I mean, I *thought* you were going to look good, but—
Christ—" He started shaking his head.

I made a face. Was he making fun of me? I felt the short
stubble with my hand, then asked for a mirror.

"What do you think?" Hector said.

I gripped the mirror in my hand. It was hard not to be re-
pulsed. It made my eyes leap out, the thick brows above them
darker, bushier, even demonic. My facial bones looked sharper,

more masculine. Could I pull this off? It didn't jibe at all with the way I knew myself, and I doubted I'd ever get used to it, but *hey*. I liked and hated it at once.

"You're going to need some sun on that scalp, paleface. Let's sit in the grass."

"But—" I looked around for a hat. I might have been standing before him without clothes.

He switched off the Laura Nyro. "Come on, fancy boy," he said, laughing harder. "We're going outside."

We sat on a patch of burnt lawn behind the office. It was a breezy, torporous afternoon. The sun was warm, coiling, boring down into the roots of my scalp. All at once I realized I was high, unbearably high. I lay back down on the grass, laughing quietly, my arms latching behind my head. Above me, wild violet clouds blew in from the Gulf.

Hector turned onto his side, looking at me, propping up his head on his palm. I heard footsteps down the sidewalk heading in our direction. I felt too stalled and contented, too lazy to move.

"Have you seen your brother?" Hector called.

"No," I said, but then I realized he wasn't talking to me. I lay flat on my back, staring up at my brother's blasted face. He attempted to smile, though he couldn't stop biting into his lip.

"When did you do that?"

"This afternoon," Hector said, answering for me. "Just a few minutes ago, in fact. I cut it myself."

The three of us fell silent. My back pinched. I tried to cover my eyes—their hazy red wetness would be sure to give us away. I sat up, wishing I'd worn my shirt, brushing off the blades of dead grass stuck to my shoulders. I looked over at Hector, who seemed amused by it all, a passing glimmer of superiority on his face.

"But why?" Peter said. "Your old haircut looked perfectly fine."

"Why *not?*" I said.

He shrugged, put off by the hardness in my voice. "It'll grow back," he said calmly. "No reason to be upset." He glanced at

Hector, blinked once, then lugged off a hose toward the junction boxes.

Hector and I were silent for a time, watching my brother work. He might have been reassuring himself. I felt hungry, diminished. I was certain of it, then: I wanted Hector as much as I wanted anything.

Chapter 15

I didn't take Peter's discomfort to heart. If anything, I felt myself becoming more and more adventurous in the weeks that followed. It was as if I'd thrown up my hands to the fear of judgment and censure. I was tired—once and for all—of reigning myself in, toning myself down. So I assembled a look. I wore faded black T-shirts with the sleeves hacked off. I wore a battered silver motorcycle jacket (borrowed from Hector) whenever the temperature dropped. I even grew accustomed to my crew cut, buzzing it short every Friday night whether it needed it or not. It seemed that I was gradually becoming my look, and I felt snappier, more streamlined and self-assured than I had in seven years, when for a brief period I'd gone through my Ozzy Osbourne phase. I was changing, crumbling, slipping away right before my very eyes. It was nothing but a relief to me. So what if I looked like a big old homo?

The truth was I'd been wanting to assume another look for years, but hadn't pursued it for fear of seeming false, pretentious, of falling flat on my face. But wasn't that part of the fun? Wasn't that what was interesting about other self-created people, the visible cracks in the armor? It seemed that all I needed was a sense of humor, a dash of smarts, and I could be whoever I wanted. What was a lifetime but a series of shifting, interchangeable masks? I could look like a biker boy today, and tomorrow a trust accountant, and the next day a geeky scientist.

I stopped before the mirror every time I passed it. *"Grrrrr,"* I growled, flexing my muscles.

What I didn't comprehend was that my dressing up could concern Peter so much. It wasn't that he'd directly addressed the issue. It wasn't that he told me to tone it down for fear that I'd put off our guests. Instead, he made his feelings known in the way he talked around everything but the clothes on my back. Maybe he was taking on the role of Sid and Ursula, feeling it his duty to keep me in line, to inspire inhibition in a personality he perceived to be reckless and underdeveloped. Or was it that my dressing this way—let's face it: hypermasculine, yet daffy— reminded him of something that scared him about himself? He certainly should have recognized he'd constructed his own look. No one wore chinos and button-downs and wire-frame glasses day after day without some degree of intention, without knowing he desired to communicate a sensibility, a point of view to the outer worlds. But was he ready to admit that? I thought now of his earlier warning about Hector the night we'd stumbled upon each other in the sample house. In the days that followed, his silence started to pique me. He made me want to dress more and more outlandishly, to tattoo my back, to pierce my eyebrow, to dye my stubbled hair aqua, cranberry—a new color depending upon the week and season.

Deep down, I wondered whether Peter was simply frightened of the confidence that had been gradually inhabiting me. Did he want some for himself? It seemed to me that he both wanted some and was afraid all at the same time, but what did I know? I'd found a way to *be* in the world, a way of letting go, abandoning myself within a certain set of parameters. It was like learning how to eat with a knife and fork. I thought about Sid, his social cluelessness and fear of outsiders. I thought about his flirtations with his female coworkers, how it was endlessly getting him into trouble, baffling him every time he was called upon it. "I never meant any harm," he'd say. "I'm not a bad guy. I only love women." He might have come from another planet, another century. He simply didn't know the rules, as if he were navigating, rudderless, through a storm-drenched sea. You had to know the rules. It might have been foolish, mistaken to crave something fixed, but it made it easier, I knew that much, and I wasn't prepared to unlearn anything I'd taught myself.

Hector and I were hosing down the lounge chairs by the pool. A girl with thick glasses and a homemade brown dress was sitting by the gate, reading about plankton in an ancient volume of *The World Book.* She peered up at us occasionally, pretending she wasn't watching.

"By the way," Hector said. "I have some good news for you."

I looked up. A star-shaped patch of cleaning fluid foamed beneath his lip.

"You know Alejandro?"

"From Fort Lauderdale? The tax accountant?"

He nodded. The banana palms creaked above our heads. "He wants to go out with you. He thinks your new look's really cute."

"Great," I said, more blandly than I'd intended. I thought of Alejandro, his aviator glasses, his slicked-back hair, the pleasing squirrely sleaziness of him. In exchange for services, he was given a free room, and he stayed here once a month, sunning himself by the pool in a micro-black bikini. He was sexier to me than I was willing to admit, but that wasn't what was irking me. It was Hector's detached, off-handed manner I didn't like: he sounded like a pimp.

"He actually said something very nice about you."

The girl looked up from her encyclopedia. Her name—Mary Grace—was markered on the olive cover.

"He did?" I said.

"He thought that you possessed a really interesting combination of butch and femme. He thought that that was a sign of an interesting, complex personality."

"But he doesn't even know me."

He shrugged, then tossed his sponge on a chair.

I followed him down the walkway. We were sitting on the floor of Hector's room, flipping through his collection of drawings—"cameos," he called them—derived from the covers of women's detective novels of the 1950s. They were surprisingly good, though I paid little attention to them. The skin of my chest itched. In my usual habit, I was only gradually becoming aware of the fact that I was harboring any rage.

"What's this talk about femme?" I blurted. "That's ridiculous. I mean, do I look *femme?*"

Hector raised his brows. "Say what?"

"I'm talking about Alejandro, what he said about me. You acted like that was a compliment or something."

Hector's eyes went blank. He remained silent for a second, then scooted over to the night table. He fumbled for something in the drawer. Not two seconds later he yanked back my scalp violently, with full force, hurting me. "Hold still, butch boy."

"What are you doing?" I cried.

He gripped the lipstick in his free hand, wielding it as if it were a scalpel. He began pressing the tube directly to my mouth.

"What the fuck?" I said, trying to push him toward the wall. He was even stronger than I'd imagined. "I told you I'd look bad as a girl."

"No one talks to *me* like that." And then he strayed from the outlines of my mouth, applying bars of lipstick across my jaw, my cheeks, my forehead, my hair.

I reached for his T-shirt on the floor and wiped off my face with it. I tossed it away. Its fabric was red, ruined.

"I'll get you in drag," he said with a cool, casual smugness. "Just you wait. I'll dress you up if it's the last thing I do."

"That's what you think," I muttered.

"Girl," he said, taunting me.

"Girl," I said, taunting him back.

I'd had about all I could stand from him. But coupled with that was another more affronting, alarming thought: he'd probably get me to do it, the jerk. I stared at his handsome, arrogant, self-satisfied face. I could have killed him.

◇ ◇ ◇

At thirteen, I was afraid of someone. I did everything possible to distinguish myself from him. I recorded my voice over and over, imagining wide flat stones on my tongue, working out the inflections, sanding over any last traces of hiss. I trudged back and forth down the length of our driveway, taking heavy, self-assured steps, bouncing just slightly from the knees until my arms swung naturally, without concentration. I did push-ups by the dozen on the laundry-room floor. I read sports page after sports page, memorizing the scores, insinuating myself into arguments in which the merit of the Marlins' MVP was in question. There was nothing helpless about me. You could say that I talked too much, that I was scattered and lacked focus, that I hungered for overwhelming amounts of atten-tion and reassurance from everyone who came into contact with me, but you wouldn't have said that I was feminine—that much I was sure.

Unlike Stan Laskin. Stan Laskin: hardware-store owner. Stan Laskin: who paid special attention to me every time I was sent in by Sid to buy switches or ten-penny nails. It wasn't that he was anything but kind. It was that his body, his entire self-presentation, soft and yielding, with its tendency toward flab, represented everything I didn't want to be. His colognes scented the atmosphere every time I waited at his counter. His glasses, all seven pairs of them, coordinated with his bracelets and rings. But most disturbing of all was the expression on his face, wounded and lamb-like, as if he were waiting for some devastating stranger to come through the door.

As far as I knew he lived alone and had never been loved by anyone in his life. His days, I decided, were repetitive, dull, and lonely, enlivened only by occasional visits to the fabric store, where he remembered all the employees' birthdays, and to the public bathroom stall where he sat six hours at a time before a vacant glory hole. After work, he'd walk through his front door, leaving his outer life behind, assuming a secret role, draping himself in chintz or black velvet, before giving hairdos to his Yorkshires or trying on his extensive collection of cloches and pins. Every morning he'd call up his mother, discussing the trip they were planning to the Lawrence Welk Resort in Escondido, California. His life had as much to do with my own as the newsletter of the Siegfried and Roy fan club.

It was a warm, overcast day in December, the weekend before Christmas. A heat wave was descending upon Dade County, moistening the foliage with dew. In Florida fashion, the trunks of the royal palms were wrapped with strings of clear lights. I hurried down the Miracle Mile with Mark Margolit and Steve Mendelsohn, two of my friends from school. At least I thought they were friends. I cared about them as much as I cared about the health of my gums, but to one another we looked like friends, and when the three of us were together no one dared make fun of us. I felt convincing with them. They believed me when I expressed my interest in Jane. Together, we talked about the color and texture of Jamaica Reed's nipples, the lead guitar solos from Metallica's second album, and the afterschool activities of Mrs. Walgreen, our Spanish teacher, who was forever tugging her miniskirt down over her hips. I wore a ripped Ozzy Osbourne T-shirt with black kohl eyeliner around my eyes, and when I looked in the mirror I even scared myself.

We walked around the perimeter of the circle, the scent of frozen pizza still rising from our fingers, stumbling to the video arcade, where we'd play a few games of Donkey Kong or Burger Time. In my thirteen-year-old way, I'd told myself I was having fun and was behaving like any boy my age was supposed to. We couldn't have been walking more than ten seconds when I saw Stan Laskin carrying boxes between a rental truck and his store, accepting a delivery. He looked relatively conventional for Stan Laskin: baggy chino pants, golden horn-rims, navy blue button-down. Except for the scrap of material—a yellow brocaded print tied around his throat. A softness slid down inside my stomach. I felt nothing but embarrassed and afraid.

"Nice scarf," Steve said.

He wouldn't look at us. He lifted up a box marked screwdrivers, watching it fall through his hands.

"Did you always like women's accessories?" Steve said.

A single drop of sweat ran down the crease of my back.

"In case you're interested," Stan Laskin said, his face the deepest crimson, "it's an ascot."

"Oh, an ascot," Steve said, highlighting his S. "An *ass*—cot."

"We better get out of here," I whispered to Mike.

"No," Steve said. "Stay." A brutal, joyous laugh tore up from his lungs. He leapt toward the stop sign and slapped its red metal face.

"Do you like to suck cock?" he said, spinning around, turning to Stan.

Nothing. A helicopter beat somewhere overhead, concealed.

"Do you? Do you like the taste of cock in your mouth?"

Stan gazed downward at the box in his hands.

"Faggot," Steve said. "Lousy cocksucking faggot."

The sidewalk might have cracked beneath my feet. More than anything I wanted Stan to dismiss us, to write us off as small, inconsequential. Instead, he turned not to Steve, but to me. He looked into my face in a more searching way than anyone ever had.

"What made you so hateful?" he said matter-of-factly.

"Me?" I said.

"All of you. I don't get it. Tell me how you live with yourselves."

Something bony and sharp pushed deep inside my chest.

"Come on," Steve said. "I've had enough. Let's check out those bitches across the street."

The days hastened toward Christmas. I completed my activities as usual: I tossed Milk Duds to Delaware, our neighbor's Boston terrier, in my efforts to teach her how to fetch. I worked through all the supplementary exercises in my algebra packet, achieving a 98 on the pop quiz. I even helped

Peter wax my father's Grand Prix, buffing its blue finish with a chamois cloth. At night, though, lying in bed, I couldn't scour Stan's question from my thoughts. I tried to tell myself that what had transpired hadn't been so sad. Everyone behaved that way, everyone I knew. It wasn't like they meant any harm. It was the way you carried yourself in the world. Otherwise, they'd pulverize you. Faggot, cocksucker, queer: these were just words—empty, stupid, meaningless words. No one needed to be defended here.

What the hell was I afraid of?

I was standing in the locker room after gym class. We were midway through the swimming unit, the only sport I could bear. Nearly everyone had already left for homeroom. The air smelled of bleach and worn elastic. I looked from side to side, pulled down my gym shorts, as the spray pounded in the shower room beside me. I turned halfway. It was Jon Brainard, a small, intense boy with blue eyes and dark curly hair, who'd just transferred from Sarasota. He was watching me beneath the showerhead, defined fingers lathering a compact stomach. He might have been my brother in another time. My skin tingled, chilled, then flushed with the richest warmth. He was rinsing the suds between his legs. I couldn't keep myself from staring back, though I wanted to stop.

"Evan," he called.

I turned. I fumbled inside my locker, pretending not to hear.

"Would you hand me that towel on the bench?"

The drain gulped down the overflow. His smile was shy, as if he were thinking something enormous, beautiful.

My toes clenched tighter into the concrete.

Many months passed before I again allowed myself to walk into Stan's store. It smelled of torn wood, matches, grass seed, pesticides—a confluence of smells that I associate, to this day, only with that memory. In my pocket, I carried an arrowhead I'd found beneath an ice plant on the Metrozoo grounds. It was my talisman, my lucky charm. I'd attributed several minor miracles to its existence—the recovery of a $50 bill and the rapid healing of a fractured ankle. My plan was this: I'd leave it on his counter in an unmarked bag without note or explanation. He could do with it what he wanted. I knew it was hopeless, and I knew it was unreasonable, but the exchange had been hovering over me, a ruined black blanket, and I just wanted to get it off my mind.

Stan was back in the supply room. I leaned the lunch bag against the cash register, then turned to make my getaway.

At once he came toward me with a crowbar. He looked kindly and quizzical, as if he thought I needed help. Then all at once his brows drew together.

"Don't I know you?"

My breathing went sluggish. I imagined him bringing the crowbar down across my forehead, splitting it in two.

"You were one of those boys," he said. "Get out of here."

"I didn't—"

"I'll call the police. Get out."

I left the store without explaining myself. It was his pain and not the crowbar that frightened me. Even then, I knew that it wasn't just about my indifference, but about every time he'd heard the word *faggot* muttered behind his back. That night, lying on the living-room sofa, I thought about the arrowhead in the lunch bag. It was a vacant, meaningless gesture that wouldn't console him, I was positive. He probably even tossed it away. But there was always the chance that he kept it, and it's serving him now, giving him luck, warding off anyone who'd hurl a word at him, or anyone who'd let it happen.

Hector and I leaned against a triple-loader at the outdoor Laundromat. We were working an entirely new look: our slacks narrow, our lashes smudgy with goo. Even our lipstick—glacial, white—coordinated with our jackets, tight vinyl numbers crisscrossed with zippers. We were space-age versions of Jean Shrimpton and Marianne Faithfull, right out of 1967. I looked straight ahead, trying to erase and assert myself at once. But I wanted to go further. More than anything I wanted to hammer through my shame, become enameled, incandescent like Hector—"Mistress Chevelle," as he called himself today. Something was off, though. If I was going to do this, I had to do it right. I looked over toward the ladies beside the dryers, taking in their weary, sardonic scorn of us. Where was that transformation that was supposed to take hold of me, whisking me off to that other sphere, where I was too perfected, too highly evolved to be bothered, beyond bitterness or spite? Was I just another failed fag, a dumb cluck, an old stick-in-the-mud?

I wondered sometimes whether, out of sheer self-protection, I'd simply never allowed myself to develop a taste for things feminine. I walked around convincing myself I wasn't the least bit interested in cooking or fabric swatches or interior decoration or figure skating, but was that the essential me? What about my predilection for finding myself in public spaces designated for women only? How many times had I wandered into a bathroom only to find an absence of urinals, only to hear a terrified voice rising over the stalls: "Is that a man in here? Oh my God, I think it's a man."

"Are you having fun?" I said to Hector. "I'm not having very much fun."

"What kind of talk is that?" Hector said.

"Maybe it's just not the right look for me," I said, tugging at my cat suit.

"You might be right. Maybe you should have done the Mary J. Blige thing."

"What?"

"You know, black girl, blonde hair. That would have worked."

"I personally think I'm the Liv Ullman type. We *both* could have done it. Did you ever see *Persona?*"

"Is anything ever right with you?" he said, flustered. "Hand me that detergent." And before I knew it he'd poured another half-box into the washer compartment. Our clothes spun wildly, suds flinging against the glass.

The truth was we needed some diversion after the events of

the week. Two nights before, the septic tank had overflowed, precluding us from doing our own laundry on the premises. Behind the office, a translucent stream flowed from the lid toward the mangrove banyans. The scent, to say the least, was less than pretty, prompting complaints from the guests.

I stared at one of the white-trashy women whose eyes had been fixed on us. "I don't like the way she's looking at me," I said, loud enough for her to hear.

"Oh, get over it. She doesn't even know what day of the week it is. She probably just thinks you're some trollop."

I fixed him with a level stare. My glance was high, my voice elevated. "Look who's talking."

"Slut."

"You're a joke."

"Whore."

"You're a joke—a dirty joke from one end of this town to the other."

We laughed, collapsing against each other. Our witnesses looked at us with a mixture of disdain and fascination. Hector clapped me hard on the shoulder. "There you go. Now you're getting it down."

A boy in a ripped T-shirt, dirty beret, and mutton-chop sideburns passed us, lugging a wash basket over his hip. His look seemed to be especially thought out, as if he'd spent a full ten minutes trying on various combinations in an effort to *seem* like he'd just thrown the whole shebang together. He had the look of someone who'd fixed a camera on himself, watching himself with every gesture, assuming that everyone else was doing the same.

"What do you think?" Hector said, nudging me in the side.

He kept staring at the boy with a flagrant, unnerving calculation. I didn't know what he was talking about.

"Our church or theirs?"

I looked him over again. "Ours," I said finally.

"No way, chica." This was new: he'd taken to calling me chica in the last week.

"What do you mean?"

"Too sloppy. *Way* too sloppy."

"Get out of town."

"Listen to me," he said, holding up his hand. "*Listen.* I'm going to teach you something. A fag wouldn't do that. He'd shave the sides of his head. He'd keep it neat and severe around the ears, and he'd wipe off the mud from those shoes."

"What mud?"

"And he isn't looking around enough. Fags always look around."

I looked at Hector, confounded. Where did this certainty come from? How could anyone possess such single-mindedness, such pigheaded belief in one's point of view?

"Watch this," he said. And before I could stop matters, he started speaking to the boy. "Excuse me, young man. *Pssst.*"

"Yes?"

"Could you tell me where you got your shoes?"

I slumped against the washer, stricken.

"Ben Southern," he said. "Actually, they've got a giant sale going on. Thirty-eight bucks."

"Really?" Hector said. "They're just the *sauciest* little numbers." He swallowed demurely. "Would it be a terrible imposition if I asked you to let me try them on?"

My body temperature surged two degrees. Either he was going to punch us out or comply.

Seconds later, he was passing the shoes to Hector.

"Goodness, they're *big*," Hector said, looking down. "My feet are just *swimming* in them. I couldn't possibly wear anything so *big*."

"You know what they say," he said shyly. "Big feet, big—"

"What's your name?" Hector's smile was huge and platinum, on the verge of ghastly. He passed back the shoes to the boy.

"Josef," he said, glancing downward. "With an F. And yours?"

"I'm Mistress Chevelle. And this is my friend, Boca. But you can call her Big Pretty."

Josef grinned back at us as he were in on the joke. He offered his hand to each of us and shook ours firmly. I was relieved. He was one of us.

"You girls from out of town?"

"In a manner of speaking," Hector said. "Slave labor."

He nodded, pretending to understand. He crunched his brow. "Well, have a good time while you're here. It was nice meeting you."

"Already?" Hector said wistfully.

"You watch yourselves, girls. Have fun on your trip."

And then he wandered off, loading the silver washer with extreme care and attention.

"See?" I said.

"See what. He's not a fag, you dope. He's fag *friendly.* He's just a straight boy who's comfortable with fags."

"What?"

"There's a big, big difference. You could get yourself into trouble."

"Oh right."

"The hair, dear, the hair."

I pointed to my wig, suggesting the crew cut that lay beneath it. "I didn't used to have fag hair."

"You weren't a fag."

"Excuse me?"

"You weren't a fag till I got a hold of you." He curled up the issue of *Women's Wear Daily* in his hand, gazed through it like a telescope. "In terms of style, at least."

The heat off the dryers was making me swoon. I pictured my knees buckling, my face crashing flat to the floor. "Oh, is this some nasty remark about my sense of style?"

"No, it's not some nasty remark about your sense of style," he mimicked. "You were making some bad choices, that was all. You looked like some sorry-ass straight boy with your hair flopping all over your ears. No wonder you weren't getting any dick."

I could have throttled him. We weren't going to get any dick looking like this, either. I stared at the front loaders, fixing my gaze on them, as if they were fireplaces—the fireplaces of Florida. I needed to turn off my thoughts. We might have been captive in Hell's Laundromat, with pool table, raucous music, bar, free popcorn, and huge TV screen across which

Morton Downey, Jr. hovered. I couldn't help staring at the well-dressed, middle-aged woman beside the soap machine. She looked around nervously, with a barely suppressed panic. Her face carried all the doubts and anxieties of an aging flight attendant, the look in her eyes saying: *Where is my beauty? Why is it disappearing from me?*

And I'd worried that *we'd* been out of place.

Hector was sitting in the yellow bucket seat, right leg crossed over the left knee. It was amazing: beneath his exterior, he still seemed butch, even butcher than usual. It troubled me that I'd actually been attracted to someone in an A-line miniskirt.

I gestured across the room toward Josef. "How would you know?"

"I *know*," he said, pointing to the place between his eyes. "You have it, I have it. It's just a question of whether you want to pay attention to it or not."

But it was never that easy. I thought about Ross-Bob Vittori, a boy from my high school, who lisped with abandon, collected Jean Seberg memorabilia, and was in possession of the longest eyelashes this side of a Maybelline model. Despite these factors, he was still one of the most popular boys in school, with no shortage of dates, asking out a different girl each weekend, most of whom had called him first. Any number of people didn't fit the bill, challenging expectations, resisting typecasting, but how could I begin to explain this to Hector? I knew him well enough: that brain was impossible to perforate.

Chapter 16

I was thinking about one of the first boys I'd ever had a crush on. It was months before William. I ran into him every day at three o'clock, on my walk home from school, on my short-cut past the U of Miami Art Building. Invariably he was sitting within the shadow of an Australian pine, nibbling at a cream cheese and olive sandwich on white bread. I presumed he was an art major. But that in itself wasn't the thing. There was something about him, a locus of energy that suggested a fiercely complex internal life. He wasn't the best-looking guy in the world, and he couldn't have been further from my type, which tended toward road thugs and serial killers, or more precisely, those who looked like them. But there was something about him. Maybe it was his chin whiskers—brown, downy— or the sketches in his notepad—fractured, strife-ridden, built from dashes, stars, and blips. I wanted nothing more than to save him from his pain. Soon enough, I was nodding to him, then he back at me, then we were actually mumbling hello, initiating that period of mutual recognition and appreciation.

It was a muggy, overcast day in early November when I

walked into Bonita's Glaceteria, a little place on Coral Way, to buy some lime-ice to cool down from the heat. I was actually in a light, cheerful mood—odd considering that I'd just been accepted to Yale, and the prospect of college unnerved me to no end.

When I looked to my right, I saw the art boy, Arden, smiling at me.

"Hi," he said.

"Hello," I answered back.

We stood there for a stunned moment, staring at each other, not knowing how to proceed. Whole epochs might have passed. Then, for whatever reason, I crept to a table by the window, covering the left side of my face with my hand. My hairline pearled up with sweat. Here, I'd had every opportunity to sit down and chat, casually, without complication. I sat there sucking at my paper straw, looking for all intents and purposes like a moron, wishing that he'd get the hell out of the place, knowing that the mere fact of his existence was just further evidence of the universe's essential cruelty and indifference.

To my dread, he stepped toward my table.

"Do I know you?" he said earnestly.

His accent was rounded, wide, as if he'd just stepped in off the prairie. He looked at me with luminous, grey-green eyes, a shade I'd never quite seen on anyone else. I'd never felt more defeated and desperate in my life. Then, as if somersaulting into a river of burning lava, I said: "Would you like to go to a movie with me this Saturday?"

He considered the offer. Outside a group of preschoolers trotted by, reciting their ABCs in both Spanish and English. "Of course."

We made plans to see Resnais' *Last Year at Marienbad,* a film about which I couldn't have cared less, but it was playing at the university, and I was certain that he'd like it. It occurred to me that this was the first time I'd ever asked anybody out on a date. I pushed past the pedestrians, knowing that my days of loneliness and emotional aridity were forever over, that I'd soon have all the sex I wanted, and more. That night, I not only cleaned out my room from head to toe, but talked to Sid and Ursula with interest and civility. I was embarking on my new life. I was in love. Soon enough, we'd devote ourselves to making each other happy, and we'd give each other back rubs, and talk back and forth, and *listen,* and once we grew a little older, we'd trim each other's sideburns, shave each other's shoulders.

I couldn't stop thinking about the sheer sonic loveliness of the name Arden. How it tripped off my tongue: a ballad, a prayer.

The day of the date, my stomach tightened as if injected with helium. I isolated myself in my bedroom, trying to relax my hunching shoulders. Only when I couldn't stand it any longer did I call Jane, asking about the appropriateness of my outfit.

"It's seven-thirty in the morning," she said. "What do you want from me, dear?"

She suggested a few pieces, a loud corduroy sport coat and a buffalo-plaid shirt, neither of which sounded particularly attractive. It occurred to me that she was more interested in seeing the endeavor fail, though she'd never admit to that.

"You know, Evan—"

"Yes?"

She yelled at Sugar Pop, her dwarf Pomeranian, to shut up. "You won't want to hear this," she said, more softly now.

"What." I aspirated the H in what. My voice took on an impatience I found myself using only with her.

"Be careful of getting your hopes up. You're not marrying him. It's only a date."

"I know that."

"I mean, you don't even know if you *like* him."

Of course I like him, I wanted to say. I'm in *love* with him. Then it occurred to me that she was just plain resentful. She wanted me to be available to her every second of the day, to go to the beach, to get her car inspected with her—all the minor, irritating tasks that she hated to do herself. The truth was she hadn't gone out on a date since her folks had forced her to break up with DeMarco, unless you could count her midnight rendezvous with Levon (aka her own private dildo). I could sympathize with her on those grounds, but what really vexed me was her unspoken belief that my attraction to other boys was a phase, that once I passed out of it, I'd come to my senses and fall deeply in love with her. *Hogwash,* I thought. *Bullshit.*

Hours later I met Arden outside the red-carpeted lobby of the campus film forum. He was wearing a checkered red shirt and a pair of overalls, the bottoms ragged and dragging. He might have been a farm boy fresh off the milking machines. A look of quiet expectation shone across his face, and all my fears were allayed.

Once seated he gazed up at the screen, awestruck, drinking in the images: the baroque hotel, the trimmed, geometric gardens, the feathered gowns of A, Delphine Seyrig, who looked as if she were listening to a ticking bomb inside her. He seemed to be so involved that I thought it best not to disrupt him, though I wanted to fuck him silly right then and there. Something twinged the root of my dick. Occasionally, his stomach would squeal, and a little belch would issue forth, but I relished this subtle indication of his humanity, relieved he felt comfortable enough to share it with me. Put simply, he was as nervous as I was.

We strolled down the storm-wet streets. The neon tubes trembled, clinging to the last of their currents. The branches were blowing. Out over the ocean, lightning pulsed twice, golden, subtropical.

"What did you think?" I asked.

"Lavish," he answered. "I never expected it to be so lavish. Those voices, those gowns."

His enthusiasm was more than I could stand. "*Tell* me," I agreed.

I had so much to say that I couldn't begin. He walked just slightly ahead of me, with only the slightest urgency, a beatific look on his face like the young St. John of the Cross. The world seemed unbearably benevolent all at once, the lightning flashing soundlessly in the distance, the palms above our heads watching, blessing us.

We stopped at a crosswalk. His smile was shy, eroding. Knowing that he wanted exactly what I wanted from him, I reached for the back of his neck and pulled him toward me—reckless, I admit—shoving into his mouth as much of my tongue as was humanly possible. His own tongue was soft, impossibly smooth, a sweet clam in a bath of brine. His whiskers sandpapered my chin. It was the most profound kiss in which I'd ever taken part.

I stepped back slightly, dazed, chilled and sweating at once. He pulled in his lips as if I'd tasted of mercurochrome.

"I'm straight," he cried.

The trees shook. My ears were humming.

"I'm straight," he cried again, as if to convince himself. Then he started running, fast as he could, down the length of the street.

◇ ◇ ◇

They'd been arguing off and on in Hector's room for more than two hours before I'd finally decided to climb out of bed. My guts burned. There was no point in trying to sleep. The moment I'd close my eyes, convincing myself that their silence was lasting this time, that they'd come to some peace, they'd start all over again, words volleying even louder than before. It was hard not to wonder whether it had been spurred on by something I'd done—or not done, as the case may be. It was hard not to feel trammeled by it all. I might have been sitting in the bedroom of my childhood, scratching my name into the headboard, bending back the balsa wings of a model plane as Sid and Ursula fought through the night in the next room.

Something was bothering him about me. Was it his perception that I'd been under Hector's influence? I sensed it, just by the passing grimace on his face as we'd walked in the door, dressed in our skirts and wigs, from the Laundromat. In that one unsettling moment, any sense that I was multiple, that I could be anything other than what he perceived me to be, shrank to near nothing.

Did I have to watch out for my brother?

He really wasn't a bad guy.

I walked out across the dark parking lot and stared down into the pool. The floodlamps burned beneath the heated water, pitching golden waves of light onto the palms, the courtyard. A cord chimed once against the flagpole. Feet thumped across the walk, and there was Hector, climbing up the steps of the pool deck in nothing but his black jockey shorts. His face was dazzled and agitated, the muscles tensing in his legs. We looked at each other for several seconds, surprised into speechlessness.

"Is my brother mad at me?" I said finally.

His expression dulled. "What are you talking about?"

"Forget it," I said. "Good of you to get dressed."

"I want to know what you're talking about."

I pulled in a breath through my mouth. "Well, it was pretty hard not to hear you two guys fighting."

His brow clenched. He seemed apprehensive and appalled all at once. "You were listening to us?"

Was he kidding? He knew as much as I how little privacy there was. Anyone walking down those halls could hear anything: burps, farts, little cries in the night.

"Do you want to talk about it?"

He wagged his head back and forth.

"All right," I said, and stood up. "Sorry I asked. I'll be out on the dock if you should find yourself deigning to talk."

He slumped down onto a lounge. The bottoms of his feet were dirty, spattered with drops of aqua paint. "It's like he convinces himself it's all about money."

"What?"

"He'll talk this way and that way about how he can't pay the bills, how it's time to start targeting a different market, cranking up the ads, but he hasn't done jackshit. He'd rather complain about it, put it off. Do you know what I'm saying?"

"He'll hear," I whispered. I pointed up toward his dark apartment.

"He actually implied that I was responsible for that tour falling apart. I mean, you know that's not true. And this is after he's been pounding my back the whole day."

A mole cricket drifted on the surface before a pool lamp. My eyes felt dry, stitchy. My throat was sore. It was minutes past 3 a.m. Suddenly I imagined this going on the entire night.

"Why don't you just get some sleep," I mumbled.

He lay back on the pink-webbed lounge. "It can all be reduced to one single problem." His voice was oddly cheery, without malice. "A single problem is all it amounts to."

"What's that?"

"The problem's that he still wants to be a good little boy. He never got the affection he needed as a kid, and that's what's messing him up now."

I looked at him skeptically. "Yes, Doctor Freud."

"I'm serious. What do you think he's doing with a girl-friend anyway?"

"You're out of your mind."

"He's just afraid. He's afraid to admit to himself he's a dirty little faggot like the rest of us."

"Oh, please."

"I'm telling you."

"And you know this for sure."

"Listen." He stood, poking a fingertip into my chest. "I know what I'm talking about. He's twenty-eight years old, and he's still talking about his parents all the time. 'Sid this, Sid that. Ursula this, Ursula that.' My God, you might think they were sitting in the next room."

I thought for a moment. There was certainly some truth to that, but only some. Wasn't Peter the one who couldn't wait to leave home, who never wanted to see them again? *I'm happy, but you're not.*

"But he hasn't spoken to them in months."

"It doesn't matter." He gestured at the first floor of the motel. A single lamp trembled on in the window, a robed figure drifting behind the curtain. "It's like this whole thing is for them. It's like he's preparing for this hypothetical time, this perfect time, when he's gotten everything down just right, so he can say, 'Look, Mom. Look, Dad. I'm not the fucked-up puppy you thought I was.'"

I didn't know what to make of it. It all sounded too cheap and easy. And believe it or not, I resented the running down of my parents, especially knowing he hadn't met them. They could be awful, the most unbearable combination of clinging and secretive, but what parents didn't cause some damage, regardless of their intentions? They cared about us in their own miserable, stunted way. How much easier it would have been to be Hector, whose own mother was a dyke, who was completely at ease with his life, who called once every week to ask his advice about her latest girlfriends. No wonder the world was much less complicated in his eyes.

Insects thrummed in the trees. Behind the clouds, the moon swelled, an amber smear of light.

"Did it ever occur to you that he could be bisexual?"

"Knock it off."

"I'm serious."

"Bisexual?" he said, shaking his head. "I don't believe that. That's horseshit. He doesn't know what the hell he wants, so instead of talking about the *real* issue, he's blowing up about everything else."

Hector squatted beside the pool, dipping his hand before the jet. Chlorine tanged the air. I walked closer to him and smelled something like gin on his breath. Was that it? Could he have been drinking and had that set Peter off?

"So do you two have sex?" I ventured.

"Sex," he laughed darkly. "What the hell's that?"

"Whoa," I said.

He looked up at me. His eyes were calm, impassive, barely concealing what he thought. He moistened the corner of his mouth with his tongue. He mumbled, "That's none of your business, okay?"

"I didn't—"

His face flushed. "I ought to beat you to a pulp."

"Hey," I said, holding up a hand. "Calm down, I—"

Tiny particles charged the air. Suddenly Hector was bending toward me. I froze, startled. Carefully, in small arcs, he started rubbing his whiskered jaw against my chin, humming something nameless. I pressed my fist into his stomach, pushing him backward. What was happening here? Then the minute I was sure that Peter had certainly seen us, Hector pulled away, grinned as if gauging my reaction, then walked toward the head of the pool.

My head was pounding. Then all the outlines colored in: the shambles of the grounds, the biting quiet between them. No wonder this place had felt so much like home.

◇ ◇ ◇

Before the night was over I'd told him everything about my time with William. I told him about the many nights spent lying awake on the living-room carpet, while William slept soundlessly up on the sofa beside me. I told him about the times I'd gathered the will to make love to him when he made it patently clear he didn't share my interest any longer, lying still, silent, refusing to respond. I told him about the sex party to which he'd taken me a few nights before I'd left, his ill-founded notion that that would pacify me. I even told him that despite our infrequency, our lovemaking was good, so unbearably good that it always meant more than it was supposed to, that soon after we'd finished, I was inevitably filled with the most numbing sense of loss, the quietest loneliness and grief, wondering why it had to be so complicated between us.

"It's funny how someone like that can screw you up for the longest time."

Hector nodded. He sat in the lounge chair across from me, wrapped in a towel. He looked off toward the umbrella pines, the broken gas lamp.

"I mean, I can't talk about this without getting all riled up. It's been months now. Aren't I supposed to be over it?"

Hector raised his brows. His mind seemed to be elsewhere. "So what finally got you to leave?"

"I don't know. I didn't really plan for it."

"No?"

"I think if I'd actually planned for it I never would have left. I'd still be there today. It's not like I had any money, or any place to go. You know the story."

We passed back and forth a single cigarette. We'd found a box of Camels on the table and smoked through the whole pack. I hadn't smoked much since my outings with Jane. My throat might have been sanded, scoured. Hector took the last drag, then tossed it off into the pool, orange ember hissing on the surface.

We'd have killed any guest who'd tried the same thing.

"One of these days I'm getting out of here," he said plainly.

My head emptied of thought. "It's that bad?"

He shrugged. "It might not seem like it, but I actually care about him."

"I'm sure you do."

"That makes it harder. That's why I've stayed around as long as I have. But, enough already. I can't be bothered with someone like that."

"No?"

"I'm better than that. I deserve someone better than that."

"Haven't you talked?"

"He doesn't talk, period. He either shouts or shuts up."

I nodded. I stared down at the shredded cigarette package in my lap, shuffling its pieces. He couldn't leave. "I'd say stick it out. Give it a few more months, then see how you feel."

"I mean, it's hard not to take it personally. If someone had told me two years ago that I'd be involved with someone who stopped having sex with me, who had a girlfriend, of all things, I'd have said they were crazy."

I nodded.

"But there's something about him . . ."

He kept talking. The night dragged on. Whether or not I listened didn't seem to be the issue. He might have been me at another time—I knew that worry, that quality of exclusion. But there was something unsettling about it too: we were all becoming too close. We might have been three wires, braided, intertwined, fully connected to one another. I looked up into the brightening sky, spotted a comet, some falling streak of light. I wasn't the right person to be told these things. Or was I? I looked at my watch: 5:45. Maybe I just needed some sleep.

"So what should I do?" Hector said. "You tell me what I should do."

I sighed. "You don't have any money?"

"I'm broke, I'm totally broke. What savings do I have? Nothing."

"Just like me."

He winced. "Two brothers in poverty."

If only for an instant, something almost unbearable drifted through my mind. I saw the two of us moving somewhere, together, New York, Seattle, London, Mexico City, changing our names, starting a life. There was nothing tying me down to this place. Peter, though upset, would eventually understand. He wouldn't be totally bereft. He had Holly, after all.

"Maybe it's just a sign of things ending. I should just buck up and dump him, but who wants to be the bad guy? Frankly, I'd rather be the one who's dumped."

The dew moistened the armrest. One by one the sprinklers sizzled on, flinging arcs of cold water across the glittering grass. I looked away from him, trying to keep the longing from my face. "I have another idea," I said thoughtfully.

⟨⟩ ⟨⟩ ⟨⟩

The three of us stood at the county landfill, tossing things into the pit. The morning was hot, windy. Wood chips sprayed from the spout of a recycling machine. Across the pit a yellow bulldozer climbed across the little hills of trash, rolling forward, backing up, rolling forward again. The machines roared and ground their gears. A spoon glinted among the mounds of used tissue. It troubled and interested me for some reason— that single instrument held up to so many mouths so many times, a little vessel of pleasure—and I was tempted to wade down the garbaged slope to retrieve it.

We were in the midst of a great cleanup. Peter had suddenly decided to empty one of the storage rooms, the contents of which had suffered smoke damage from a fire months before my arrival. The clothes, in particular, stank. Though we'd washed them in everything from Borax to bleach, they resisted our efforts, clinging in defiance to their new soiled selves. The scent nestled into their very fibers. They weren't even worthy of the worst thrift store. I wasn't sure why this task couldn't have waited, especially since high season was only weeks away. I, for one, thought someone should have been staffing the desk, but I didn't voice my concerns.

A good 90 percent of the clothes had been Hector's. With an exaggerated flourish, he tossed each article into the pit. His sunglasses—aviators that had once belonged to me—reflected the striated clouds, the chaos around us. He behaved as if the whole experience were of great significance, an elaborate ritual. He paused to remember each piece—a sock with blue sparkles, a pink kimono, a T-shirt with a faded drawing of Mao Tse-tung—as if each one had an intricate history attached to it. Then he sent it flying out over the ledge.

He draped a worn chartreuse shirt over his arm. Its collar was pointed, its buttons huge, even silly, the size of silver dollars. I couldn't stop looking at it.

"What?" he said to me.

"That's an amazing shirt. You're throwing that out?"

He shrugged. His face feigned indifference. "I was wearing this shirt the night I went out with Jonas Pike. We were walking down the aisle of the St. Mark's Theater, and everyone, I'm serious—I mean, fucking Joe Dallesandro was there—*everybody* was staring at me."

"How come?" I said.

He shrugged again. "I don't know. I might have looked fierce. Or I might have looked like a street person."

I glanced over at Peter. His face was drab, pensive. He made a point of extracting himself from our conversation.

"Could I have it?" I asked.

Peter exhaled, as if he'd reached his limit with us.

"What's wrong with keeping one thing?" I said to him.

Peter said, "It's ruined. It smells. What are you going to do with it?"

"I don't know," I admitted, then stared down at the muck on my shoes.

I watched a truck dump a fresh load onto the desolate slope. The gulls were screaming above it. The truth was I didn't want to rile him anymore. He didn't deserve it. All morning I'd convinced myself that his mood had been prompted by seeing Hector and me by the pool. It was ridiculous, but it preoccupied me, threading in and out through my thoughts. Not to mention that I wasn't fully myself. We'd gotten in at six, and I'd had but two hours of sleep. I imagined circles, the deep violet of bruises, beneath my eyes.

"Maybe you're right," Hector said, still clutching the shirt. "Maybe I should hold onto it for a while."

"That's it," Peter mumbled.

We both looked at him, utterly blank.

"Do you want to see what I think of my clothes? I'll show you what I think of my clothes." And with that, he dumped out his garbage bag, watching its contents sliding down the slope.

"I'm impressed," Hector said, deadpan, with raised brows.

I didn't know how to react. He was more bothered than I'd imagined.

"He doesn't have a fleck of fun in his body."

"Let's go," I mumbled.

"Come here," Hector said to me. He stepped closer to the edge of the pit. The marl loosened beneath his shoes. "Just come here for a second. This is amazing. There are twenty different versions of the same blue chambray shirt."

I did as I was told. Hector was right. The shirts lodged against the side of an old washing machine.

"We don't like to be creative," Hector instructed. "We don't like to take risks or exercise our imaginations. And when we go out to replace our clothes, we go straight to the Gap and say, 'Six stonewashed chambray shirts. Size Large, please.'"

Peter's eyes were shot through with an enormous sadness. I wondered whether he was going to start yelling. Instead, he strode toward the van in silence, waiting for us to finish up.

"Oops," Hector mumbled.

"Now we've done it," I said.

Back at the King Cole, we immersed ourselves in the most taxing assignments, a penance of sorts: Hector attended to the twenty blinks on the answering machine, while I helped replace the charred wood of the storage room. I couldn't stop thinking about Peter, though. I couldn't stop thinking about his reaction to the shirt. Didn't he understand that things could be more than themselves? Wasn't that why we honored them, hoping to reclaim them: little emblems of change, loss? Why else was he putting so much effort into running this pit of a motel, a motel with its clerestories and tinted terrazzo—all of which embodied something that was new during the era of his childhood, when the world still seemed ample with possibility?

Or maybe his feelings were about something else entirely.

He watched me working. In truth, my skills were less than stellar. I'd bent nearly eight out of every ten nails I'd tried to drive into the plywood. They littered the floor, making a wreath around my shoes, tokens of my distraction.

"Could you hold the hammer right?" he said finally.

"I am holding it right."

"Come on," he said. "Grip the base, not the neck. That's it. Swing back, then aim."

I followed his instructions. Once more, the nail bent, splitting the wood.

"God-*damn*," he cried.

I wouldn't look at him. It was the first time he'd actually raised his voice to me alone, and the sheer force of his outburst, the pent-up pressure behind it, scared me, caught me off guard.

"Maybe if you started behaving like you dressed," he said, "you'd get it right."

501s, black T-shirt with cutoff sleeves. My leather motorcycle jacket lay crumpled in a heap beside me. There it was:

the issue of my look again. "What's wrong with what I'm wearing?"

"I'm sorry," he said. "I didn't say that. Forget that I'd ever said anything like that."

What *was* this crap about my clothes again? Was it jealousy, a projection of his fears? Or was he still hearkening back to the drag of a few nights ago? Outside, the sun lay burning, trapped behind a curtain of dirty clouds.

Maybe if you had it in you to fuck—

"Are you upset?" I said after a while. I'd had enough of this shit.

"I'm not upset. Why would I be upset?"

"You certainly sound like you're upset."

"You're way too sensitive," he murmured. "Here," he said, passing a Coke bottle to me. "You must be thirsty. Drink some of my soda."

I shook my head, declining.

"Drink it."

"I'm not sensitive."

"No, no, you're not at all." He smiled, attempting to diffuse the tension in the room. "My God, you're still that touchy little boy."

I went back to work. I gripped the hammer like he'd told me, this time driving the nail straight through the plywood without splitting it. I resisted the urge to say, *"See."*

But I didn't have to. To my surprise, his eyes held within them a sadness, a regret.

"Listen," he said, stepping closer to me. There was a new smell about him: pine, citrus, shards of burnt wood. He exhaled. "I'm sorry. I'm really, really sorry. I'm under a shitload of stress right now. Florida tourism's down 40 percent from last year. If I don't have a good season, I'm going to lose the place."

He had a point. In the last month, our regulars, many of whom were from England or Germany, had been canceling left and right after the murder of a British couple at an I-4 rest stop. It was as if the very name of Florida had instantly become the most fraught of metaphors: a brutal, ruthless jungle where innocent tourists were hacked to death.

Was this what all his tension was about?

"How have things been between you and Hector?" I asked.

The mere mention of his name, the mere yoking of them together in the same sentence, aroused a perceptible change in him. He might have been a cat: I actually saw his pupils shrink, then swell.

"What has he said?"

"Nothing," I answered immediately. I'd done it now. What was the matter with me? My face flushed hotly.

"Everything is fine with us," he assured me. "We've had some troubles, but everything is generally fine."

"Great," I said dully.

He smiled at me. I brought the hammer firmly down on another nail.

Chapter 17

Already I knew it was going to be one of those days. Sometimes you know it the second you wake up, if only by the feeble slant of light on the furniture, the smell of mildew in the room. Other times you know exactly what's wrong.

For the past day we'd hosted Fulvia Diaz, editor of a widely read travel guide. As a rule I hated these people. A tiny woman in tennis whites with a nasty helmet of hair, she seemed to be completely at home in her role as a walking irritation, expecting, even demanding me to be exasperated with her. Not only had she asked to use the desk phone for six personal calls, all of which were of a half hour's duration, but she'd ensconced herself in the lobby, holding court as it were, asking leading questions of our guests ("Was *your* shower hot enough this morning?" "And what about that continental breakfast?").

I'd had about as much as I could stand when Peter phoned from another line.

"Still there?" he murmured.

The TV blared. On The Weather Channel, Vivian Brown described a developing winter storm off Cape Hatteras. I whispered, "Yeah, but she's going to check out the beach in a few seconds."

"Tigertail?"

"Yes, yes."

"You told her about the shortcut?"

"No, I told her to crawl on her hands and knees through the swamp."

"What?"

"Peter—"

I stepped back behind the desk. She walked across the parking lot, head down, chugging her arms. She opened the door to her rented Lexus.

"So I take it everything's going well."

"Oh, she's just as pleased as pralines. She's got the nicest suite in the place, all the free gin she can drink, and she's tied up the line for hours."

"That's fine," he said. "A lot's riding on her. At this point we need all the good press we can get."

The storm swirled on the TV weather map, a furious, spinning comma. Meanwhile, it couldn't have been any more hot and torporous here. The liriope wilted in the heat. Even the motors of the air conditioner felt sluggish.

"I, on the other hand, think the Vatican should start canonization proceedings on me."

He started laughing.

"I'm serious. She's been relentless, a real pain in the butt."

"Come on now."

His laughter only sparked my aggravation. "Why did you give me the desk, today of all days?"

"What did she say?"

"Oh, some crack about hospitality management. It doesn't matter, it's just—"

"I apologize."

"It's—"

"I *said* I apologize."

"Well—" I gazed up at the weather instruments—thermometer, barometer, rainfall gauge—over the desk. "I just hope I never have to see that walleyed shrew ever again."

I turned. My whole body went cold. There she was, standing before me with shining forehead. A manic smile spiked her face.

"Better go," I said, then hung up.

She passed her key across the desk.

"How much of that did you hear?" I said, too shocked to be polite.

"I've seen just about as much as I need to see, thank you."

My tongue felt frozen in my mouth. "Is something the matter?"

Her jaw clenched, then relaxed. She seemed oddly relieved, as if I'd delivered what she'd truly wanted. "I said, thank you. I'll fax your entry by the end of the week." And with that, she turned and left through the door.

I held onto the edges of the desk, immobilized. My hands were trembling, wet. My toes felt icy inside my socks. Once a few minutes had passed I walked up the stairs to Hector's room.

"Open up," I said.

"What's the matter?"

"I think I really fucked something up."

The door opened, and he led me to the couch. I was beside myself, mixing things up, halting, recasting my sentences. All the while Hector lounged on his side in a red union suit unbuttoned to his stomach, absently rubbing his crotch, his chest. A lazy, half-smile settled on his face.

"Get over it," he said finally.

"What?"

"She's not going to run us out of business, and if Peter wants to believe that, that's his problem."

"But he needed this to work out, and I had to open my great big mouth."

"Listen to yourself," he said with some irritation.

"What?"

"Why are you so freaked out?"

I exhaled through my nose.

"He should have been working the desk," he said, "and you know it. Why was he letting Little Miss Travel Editor walk all over you?"

"So—"

"So he could absolve himself of responsibility if something went wrong, okay? I'm tired of watching you running yourself down like that. Here," he said, flinging something onto my lap. His grin was sly, complicated. "Enough of that horseshit. I've been cleaning up. Look what I found."

A dog-eared magazine lay across my knees. Beneath its title—*Man's Favorite Sport!*—two dark-haired men, stripped to their waists, lay embracing on an unmade bed, open mouths locked together. In the corner, within a yellow starburst, appeared the words: XXX Rated, Non Violent Explicit Pictorals— Adults Only.

Something frigid pooled inside my stomach.

"Look inside," he coaxed.

My face flushed with blood. I wouldn't look at him.

"Come *on.*"

I finally flipped open the magazine. On the first page, the older guy, a big, muscular lug with stubbled jaw, sucked the dick of the younger, a weasly type with tattoos and a ruddy dick. On the next page their roles were reversed. On the next the older, now in a ribbed sleeveless jersey, was crouching on his hands and knees, face to the floor, reaching back for the kid to plow him. The shoot might have taken place in some Long Island motel room, the dark paneling, macrame wall hangings, and leopard bedspread adding a cheesy kind of authenticity to the scene. I imagined a nuclear plant humming across the street, steam billowing out over a glassy bay, a dead fluke floating on its surface.

It wasn't long before Hector was seated next to me, knee pressing into mine. I didn't know whether to inch away or to lean my weight into him. I went with the latter. Heat swarmed in my groin. "What were you doing with this?"

He shrugged. "Doesn't everyone have a little stash?"

My chest hammered. If I were only at ease, I would have enjoyed this. It wasn't like I'd never looked at this stuff before. But it was different to be looking at it with Hector beside me.

"Now that's some killer porno."

He couldn't have been more casual. He might have been some old man showing off his fishing gear.

"I mean, look—not a pretty boy or a gym rat in the bunch. See that mussed-up hair, that little scab on his back?"

I nodded.

"These new photographers, this slick shit—they would have airbrushed that out. And that's why the new porno sucks."

The magazine's narrative continued. On the fourth spread a skinny young guy in a brown UPS uniform barged in, to the amusement of the two guys on the bed. I paged forward, absolutely immersed. Someone might have been speaking directly into my ear: a murmur, a whisper. And then it occurred to me that the visitor was none other than Hector himself.

I was absolutely speechless.

His knee ground deeper into my leg.

"What the—Oh God!"

"Well," he said, a little sheepish, flustered. He pressed his fist to his mouth. "Are you surprised?"

I gazed at his torso, the ropy, idiosyncratic dick. That smile— oddly complicated, disarming. His image shivered with life. It was hard to connect the Hector beside me to the Hector in the magazine.

"You never told me about this," I said finally.

"Yes, I did."

"Did not. You never said a word."

He wagged his head. "If you only yanked your head out of the clouds—"

I shouldn't have been at all surprised. But it did surprise me, and I couldn't help but wonder why he'd kept it from me. Some things you don't forget.

It turned out that Hector, twenty years old, had moved out to San Francisco to stay with a trick he'd met on the 21st Street Beach. It didn't take long to realize that the trick was full of hot air, that he already had a boyfriend, and Hector was out on the streets, with five dollars in his pocket. He'd wandered into a bar in the Tenderloin, where he was approached by a middle-aged man with a pocked face. "I'll give you a place," he said, "if you say yes to some pictures. Naked, I mean." Desperate, he went home with the guy, who, to his astonishment, led him to a room of his own. But the guy had big plans for Hector. Within weeks he was appearing in two videos a week, and was making enough as a hustler to live in North Beach, in his own two-bedroom apartment, with enough hibiscus and bougainvillea to remind him of his mother's yard in Hialeah.

My left eyelid pulsed. I'd seen him once before, maybe many times. Wasn't he Al Parker's partner in the video I'd once watched at the arcade?

I paged ahead, entranced. All that brightness and heat, all those urgings toward—*Come here,* they said. *Come with us.*

Hector laughed, testing my vision, moving his palm before my eyes.

Then footsteps down the hall.

"Shit," I whispered.

"What's the matter?"

"Is it Peter? It's Peter, isn't it? Shit, fuck."

We sat in absolute stillness, listening. Coins fell; a soda can knocked, tunneled through the machine. A ziptop stripped, then mouth to metal. Fizzing.

"Guess not," I said, rubbing my face with my palms.

"Easy." Hector clamped his fingers around my wrist. "Easy."

◇ ◇ ◇

I waited till I was alone.

I dug down deeper in my bed, relaxing.

What other feeling could measure up? What other thing could smash me apart so beautifully, thoroughly? I might have already pulled the needle from my vein, drawing it out, waiting for its effects, heat seeping into my muscles. Once I said yes to it, that was that—loneliness, fear, death, loss: all of it gone, running off into a wilderness. I was solitary, myself, a pure, driven thing. No past, no future. I imagined lying over him, holding onto his hands, tongue working, eating up a trench from his belly to his throat. His skin tasted of salt water, leaves. His dick pressed upward into my chest, grinding.

Why else was he showing me his pictures?

I couldn't help but laugh sometimes.

I wandered into the bathroom, wet washcloth to my face, breathing. I glanced up at myself in the mirror. My bottom lip, fat, ticking; my face, older, paler, harsher than I'd expected.

Seventeen: slouched beneath the dark palms, waiting for William to walk across the lawn.

My hand wandered through the curling hairs of my belly. I cradled my dick, testing its weight, heft, fullness. I felt my stomach again. The skin was hot. Groping higher: something swollen, tender. A hardness. Scab? Blister? I kept pressing, probing it with my fingers.

◇ ◇ ◇

"Did you see this?" Peter asked.

We were standing behind the front desk, 7:07 a.m. Peter fumbled through the rack of incoming mail, gestures animated, jerky. I smelled the coffee on his breath. He behaved like he'd been up and around for hours.

In my hands I held the fax from Fulvia Diaz.

While most renovations wipe out the past, Peter Sarshik's King Cole Motel serves as an homage to Clem Thornton's former Boca Palms showplace. Not only have the odd details been lovingly restored (stucco friezes of gladioli and water jets, starfish, seaweed etched into plate glass), but there's enough decay in evidence—e.g., rust stains around the pool, sulfurous tap water—to make it all seem real. Check out the pastel disks of the walkways. Check out the aerodynamic design of the Nurmi wing (tell yourself it isn't moving a million miles an hour). Have a blended drink at the pool bar. And be sure to introduce yourself to Evan, the handsome, affable desk clerk.

"I mean, she really got it," Peter said.

Could she have mixed something up? What stucco friezes? What seaweed etched into plate glass?

"This'll help us. I *know* this'll help us."

I gazed out at the browning papyrus through the window. The light outside was glassy, overcast. She had to have mixed something up. "I thought I'd pissed her off."

His eyes hazed over. "You never told me that."

I read through the fax again. At least she'd called me handsome. "Did you have sex with her or something?"

"Funny."

"Well—"

"I mean, she mentioned your name. I thought you'd be thrilled."

I yawned, shrugged. "I'm thrilled."

The truth was I hadn't been getting enough sleep to care very much about some travel editor's opinion. I lay in bed, wide awake, four, five in the morning, thinking about Hector.

He looked at me strangely. "I'm going outside to work on the storage room. I've been on a roll. Call me if you need me."

I stared outside at the gleaming inadequacies. The pocked leaves of the aurelia. The yellow mineral stains on the walls, fan-shaped from the sprinklers. *Some*-one had to have had sex with her. Not two minutes after Peter's departure the phone rang. I lunged for it, alarmed. "King Cole, how may I help you?"

"Peter?"

Silence, breathing. A woman. *Holly.*

"Listen, I thought it would be nice if you came over Friday night. I mean, Ory's going to be with my sister, and I thought we'd grill some shrimp. We'll have a nice quiet night together. How's that?"

A lump in my throat. I cradled the handset, frozen, until I was able to breathe again. "Sure," I said finally, "I'd like that."

Silence again. In the background, Ory chattering about box turtles. "Do you have a cold?"

"No."

"Good. I'll see you Friday, then."

My head tingled darkly. I hung up the phone, rapt, listening to Hector's bare, perfect feet on the floor above me.

Chapter 18

The swelling still hadn't subsided.

I kept telling myself not to panic. How many times had I acquired a cold, rash, or virus only to watch it fade, to learn it was just what it was, not a harbinger of something larger. It was life: one got sick, then healthy. Sick, then healthy. Who could even pass through a single hour without battling all kinds of imperceptible threats? Cooling systems, doorknobs, mosquitoes, standing water—all of them birthing pools for potential hazard. If only I *saw* what was happening, saw how efficiently my body was burning, fending them off, I'd have much better things to think about. Instead, I'd willed myself indomitable. I'd gotten to the point where I'd *refused* to get sick, where I actually believed I'd acquired the ability to purge illness from my system, if only to prove to myself that I was well.

Didn't I have a little swelling once before? Didn't I think it was something greater, before it passed on to nothingness?

Once I'd welcomed the first signs of a cold. Sickness was a tent, a house, a warm dark blanket wrapped around my aching bones. Game shows droned on the TV. Palms blurred through the windows. Ursula wandered in and out of my room, cool hand to my scalp, passing me a cup of broth or pineapple Jell-O. She liked these times as much as I did, her worries focused to a single point. There was nothing else in the world: no Sid, no Peter, only *her* care and *my* sickness. Compassion, an absence of complication. We were never any closer than this.

It would never be so simple again.

When my worrying had gotten out of hand, I decided to approach Hector. I stood outside his apartment door, walked away, then back again. Would he think I was needy? Were my visits too obvious, or frequent? I stood there, paralyzed, mouth sour, listening to him puttering with some papers. Finally, I knocked.

I said, "Could I show you something?"

He nodded. He was standing, thick arms folded, looking at the snapshots he'd just tacked up above his desk. On the top, Julia, his mother, standing before the exploding Mount St. Helens—her smile huge, red, lipsticked—volcanic ash clinging to her shoulders. Beneath her, two men on a beach—shirtless, muscular, eyes flashing with laughter—arms wrapped tightly around each other. Beneath them, a young black man—almost pretty—with solemn blue eyes and beaded necklace, squatting before the great globe of the Unisphere in Flushing Meadows Park.

"Who're they?" I said, pointing to the couple.

"Don and Miguel."

"They're adorable."

He nodded. He passed through the stack of snapshots, assembled them with a rubber band, placed them in a drawer.

"I mean, they're not kids, but they're really, really handsome."

His smile clenched. He looked amused. "I knew them for ages. Miguel, the shorter one—he was my lover for two and a half years."

"Really?"

We both looked over at their picture. Together, they seemed so radiant and self-contained, so oriented toward a future, that I couldn't help but feel included. They unsettled me, too. They reminded me of the fact that I'd never believed in the possibility of my own future, how my lack of faith had infused all my decisions, a low-grade fear and rage burning at the heart of everything, from why I'd stopped going to the dentist to my lack of organization to my hasty decisions about college, money, boyfriends. Wasn't it better to extinguish oneself than to lose one's light, little by little? Wasn't this what all those silly rock songs told us? But looking at them, I felt differently. *It isn't so bad to get older.*

I said, "Why is it we only see pictures of young men? All these magazines. You might think queer life was only for kids. What about the older guys?"

"What older guys?" Hector mumbled.

"Hmm?"

"They're dead. Don and Miguel—all these older guys are dead."

My stomach pitched. I thought of their contentment, their absolute confidence in each other. They'd known what they'd wanted: how could anything *not* have gone their way? Something fleeting coursed up the column of my spine. I might have been lifted, for the briefest instant, off my feet.

Outside, the palms were drenched with an oddly golden light.

"What were you going to ask?" Hector said.

My swelling pressed against the waistband of my jeans, resisting it. Blood hummed, murmured within my veins. I looked at him: there really wasn't very much time.

I'd make my move on Friday.

"Would you mind cutting my hair?"

"I'm tired," he said.

◇ ◇ ◇

My haircut was growing out, stray strands curling over the tops of my ears. It required more maintenance than was initially promised. Though it didn't need to be combed or washed every day, it looked dingy if it wasn't cut once a week. I looked more like my old self, the diffident, milky self I'd been before Hector had gotten a hold of me. But it didn't matter now. The swelling on my belly was healing, along with all those ghastly feelings I'd attached to it.

Still, I felt distracted, possessed by an emptiness I couldn't name. Wasn't there someone, someplace in the world, who was being told that he or she was dying right at this very minute?

Late Friday afternoon I walked into the Nurmi wing, where Hector had room duty. He was studying the bottom sheet of a bed, checking it for stains, sand, crumbs, or offending odors, deciding whether or not to change it for the next guest. I knew the ploy; I'd practiced it myself on occasion, though it was a lousy one. From the boom box, Laura Nyro wailed at top volume, pounding out parallel triads, Motown-style, on the piano.

I stood inside the doorway, watching the deliberations crossing his face. Then he glanced upward, startled. "Would you mind cutting my hair when you get the chance?"

"Huh?" He turned down the volume.

"I said—" And I repeated my question.

His brows lifted. He swigged from a can of watermelon soda. "I'm really busy."

His response, however subtle, carried an accusation: I was demanding, pushy, self-absorbed. But I'd never asked him for anything.

"I mean, could it wait?" he said, face thawing. "This is a bad time for me. Maybe Tuesday?"

I tried not to be miffed. I pulled one side of the bottom sheet, helping him fit it around the corners of the mattress. He replaced Laura with Kate Bush's *Lionhearted* album. "What about that barbershop in Naples? Have you heard anything about it?"

"Porkchop's?"

"Yeah."

"He's pretty good," he replied, glancing up. "And cheap. I've gone to him one or two times myself."

"Well, thanks," I said, too loud, forced.

I walked down the hall. It hadn't occurred to me that I was

asking for much. Five minutes, not even that. After all, wasn't he the one who'd insisted I'd look better with a shaved head? And wasn't I the one who'd been sprucing up his rooms, which had seemed increasingly flagrant in their ineptitude, just to keep him in Peter's good graces?

I stood at the window in the eastern stairwell. I watched Peter standing in the parking lot, waiting for something. I couldn't stop staring at him. It seemed to me that his entire story was encapsulated in his waiting, from his jerky glances toward the road, to his nearly constant pacing, to his wringing hands, which he kept twisting and pulling as if they hurt him. He was nothing but uncomfortable in his own skin, and it was the loneliest thing I'd ever seen, and it repelled and frightened me, knowing that we were a part of each other.

When I couldn't stand it anymore, I trudged down to the office, swiped the key ring off the rack, and walked outside. Over the Gulf, clouds hurried toward the south, swarming, tornadic.

"I'm taking the van," I called to Peter.

The breeze lifted, blew through his thinning hair. His eyes looked impossibly green against the palms. "Where're you going?"

"Haircut." And before he could insist I didn't need one, I shifted the van into reverse, and headed north.

◇ ◇ ◇

The sky darkened as the squall line approached. I was lost somewhere inside Golden Gate Estates. All the streets bore numbered names, qualified by quadrant directions (Northwest, Northeast, etc.), and I couldn't quite remember whether it was SW 130th Street or SW 130th Place. I pored over my memory of Peter's address book. It troubled me to think that anyone actually lived here. Like its better-known sister, Cape Coral, the landscape was jungly, dense, overrun with escaped tropical species—Brazilian pepper, Chinese tallow, punk tree— not a shred left of indigenous beauty. It was the kind of place that wasn't civilized enough for comfort, nor remote enough to point up the pleasures of solitude. The axle bumped over a tiny sinkhole in the street. There was no point in continuing on.

Just then I spotted her gold Tercel. It sidled up alongside a long, narrow trailer in which all the lamps inside were on. A funnel of light illuminated the front yard. To my surprise, Ory, her six-year-old, was sculpting sandcastles beside a weaving pyracantha bush.

I slowed the van to a crawl. "Storm's coming," I said through the window.

"Lightning," he said, pointing a plastic shovel to the sky.

"Yes. It's dangerous. Do you know what happens if you get struck?"

"Boom," he said, throwing up his hands.

"Does your mom know you're outside?"

The boy nodded avidly, then smacked at the sand with his shovel.

"Ory," Holly said. She stood at the screen door in a black T-shirt, cutoff jeans, and motorcycle boots. Her hands were fisted on her hips. She squinted. "Who're you talking to out there?"

I couldn't leave now. In truth, I'd only wanted to see where she lived. I'd only wanted to see the trailer, then get the hell out of there.

Her smile revealed her upper gum. "Peter?"

I froze, stricken.

She stepped closer to the van. *"Peter?"*

"It's Evan," I said finally, and looked away.

"Oh my God," she said, breathless.

"What?"

"I didn't have a clue. I've only seen you from a distance."

I shook my head.

"I mean, your hair's shorter, and you're a lot younger and all that, but—" She exhaled through her mouth and stared. "Say something."

I frowned, waggled my head.

"*Please.* Say something."

I mumbled, "What do you want me to say?"

She started laughing, a little pained. Her eyes were vibrant. "You even *sound* like him. Oh my God. This has to be, like, the weirdest experience of my life."

We stared. I had no business here. I should have gotten my hair cut.

Her face quieted down. The wind picked up, palmettos scouring the surface of the trailer. "Do you want to come inside?"

"No," I said. "Just out for a little drive."

She laughed knowingly. Her absolute familiarity with me was both unsettling and comforting. "Yes, Evan. You just happened to be driving through beautiful Golden Gate during a severe thunderstorm warning, a full thirty miles from the King Cole."

"But—"

"Oh, just for a minute. Come."

She placed her arm around me as we walked toward the door. I wiped off my boots on the grass mat. "It's so good to finally meet you," she said.

Inside, the trailer was as long and narrow as a boxcar. Nearly everything had a dual purpose: a sofa that opened up into a bed, a coffee table that doubled as a chest. On the table stood a tiny lamp, no taller than a wine bottle. The whole space was possessed by the spirit of order, a spirit determined by its limitations: one thing left out and the place would be a mess.

"So's it time to go to bed?" she asked Ory.

He was sitting on the floor, looking up at me on the sofa, curious and amazed.

"Ory?"

He stuck out his lip, showing off the linings of his eyelids, then shook his head no.

"Stop that," Holly said. "Don't make monster faces at Evan. He's our friend."

Ory's face relaxed. He reached up, fingers scrabbling toward my belt loop.

"Oh," Holly said, and smiled. "I know what he wants."

I stood, picking up Ory. He was almost weightless, lips moist, sticky against my cheek. I kissed him back, bouncing him slightly. I wished I felt more at ease. His grasp tightened around my neck, flooding me with self-consciousness.

"Okay, that's enough now," Holly said. "Time to say good night. Time for bed."

"Good night," he said to me.

"Good night, Ory," I said.

I watched them walk hand in hand down the hall. I wandered over to the mini-china closet, an oversized toy, and glanced at the clear green tumblers on the shelves—the free kind from service stations—while Ory fussed and sobbed in his room. I looked at his pictures on the wall. Ory, at one, fed by an unseen hand, chocolate syrup smeared all over his mouth. Ory, at two, standing at a dock, eyes shining, holding a minnow in his palm. Ory, at three, in a straw Hawaiian hat, brim swallowing up his head. I kept staring at his face, the narrow forehead, the benign smile, pure and unassuming as a dolphin's. My stomach hurt. A queasy notion passed through my mind: Ory was my brother's son.

The rain picked up, pelting the windows. This was Peter's separate, hidden life.

I roved down the hall to Ory's room. He was still crying, squealing, voice pitching higher with each explosion of thunder. Water pooled on the sills, seeping through the cracks. Holly perched on the edge of the bed, eyes merry, twinkling, but clearly within two seconds of coming undone. I stepped through the dump trucks on the floor, past the wooden blocks and the spotted pink anaconda. Bright tempera paintings covered the walls, edges curling inward.

"He's scared," Holly said.

"Am not," he said, face pressed to his pillow.

"Are too."

He gazed up at me with a single eye.

"But you liked it outside," I said to him.

He pressed his face to the pillow, shook his head no.

"Be still," I said, then turned off the lights. "Be absolutely still." I motioned to Holly, and we climbed into bed, lying on either side of him, bodies tight. Ory flipped over on his back. The trailer rocked and pitched, wind nearly wrenching it off its footings. The lightning was upon us now. I pictured the palms outside flaring up, one after the other, blazing around us like torches.

"Shhhhh," I whispered. "It's taking our picture."

The room flashed. Ory frowned, whimpering.

"Look, the sky's taking our picture."

It flashed once more, and then again and again. Ory's eyes widened in the dark. And the three of us leaned into one another, breaths falling into sync, various smells commingling. Warmth passed from body to body, a single unit now.

Gradually, the storm subsided, thunder fading to a distant hush. The branches outside stilled, dripped. Moonlight poured through the room, illuminating Ory's mobile, his finger paintings. Down the hall clothes tumbled in the dryer.

"Thank you," Holly whispered.

"I can't believe he's actually sleeping."

"He likes you." She sighed hugely, then held herself with her arms. She lay absolutely still, eyes closed. I imagined a heaviness—the weight of a truck tire—pushing down upon her chest.

I whispered, "Are you okay?"

"Listen," she said, "do you mind if I kick you out?"

"No, no. Not at all." And I didn't, actually. The roads would have drained by now. It was time to get home.

She turned on her side. "Am I being rude? Tell me if I'm being selfish."

"Don't worry about it."

Her smile was enormous, melancholy. "I'm glad you understand. This was very nice." She reached over Ory and latched her damp fingers through my own. "Let's get together sometime soon, okay?"

I nodded.

"And tell your brother I'd love to hear from him."

I nodded again. My chance: should I tell her about the call, that I'd pretended to be Peter on the phone? I straggled by the potted fig, rubbing my thumb across a dust-coated leaf.

"What's the deal?" she said in a hushed voice, as if talking aloud to herself.

I turned to look at her again. Coward: I didn't say a word.

"It's just—" She stopped. She seemed hopelessly, utterly baffled.

"He cares about you," I said, surprising myself.

She shook her head. "It's not like I'm going to get anywhere with him. I should have known what I was getting into."

My ear felt hot, as if I'd knocked it against a post. To myself, I counted backwards from 100, trying to calm down: 99, 98, 97 . . . "I mean, he really cares about you more than you know. He's crazy about you. You're all he ever talks about."

She glanced downward at her crossed legs. A dog barked at regular intervals in the distance. "Really?"

"Yes, really."

"But—"

"But what?"

She lifted her face and looked at me. Her eyes were dolorous, hopeful, full of feeling. "What does he say about me?" she murmured.

I touched the cooling silver of her bracelet. Her wrist felt warm as if she were running a temperature. "You have to ask him that yourself."

She sighed. Her eyes rested on the sleeping boy beside her.

"Tomorrow night," I said. "Come over tomorrow night. Surprise him. Come for dinner. He'd love to see you, I know it."

"Okay," she said quietly. "You're right. You're absolutely right. Why have I been such a wimp about everything?" A triangle of light illuminated her face. Her eyes looked calmer, grateful. I might have granted her a wish.

I walked back to the living room, where I glanced at the TV. I knew it now: everything would work out for the best. I'd get Hector, Peter would get Holly and Ory. I'd make sure of it. We'd all be thankful and relieved, kinder, calmer. Another front was lining up over the Gulf, weather map pulsing, all greens and reds, blinking like a Christmas tree.

◇ ◇ ◇

His plan was this: he'd walk into our respective rooms, pause before our sleeping bodies, then smother us with a pillow. He'd listen to the gulp, stammer, and wheeze of our closing-down systems. Then silence. An absolute reverence. I'd be the first, the harder one. I'd resist, yelling out, driving my fists into his chest. Hector, on the other hand, would be the shocker. He'd take to the pillow, almost tenderly, like a lover, almost welcoming that choke, that heightened sensation before the heart stills then floods. Peter would pause, pondering the drip of the bathroom sink. He'd call up the police. He'd fix himself some coffee, basking in the numbered minutes of his freedom, bare feet up on the coffee table. Minutes later, he'd hear the squad cars pulling over the potholes in the drive. Daybreak.

I woke up, panting. I crept to the window, eyes foggy from sleep. The yard was a reservoir, a lake. Paint cans floated across its surface, loose boards and boxes, all of them drifting, drawn by the imperceptible suck of the culvert.

In the morning, Peter and I sat at the office table, silent. My T-shirt clung to my back. He reached for the box of corn flakes. He poured them into a bowl, spooning them into his mouth, determined to finish them off, not allowing himself to acknowledge that they were stale, virtually inedible. I knew that he was losing money by the day, but this was about something deeper. He might have been our father. I saw it all: his self-denial, his secret cultivation of martyrdom, his exquisite selfishness, his stubborn indifference toward those affected by his decisions. My rage pushed up against my chest, a hard metal plate. I stood, then glanced at his thinning crown before I left the room.

I had to stop. I walked through the corridors, listening to the water streaming through the rainspouts. I thought about what I'd liked about him, what made him interesting, valuable.

I thought about his complete devotion to restoring the King Cole property, his ability to bestow all his attention upon a single window, sanding its frame for days on end until it was nearly perfect. I thought about his various interests—the paintings of Richard Diebenkorn, the designs of Luis Barragan—how he most likely knew more about these things than anyone else on the planet. I thought about his measured, good-natured rapport with our guests, how he'd once sat for two hours with an elderly couple after the man had experienced chest pains, convincing them he was actually interested in the subtleties of fly fishing, all in an effort to calm them down. But I couldn't hold all these thoughts in my head at once, and the pictures were already crumbling about the edges, no matter how hard I tried to keep them intact.

Why is it that I hate you so much?

He was everything I didn't want to become: stingy, closed down, secretive.

I slouched around the pool that night, watching the lights blazing beneath the water. The rain had finally stopped, the ground swollen and sipping. Water lapped over the edge of the pool; the overflow made gulping sounds. Holly's gold Tercel was parked haphazardly on the grass beneath the royal palm, and I gazed up at the light in Peter's window, wondering what was happening between them—love or argument, anguish or boredom? A tiny plane jetted across the dome of the sky.

Then something popped.

I looked up. In an instant a spark sizzled across a wire, traveling between the light pole and the office. It was all of ten feet. It happened so fast that I doubted myself—flashes: detached retina?—before it happened again. I couldn't stop watching. That subtle blue movement: it was as pretty as it was unnerving. My eyeballs ached from its brightness. And then the line sparked again.

What dark fortune: my luck couldn't have been better.

I pushed at the door to the stairwell. I bounded up the steps, two at a time, then ran down the hall to Hector's.

"Hi," he said, eyes foggy, half closed. His T-shirt said

PUNCTURED. He looked like he was about to lean forward to kiss me. He grinned. The sweet smell of hashish fermented the air, drifting out into the corridor to be taken into the valves of the air conditioner.

"Did you look out the window?" I said.

His face dulled slightly. "What?"

"Come here." And I grabbed him by the arm, pulled, stepped over the rumpled clothes on his floor. We stood together at his window, watching the wire, hushed, expectant. The quiet blue flashes lit up his face. We were motionless. Were we just seconds away from feeling the floor heating up, burning through the soles of our shoes?

"Shit," he said.

I folded my arms across my chest. "We have to tell Peter."

"He hasn't seen it?"

I shook my head, hard. "No. We have to tell him. Now, right now. *Move.*"

And before he could say we'd handle it ourselves, I was leading him down the hall, nearly pulling him toward my brother's door. My chest pounded. My forehead boiled. Hector reached for the knob without bothering to knock.

"Peter, there's—"

I stood directly behind him. He didn't process it immediately. Peter lying atop Holly, movements furious, ass gyrating, clefting like an opened fruit. They didn't stop. Peter glanced over his shoulder. His hairline filmed over with sweat. A rank human sweetness saturated the room: it almost had a taste. Holly's nipples were unusually large and dark, the deepest pink, unutterably foreign to me. She seemed to be too embarrassed to cover herself.

Silently, Hector closed the door.

The line stopped sparking only two minutes before the fire department arrived in full force, radio blasting, beams of red light whirling about the courtyard.

It didn't happen till the next morning, but when it did, it was worse than I'd imagined. I watched it all from my window: Hector standing on the second-floor balcony, gazing down at Peter, whose arm held her close to his chest, escorting her to her car. "You're an asshole," Hector called out hoarsely. "You're a low-life fucking asshole." Peter looked up once, stricken, then looked back at Holly, who covered her face before opening her car door. Was this what I'd wanted? It hurt me as much to see it. I felt it deep inside my soul, burrowing.

Chapter 19

I didn't think he'd still count. I didn't think I'd still think of him, but I did, often in the least expected moments. I might have been walking through Port Royal, immersed in the particularized order of a rose garden, and—*bam*—there he'd be in black leather and chains, throwing stones at me. Or a little farther up the street, squatting atop the bank in the lewdest position, dressed in harness and jockstrap and pretty clothes. I'd be startled for an instant, a dense high crackling like a brush-fire inside my head. And then it would pass. He was back in Miami, working the camera at Channel 7, forever settled in his banal, tired habits, which he'd embrace for the rest of his life.

I wouldn't see him again. Of that much I was sure. I wasn't so deluded to think there had ever been a chance anyway. Together we amounted to nothing: two specks, ground glass, empty bags blowing across a backyard lawn. At best, we were only an idea, and though the idea might have thrilled us with its daring, we were hardly daring. I couldn't say our time together had been a mistake, but some things are better left an idea.

Still, if I thought hard enough, I could conjure him. The

texture and taste of his back, sweaty and rich, as he came in from the garden. The trembling board of his stomach, brown, vascular, from light years of situps. In my mind I could play him, use him like a doll. My fury spun wild. I could poke out his eyes. I could spray him down with paint. I could strike up a match and toss it at him, watching him running through the woods with his hissing scalp, miles and miles, looking for water, screaming my name.

I walked up Tamiami Trail, two in the morning. Cars careened up the highway, broken fenders dragging up little storms of blue sparks. It surprised me that he still mattered. He kept flaring up: a gas fire, a torch in the center of a cracked path, forcing me to reckon with myself. It seemed to me that I'd been shutting down, that I'd once again relegated myself to monkdom. Sometimes it seemed that the issue of sex had all the force of something much larger than myself, a huge moving glacier that threatened to run me over, consume me with its force. What the hell was I so afraid of? I could convince myself that the search for a lover—or frankly, just someone to fuck—was fraught with such risk and pain that the inevitable mess wasn't worth it, that it was easier to stay enveloped in my own fog, beating off to muscled images from magazines that had nothing to do with reality. Was it that I was truly afraid of happiness, of what I really wanted? Of what was so easily within reach?

I was sitting across the street from a park. The palms were totem poles, their shaggy petticoats hanging lushly in the dark. It was getting hotter. Humidity funneled up from the tropics, coating everything with a slick wet net. Everything smelled of moisture—the grass, the trees, the streets, the buildings. I glanced down at my arm. I wouldn't have been surprised to see a fresh mold growing on my skin, thick enough to be scraped off with a butter knife. At times like this I saw the whole Florida experiment as one vast error; the notion of an entire existence modeled after the one in the North seemed doomed to failure.

Two teenagers were running across the grass, diving near the sprinklers to cool themselves down. Deeper in the woods

I saw the outline of a man. He situated himself in a glade of mock oranges, half hidden beneath a limb, only his vaguest outlines visible. He was tall, sturdy. I tried not to stare at him too intently. I pretended to watch a cargo truck with huge yellow letters bucketing down the street. When I looked up again, I noticed that he'd taken one step closer. There was no question that his eyes were fixed upon mine.

I knew what was happening. Behind him, submerged in the dark trees of the park, were other men, all watching, waiting. It seemed nearly incredible that I'd delivered myself here of all places, but I wasn't about to question the destiny of things. I stood, conscious of the leaden weight in my legs, my trembling hands. Before I allowed myself to recognize my fear, to dwell in the moment of my essential ambivalence, I was walking toward the stranger, staring directly into the glare of the streetlight.

"William," I said aloud.

My words caught like crumbs in my throat. He pulled me toward him. In no time at all he'd taken off my shirt, and I was lying down on the grass beneath him, the stones digging into my back. His tongue was rough in my mouth. He worked a dry finger inside me, and I drew in my breath, resisting. I wasn't sure if I wanted this. He was going to murder me, I thought. We were going to be caught or he was going to murder me. I shut my eyes. I saw myself in a plane, looking down at a scar in the earth, an open pit filled with water the color of sewage. The plane circled the pit. A parachute opened, and then I saw myself slipping deep into the water. The stranger lifted me to my feet. He smelled of solder, burnt things. I looked into his grinning face, the gap between his teeth. I felt oddly moved by that for some reason, and he reached for my dick, holding it tight, tighter, and that did it—I crumbled, my back going tight, my legs giving way, and then the release.

I slouched against a palm, listening to the struggle of my breath. The man's footsteps crunched on the gravel. I recognized something, though I wasn't quite sure what it was.

Where was I? I stood in the shelter of the glade, watching the man stumbling back to his car. I tried not to be absent. I waited until he was completely out of sight, then wiped myself off, walked over to the Trail, and hitched a ride back to the King Cole.

◇ ◇ ◇

I stood on the abandoned golf course, watching Peter dismantle the old cabana, an outbuilding from the Clem Thornton Boca Palms days. The building inspectors had been hounding him for months, insisting it a hazard, in danger of collapse. I didn't know what had possessed him to finally take on the project now, at nine in the morning, in 88 percent humidity, but nothing he did alarmed me anymore. He worked the prybar into a seam and pulled. The rotten plywood crumbled like foam in his hands. I thought of people who'd become possessed of extraordinary capabilities in times of crisis, sandbagging their properties for thirty-six hours straight to save their livestock from flood. His energy reminded me of them, though I didn't know who or what he was protecting.

I stepped beside him and pulled at a loose sheet. Grit blew through the air, catching in my eyes. I blinked it away. He kept pulling down the structure, holding in his breath, deliberately ignoring my presence.

"Not like that," he said finally.

"What?"

"See what you're doing?"

"What?"

"You don't have the right tools."

Termites crept over the brittle wood, tensing their clear, sticky wings. "Calm down, will you?"

"Gloves." He pointed at the nicks in my fingers.

"I didn't bring any."

He batted a mosquito from his brow. "Listen, why don't you check out the pool?"

I tightened my fist in my pocket.

"I'm serious. It's been raining for days. It's bound to need some chemicals."

His eyes were vivid, sea green behind his safety glasses. He was wary of me now. Would we talk about the other night? Did he have any idea I'd partly set it up? Secrets, secrets.

I trekked across the grassy slope. I imagined him nameless, a worn silver surface where his features had been. He wasn't himself anymore. He was emptied, a phantom. And all at once I knew what he was becoming for me. He was everything that stood between me and what I'd longed for, everything I'd ever lost and never had. He was my relationship with William—*failure*. He was my relationship with my parents—*failure*. He was my fear of the future—*failure*—my shame, the absence of love and trust—all of them tied up together in one sticky knot. But I wasn't about to start fussing with it now. I might have been a whirling hate machine, hot wind blowing through my blades, spinning me around so fast I could have lifted off the ground, and then what?

◇ ◇ ◇

A little after midnight I spotted Hector within the illuminated rectangle of the pool. He drifted around on a red rubber raft, turning imperceptibly like the hand of a clock, nudging himself from the sides with the ball of his foot. I couldn't stop watching him. I eyed him from the darkness of my room through the torn fronds of the travelers trees, murmuring his name.

I walked to the pool in my green swimsuit. I stood on the ledge for a moment. The water bubbled, teeming, alive, a container of light.

I'd waited long enough.

I dove in. I swam all the way down to the pool lamps, kicking forward, then up, up, water *whooshing*, churning inside my nostrils, ears. My eyes burned. I moved beneath the raft—a submarine!—and knocked him off. "What the fuck," he cried.

His arms thrashed. His drinking glass sank—dream-like, slow-motion—to the bottom. I grabbed for his swimsuit, pulled it down, as he fought me off, pounding my back, laughing, bewildered. We faced each other. I reached for his dick and looked in his face. "What?" he said, shier, more vulnerable than I'd expected. *"What?"* I squeezed him tighter. A tingle in my groin. "Give up," I said. "Give it up. Let go. This isn't any surprise. You know exactly what you want." He sighed all at once, eyes closed, a little smile on his lips, shoulders letting go, dropping forward. He laughed softly. I pulled him toward the shallow end. I had him now. My moment: I wasn't going to waste it. I knelt, water sloshing around my neck, and took him inside my mouth. I sucked in a breath through my nose, throat full. Good, so good: I raised my chin. I rubbed his stomach, squeezed the tough pink nub of his nipple. Skin, musk, hair, the moist rich darkness—everything focusing, everything centering in us. He bit into his lip, winced. "Yes," he said, and swayed above me. "Ah, yes." My head knocking his belly. His palms pressing harder to my ears, blocking out the sound.

A rushing inside my head: a downpour.

How long did it last? An hour? Fifteen minutes? Five? Time dilating, opening up like an aperture.

The backs of his legs clenched. Something scalded my shoulder. When we finished, we both started laughing, soft at first, then louder, more raucous. We shook the water from our hair. "Jesus," he said.

"Oh God." I backed up to the rungs of the ladder and fought for my breath. What had I done? I couldn't believe what I'd done.

"It's all right," he said. He kept blinking, rubbing his temples with his fingers.

I exhaled through my mouth. The windows around us were dark, curtained, everyone sleeping soundly in their rooms. The fans of the air conditioners rattled in unison. I heard voices in their drones, scraps of songs, harmonies. Stars blazed, rotating above our heads. "So I'll see you tomorrow, then."

"Good night, you."

"Good night." I swam to the opposite wall—heart banging, triumphant. I pulled myself out of the pool, and ran, shivering, all the way back to my room.

◇ ◇ ◇

I couldn't sleep. I lay on my humble bed, sheets kicked to the floor. Floodlights poured through the curtains. The room felt hot, sealed off. My mouth tasted like a bandage. A thousand thoughts stampeded through my head. I pulled on some shorts, hooked my flashlight to my belt loop, and left.

I walked down the Trail. I walked to the west, through the vast, vacant city until the sky blued, until my feet hurt in my shoes. Branches bearded with moss. Ghosts crashing in the trees. Shapes, souls. Something was ringing inside my head, a fire alarm: *You can change your life, you can.*

◇ ◇ ◇

The van lurked behind the office. We swung onto the back-seat, leather scorching our legs. Two p.m. Roasting, a sauna inside, the floor cluttered with coupons, wrappers. Our sun-glasses steamed up. I crouched, facing him on the seat, palms pressed to his jaws. Air stifling, too thick to breathe. I pushed my tongue between his lips, tracing the ridges on the roof of his mouth, the softness, his teeth.

I cradled the pouch of his jockey shorts.

"Here?" He laughed, bewildered, as if afraid of me. "You've got to be crazy."

"Yeah, here," I said.

He cleared his throat, swallowed. He shook his head. Then he unzipped his own pants, lifting me inches above his lap.

A stab. I yelped, clenching, breathing, then balancing my-self, grabbing onto his shoulders. His skin whitened beneath my fingers. I coughed. Little by little, we started moving. Wet, sloppy inside. Sweat rivering down my torso.

"Like *that?*" he said.

"Like that."

The axles flexed. We kept moving the van that way, squeaking, working it, almost laughing at our audacity.

◇ ◇ ◇

"Are you all right?" said Peter one day.

"What do you mean?"

"You look a little strange," he said, tilting his head, considering. "Around the eyes. Have you been getting enough sleep?" His breath felt warm, like the heat off a candle, on my cheeks. He stepped closer, so close that I almost fell backward.

◇ ◇ ◇

Hector and I floated in the pool one night. No talk. My suit floated off on the surface, an empty bag. Our mouths fastened. We were circling, hands pushing at each other, muscles tensing. I wanted him closer. I studied his face: that scar beneath his ear, those fleshy pink lips. How to get him closer? How to get deeper inside the body? *Our* bodies. I tried hard as I could to inhabit it, *us,* closing my eyes, frenetic. A fluttering in my gut. *Deeper,* I thought, concentrating. *Deeper.* A well: the water inside the well. Icy, burning. *Down, down, down the dark ladder.* His stubbled jaw rubbed against the grain of my chin. Shuddering, my eyes opened. I pictured something rising off Hector, a dark violet cloth, the size of a handkerchief, floating upwards.

It occurred to me we were most likely causing someone pain.

We were up to our shoulders in water, chlorine burning in our nostrils. I pressed my mouth to his shoulder. I might have bitten right through to the bone, hurting him, leaving a mark like a tiny animal trap.

I glanced toward the nearest wing. There were rustlings from the rooms, vague murmurings and the occasional cough. A jalousie window cranked closed.

"Did you hear something?"

His brows drew together.

"I'm serious. I think someone might have been watching." I looked off toward the buttonwoods, the acacia, the loquat. Peter? "Hey, somebody there? Who's out there?"

His eyes were solemn, dignified. Garbage trucks lumbered down the Trail. And, if only for an instant, looking at the smudgings of his cheeks, the slight sag beneath his eyes, I imagined him older, sixty. "Everyone's been in bed for hours. Stop worrying."

"I'm not worried," I said.

He hefted himself up onto the raft, belly scuffing against rubber, hands scooping, paddling away from me.

Chapter 20

Day 21. Agitators, vandals; we did it anywhere, in the most outlandish places: the utility passage, the floor of the conference room, the hood of a guest's sedan within full view of the pool. Always testing our nerve. Always amazed by ourselves. My body authoritative and deft, my thoughts fluid. I was beside myself with—what? Bliss? Joy?

◇ ◇ ◇

My head buzzed. I imagined him standing behind me, arms around my chest, chin wedged between my shoulder blades, wiggling it, telling me to trust him; yes, of course, he felt just like I did, of course. He was crazy about me. I meant the world to him. His breath heated my spine. I curled back into him, eyes closed, purring like a cat. But why so many fragments, scraps in my head? Why this persistent, gummy absorption: the almondy taste of his fingers, the smell of his scalp already growing fainter and fainter?

◇ ◇ ◇

Hector crooked his elbow over his face, feet wide apart, in imitation of a vampire. Together we stood outside the laundry room. The dryers rushed and spun inside, throwing out their heat.

"Dracula?" I said.

He made biting motions toward my neck. He raised his upper lip: fangs, plastic Halloween fangs.

"This is supposed to be funny?" I said.

"I'm used to seeing you only at night, that's all."

It occurred to me that I'd been avoiding him outside of our "dates," for lack of a better word for them. Just the merest sight of him had started jostling my demeanor. "Shhhh—" I pointed to Peter's hunching back through the office window. He leaned forward over the desk, talking on the phone, taking notes furiously upon a legal pad.

Thumb pressed to the roof of his mouth, he pulled out the fangs with a quick suck. "I thought you were through with being afraid."

My voice stopped in my throat. Instantly I saw it: he wasn't anxious about me at all. His stance, his wry, ironic gaze—it was as if nothing substantial had changed between us.

"I've got rooms to finish," I mumbled, then hurried down the walk.

"Evan, wait, *wait*."

I sighed hugely. I didn't turn.

"Do you want to drive into Fort Myers this afternoon?"

The glibness. How could things be so easy for some people? Whoever said life was supposed to be so flippant, so casual? My eyes fixed upon a sea-almond pod in the dirt. "Some other time."

Nights later, I came in from the pool, hair wet, shivering. I lay facedown on my bed with my clothes off. The air conditioner ebbed, droned. I couldn't catch my breath. I had every reason to be ecstatic, energized, relaxed: didn't I finally have what I'd been longing for? Didn't I finally know the elusive pleasures of the body? How far away those days with William seemed. How far away those days of loneliness, panic, yearning. Yet even the most fundamental tasks required a terrific will. No energy. I couldn't even finish my sentences. They stalled on my lips, dissolving in my mouth like sugar cubes, while my listener waited for me, puzzled, impatient. My room was a mess, my floor strewn with T-shirts and towels. I hadn't gotten my hair cut in weeks. No books, no tending trees. I'd become so lax in my duties that I was surprised that Peter hadn't let me go by now.

I cleaned the first-floor rooms one day. One of the guests had left behind a pack of Lucky Strikes, and I started smoking them, one after the next, as I vacuumed the worn carpet. I left my cigarette on the air conditioner. Not three seconds later the curtain above it started smoking. I tore it off the rod, stomping it, swiping it with my sneakers until I was certain the fire was out. The flames had chewed and charred it, eaten off its edge. It seared my palms as I tucked it the closet. I sprayed a half-can of Glade around the room, and still I smelled the smoke, gloomy and acrid, stinging the membranes of my nose.

◇ ◇ ◇

The old sample house glowed. We'd brought with us four orange flashlights, and I'd propped them together on the warped floor: a centerpiece. They cast their warm glow onto the rotting studs, the unfinished ceiling. Fat sacks of Dursban hulked beneath the windows. We'd just finished, and we lay there on the floor, lingering, listening to the ospreys in the swamp—a departure from our routine.

I was lying on my side, running my thumb along his jawline. His face looked unusually pensive, aquiline.

He turned on his side. "Well, you're affectionate this evening."

The tips of my ears blazed. A judgment? I felt foolish, as if I'd violated some invisible code.

"I'm sorry. That wasn't very nice. It's just—you care about me?"

"*No,* like—" I sat up. Blood rushed from my head, blackness falling before my eyes.

"We have to talk."

I looked at the ceiling, willing any reaction out of my face. I was motionless now, a puppet, a cartoon, a stick figure. I steeled myself.

"I'm worried about you," he said finally.

"I'm perfectly fine."

"It's like this means too much to you." He shook his head, faltering. He dragged his tongue across lower lip. "You're a very sweet boy, a very good friend to me. But you need to get harder, tougher."

His voice was impossibly quiet, almost tender. One of the flashlights toppled on its side, beam swinging across the ceiling, down the wall, to the floor.

"I don't understand."

His eyes darkened, burning now. "We're having sex, all right?" His voice got louder, tinged with a warning. "It's just sex. I'm not your boyfriend, I'm not your lover."

A welling, a heat gathering in my throat. "I see," I said finally.

He nodded.

"And you're making this decision for the both of us?"

"I just want to make sure we know what's what."

I couldn't hide it any longer. I flexed my toes until they popped inside my shoes. At once, a door yawned open beneath me. My stomach fell. Bright lights flashed above, taking my picture. I felt astonished and exposed, to him, to myself.

I wanted to pummel his back until he wept.

"Are you okay?" he said.

"Have a good night, pal."

My back teeth might have cracked apart. *Sweet boy,* I thought. *Good friend.* I shook my head, left the emptied house without another word.

◇ ◇ ◇

Hope: a pop, a lightbulb blowing out.

◇ ◇ ◇

I woke at three one morning. A party was in full swing across the courtyard. The door was off its hinges; inside sat a boom box on the bathroom counter, bass line thudding. The proceedings spilled out onto the grass. The kids stomped, throwing back their heads, flailing their arms. An occasional scream lashed the gusty, gelid air. A girl ran out the door followed by a guy with the widest shoulders I'd ever seen. He tackled her to the grass, and amidst her protests, poured beer foam down her impossibly white back.

The idea of a party at this minute in the world seemed completely beyond my comprehension. I fell back asleep.

I cleaned up the mess first thing the next morning. My rage and longing fueled me, helping me work faster and faster. An unrolled condom stuck to the headboard like something ghostly, mysterious: a jellyfish. As I cleaned, the radio announcer described the late-night shooting of a local teenager in the Crossroads Mall parking lot. His voice was flat, clinical, as if he were reading off a grocery list.

When I finished, I sat at the desk, reached for a piece of motel stationery, and started writing as fast as I could.

Hector,

How not to sound like an asshole, a fool?

Question: what is it you feel for me? When I look into your face, I think, well, of course, of course. And then I'll see you walking across the blacktop, cocky, not even a hello from you. And what you said the other night: fuck you. Do you think we're going to keep this up?

Your indifference makes me want to yell.

I want to smear myself in it to show you what it looks like.

I'll get up again: don't doubt that for a second. As for you—

I can't get anything done.

I read what I'd written three times, crossing out words, writing over them. The pen pressed deeply through the paper. Idiotic, ridiculous: nothing sounded authentic to me. Then I ripped the page in two and flushed it down the toilet.

◇ ◇ ◇

Hector was up earlier than expected. He strode back and forth from the Dumpster to the stairwell, gestures infused with an unexpected energy. This wasn't like him: he usually didn't get moving till ten or later, not till his two cups of *cafe con leche.* After a few minutes I followed him up to his apartment. Everything was packed up in boxes along one wall; snapshots were stacked on the desk.

Something gnarled in the root of my neck.

"Want this?" he asked.

He offered me the chartreuse shirt with the pointed collar and oversize buttons. It was the very shirt we'd retrieved from the county landfill, to Peter's protests, many months before.

"Why would I want your shirt?"

"What about these things?" He walked across the room, picked up a magenta House of Field shopping bag. Inside an assortment of gadgets, postcards, magazines, doodads, gewgaws.

"What's going on?"

"You're going to freak," he murmured.

"What?"

"Peter's onto us."

"Peter?"

"Peter knows that we've been fucking around."

Something rumbled in the distance—a plane crash? Forest fire? I watched his wiry back through his white T-shirt, the muscles rolling gently in his arms. My adrenaline surged. I brought up my hands to my face.

"He sat me down last night and said that he'd heard us together in 209."

I whispered, "But that was last week."

He nodded firmly.

I tugged at the skin on my wrist, twisting it. "Oh *God.*"

"It's no big deal—*really.* He seemed perfectly sane about it."

"But—"

"He just wants me to leave."

The laugh that came out of me was ridiculous, raw—a splutter.

He fastened the buckles of his knapsack. He lifted it once,

testing its weight. "I'm going back to New York. I've already made the arrangements. I'm staying with my friend Juany."

My eyes wandered about the room. The thought of it emptied seemed outrageous, dreadful to me. The gnarl spiraled deeper into my neck. "You can't just leave," I said.

He moistened his lips. "I talked to my old boss last night. Believe it or not, I have my old restaurant job back." He smiled now, the brown of his eyes brightening, pupils haloed with amber. "Actually, I'm really looking forward to it. It'll be good for me."

My eyes fixed on the wall where his snapshots had been. Already they'd left crisp white squares where the sun had yellowed the paint around them. I'd memorized their positions: Don and Miguel, Julia before the steaming volcano.

"What's the matter?" he asked, glancing over his shoulder.

I grabbed his forearm, looking him straight in the eye, and twisted it behind his back. He gritted his teeth and winced. The cords of his veins tightened in his arms. "You almost seem grateful," I said.

"Hey," he cried.

He shook me off, frowning, stomping off. He raised his brows, face cautious, bitter, aloof.

I studied his scuffed boots on the floor. Against my wishes, my eyes started to fill, flood. I pressed the small of my back into the wall. "Jerk," I said, sliding slowly down to the floor tile.

"Don't—" he said.

I sat there for a while, watching him rolling his shirts. I'd ruined things. So why not push it further, see how far I could go? I'd crawl around in the muck if I had to. A snake in the slough, a vole. *Let him be disgusted by me.*

"I'm coming with you. I'm going to run up to my room to pack some things. What should I bring?"

"Stop—"

I folded my arms. The light in the room shifted, leaves quivering outside, golden, polished, as if a front were passing through. Drier weather.

"So I was just dreaming this up, then?" I said finally.

"Evan," he said, a kindly, pitying look in his eyes.

And then I knew. Something thorny pierced the surface of my skin, right through to the center of my chest. My heart felt hot, too big for my body. A cold breeze sluiced through the room.

He picked up his boots, then tossed them off to the side. "My plane's at six-thirty. Would you do me a favor and let me finish, and then we'll talk about this?"

I wouldn't look at him.

He wrapped his arm over my shoulder, holding me tight. I tried to shake him off, but he only gripped harder. His shirt had a smell: dust, fabric softener, cigarette smoke. I almost kissed him on the mouth—a challenge, a protest—before he let me go.

"Meet me at four outside the office. We'll say our good-byes then."

"So this is it?"

He shrugged. "Evan, this isn't the end. Get a hold of yourself. Buck up."

I walked out the door. I wandered through the woods for hours, walked all six miles out Pan American to the ruined marina. The water in the cove looked smoky, brackish. A dead fish swelled on the surface like a piece of foam. I pulled up a weed and tore it apart in my hands.

When I made it back to my room, my body felt emptied, oddly spent, cleansed. But tired, terribly tired. I stepped before the sink and splashed water onto my face. My eyes were red, my muscles sodden. There was something on my bed: Hector's House of Field bag. One by one, I laid the various articles out on the floor with a kind of awe—a map of Las Vegas, Laura Nyro's *Gonna Take a Miracle,* a leather wristband, a postcard of the Lady Bunny milking a cow, a Crown and Anchor Townie Pass, shirts, jeans, hats, belts—trying to make sense of them, pondering their connections.

◇ ◇ ◇

He was gone, once and for all: I'd finally admitted it to my-self. He was lost: the one I'd been before I'd left home, before William. It was hard not to think him stupid, insignificant. It was hard not to wish him out of existence. The one who believed he held a secret so extraordinary and vast that he couldn't possibly tell anyone, not even his best friend, Jane. Who believed that once he broke away from his parents' judgment and silence he'd find someone to love, and love him back, and his real life would begin. Who felt an inordinate pleasure, an electrical current, when another boy just happened to brush up against his shoulder. Who believed that once he moved past his initial awkwardness and grief and grew into himself, his life would continue to offer him reward after reward.

I thought of his eager, dark face, that enormous secret behind his eyes. I didn't know what to call him anymore. Dead now. It seemed remarkable to me that he'd ever been called Evan.

◇ ◇ ◇

At four o'clock I stayed behind in my room. I busied myself with my reading, wearing my chartreuse shirt with the pointed collar. I glanced once through the blind. He looked up toward my window, before he swung into the cab's backseat. I turned away, imagining its lozenge-shaped taillights growing smaller down the driveway. I was determined not to watch. *Go, just go. Enough already.* I refused to have another ending in my life.

Chapter 21

I stood at Peter's open door, holding onto the frame. He sat
upon the bed in jeans, unbuttoned denim shirt, and cricket
cap—all of which appeared to be too small for him. Were they
Hector's? His chest pearled with sweat. Outside the window,
an elaborate white bird—an anhinga?—took off for the sky.

"Do you have a minute?" I said.

He nodded evenly.

All I needed was to look at him. Something rumbled and
chugged inside my chest—orange, molten. I couldn't let it out—
wouldn't unless I had to. "I'm not very good at these things," I
said, wetting my lips, standing at the window. Around the pool
a towheaded boy pulled a red wagon with a missing wheel, its
back axle scraping the asphalt.

The small of my back needled. "What's wrong with you?"
I said.

He blinked. His eyes brightened, their rich green going
bluer all at once.

"You let Hector go, just like that," I said.

"You were doing all his work for him."

"That's not why you fired him. Hector, Holly. What's going on in your head?" My voice sounded hoarse. I started shaking inside, just slightly, cold now, as if I'd downed a pint of something frozen. My arms prickled. I kept them hidden behind my back so they wouldn't give me away.

"Keep it quiet. There are guests in the next room." His jaw shifted. He pushed it out, attempting to harden his face. He glanced down at the bed, the stained sheets on which Hector and I had lain a few short weeks ago. "What's the gist of all this?"

"Secrets," I mumbled.

"I beg your pardon?"

"I can't live like this anymore."

"Secrets," he repeated.

He stood before me with his hands in his pockets. His face was dark. I couldn't tell whether I was making any mark on him. I pictured myself holding a struck match in the room, and the whole place blowing up from what it contained.

"And you?" he said.

"What?"

"What makes you think you're any more direct than I am?"

The skin vibrated around my lips. My mouth parted, astonished, as if someone had punched it. I imagined it swelling, a rich hurt purple.

"I'm not like you," I said.

"You don't have any secrets?"

"I'll tell you anything."

He walked to the window, hands working in his pockets. "So what about Hector?"

◇ ◇ ◇

We floated around the motel pool for as long as we could stand it, determined to push ourselves. It was dark. We tried to talk about Mom and Dad; we tried to talk about Hector—but thick with emotion, we couldn't say much. Our tongues fattened in our mouths. Stubbornness. We stared at each other, lockjawed, ashamed. The pads of our fingers wrinkled. After an hour, we hefted ourselves up the ladder.

Secrets, secrets: welcome to Sarshik's House of Secrets.

The sprinklers cooled the flower beds, the little piles of mulch. We walked up the outside steps to the second floor. On the landing, Peter stopped and turned to me. "Didn't I tell you he was going to be trouble?"

"Who?"

"Hector."

My thoughts stalled. A gibbous moon hung suspended in a cloud.

"Didn't I? Didn't I try to help?"

We stood together on the landing. I wanted him to stop, to talk about something else, *any*-thing else, when all at once he was looking at me, eye to eye, standing even closer. My scalp tingled. A pungent, sweet scent wafted off his shoulders. He put his arms around me, embracing me in spite of all my tightness, my resistance. His breaths were warm, oddly comforting upon my neck. He was alive, thrillingly human and real. I gave in to him; I held him tighter. Blood hummed beneath his flesh. My love was so fierce that I felt giddy with it, woozy, a little sick. Then it all started pouring: how I'd have done anything to be him once; how I'd have copied his handwriting, dressed like him, spoken like him; how I'd have waited outside the bathroom door for him just to catch his gleaming wet flanks; how I'd even have died for him, jumped off the roof, or at least pretended to, laughing, the city stretching out just for us like an offering, a bed of candy.

I looked down. Below us, a rolling, scraping sound, and the child I'd seen out the window earlier was pulling his broken red wagon again. He stopped, turning his face up to us (eyes shocked, pale; strawberry-blond bangs) as if he'd listened to our every word. He sat on the curb, put his head down, and pressed his hands together.

An edgy muteness from Peter. He looked away from the boy, shy now, reserved.

"What?" I said.

The streetlight shined on Peter's forehead. He lifted his face to me, wearied, corners of his mouth raised. A smile?

"Why didn't you tell me about Ory?" I said quietly.

He tilted his head as if puzzled.

"Ory," I said. "Your son."

The muscles relaxed in his jaw. His tongue pushed his bottom row of teeth. An "uhh"—something abrupt, strangled in his mouth, then just as quickly he stopped himself, swallowed, squinting. He moistened his lips. He looked at me harshly, briefly. He took a firm, calming breath, then walked up the steps.

"Peter."

He turned right, striding down the long dark hall, shoes trundling.

The soles of my feet trembled. I followed. "Wait."

He paused outside his room and stared downward at the knob. He wrenched his head to the left, opened the door, walked inside. Shut now. The deadbolt clamped. A hushed, liquid wind passed over the roof, then stillness, rest, a single cricket screeking in some corner.

◇ ◇ ◇

Days passed.

I spent most of my free time walking, trudging out through the sawgrass behind the resort. The sky changed as many times as my moods, one evening a brazen pink, the next the deepest indigo: clear funnels—waterspouts—swirled deliriously above the coastline. The longer we were apart, though, the more I dreaded seeing him again. No resolution, no change. The days felt wide and ponderous, emptied cathedrals in which a clock ticked. I walked deeper and deeper into the swamp. The muck—the color of pumpkins—sucked at my sneakers.

A postcard of an East Village restaurant arrived for me in the mail. Postmarked from Hialeah. I stopped my packing, looked at it for the longest time: a dark cellar with cherry-red upholstery, ceiling strung with a thousand blazing white lights. I projected an ebullient crowd into those rooms: glasses clinked, curries spiced the air. Hector weaved in and out through the cramped tables, brow creased, superior in expression, holding a tray high above his shoulder. Someone was laughing. And just as quickly everyone was gone, their collective absence making a rushing sound like space.

He'd scribbled on the back: a temporary address, then *Forgive me. I miss you.*

Part Three

Chapter 22

With the little money I had, I rented a car and drove off for Miami.

My first stop was the airport. A red radar grill spun ominously on a pedestal. Pulpy clouds shredded across the sky. Out where the runways ended I knew of a place where you could watch the jets landing. I'd spent hours there when I was twelve. I'd ride my bike after school, all ten miles up Dixie Highway, in and out through the bus exhaust and the brake lights, timing it so I'd get there in time for four o'clock, when the L1011's from New York and Philadelphia and Detroit and Chicago landed one after the other in a great continuous chain. All my anxieties—about my parents, school, Peter, my growing yet unnerving interest in my friend Luke Oosterhuis, about whom I'd started to fantasize—all of them seemed to disperse as I lay motionless on my stomach, staring up as the landing gear descended, that massive sound rumbling in my bowels. I stopped the car, got out. The bare flesh of my arms prickled. When I screamed, only a dry noise came out of my throat.

There were other places. I drove past my high school, through Coconut Grove, underneath the dual signs of the Everglades Hotel and the Coppertone girl. I drove past Dadeland, the Woolworth's, Miamarina, the old Dusty Cartwright Dairy Bar—now shuttered and festooned with graffiti. I drove past the islands—Rivo Alto, Star, and San Marco. I drove down Coral Drive, which only a few short years ago had bisected a drained swamp, an empty prairie, but was now surrounded by vast tracts of Lennar Homes. I should have been troubled or angered, but the truth was the land had already been wrecked, and if it wasn't this, it was going to be something else: a dog track, a shopping mall. a gambling casino, a jetport, a virtual reality entertainment park.

Welcome. Welcome to South Florida.

My thoughts scrambled. The houses I passed seemed to take on richer colors, yellows and deep blues, until they weren't houses anymore but complete worlds in which I imagined intricate dramas were being played out. In the first house a second-grader was sitting at the kitchen table with her mother, explaining to her with great kindness and trepidation that she couldn't bear living with her new stepfather. In the second an oral surgeon was lying atop his wife, whispering in her ear that he loved her more than anyone in the world, even though in two short weeks he'd be charged with fondling a female patient seconds before he extracted her wisdom teeth. In the third a teenager smoked crack for the very first time, curled up on the bed of his childhood, shocked and frightened by how much he liked it, how much it admitted he wanted to be extinguished. In the fourth a young couple knelt before a framed portrait of Jesus, holding hands, their heads bowed, murmuring, petitioning God to return the world to the safe place it once was.

I drove by Kevin St. Ledger's old house on Avenida Santurce. I thought about my father's initial explanation for its suddenly emptied rooms. "Kevin blew away." It wasn't till I was six or seven that I'd realized he'd said something else entirely, that I'd misheard him: "Kevin *moved* away." But it wasn't quite the same. For years after I refused to let it go, the image of the weightless, mysterious boy drifting, scuttling upwards over the neighborhood like a leaf.

◇ ◇ ◇

William's lawn was as lush as it ever was, washed and pristine, smelling of minerals, fertilizers, hose water. The house had been painted apricot. The sprinkler heads pivoted and locked above the grass line, coughing once, misting. Leaves glistened. A tiny red bird flitted her wings inside the head of a palm, frantic and joyous at once. I slumped further down in my seat, fingered the letters of the steering wheel. A thin dust powdered the radio dials, the stickshift knob, the air-conditioning vents like a coating of sugar. I brought it to my lips and tasted. Was I ready to do this? A quick cramp in my side, a stitch. I slumped even further. Did I need any more grief in my life?

Then I started up the walk and knocked at the storm door. Prisms sparkled in the arcs of the sprinklers.

"Hello, William," I said, my head down.

"Evan? *Evan?*"

"The one and only," I said with a weak smile.

"What on earth are you doing here? Come inside. Come in, you, come in."

He laughed ruefully, warmly, a relief. I concentrated "authority" into my expression, but it kept falling from my face, my loneliness welling up inside. But he seemed to read my thoughts. Did he feel it too? He put his arm over my shoulder and drew me into the house.

"You've lost some weight," I said. "You're looking good."

"Thanks." He stepped back from me and appraised my new look: the shaved head, the hacked-off sleeves. My forehead went hot above my brows.

"How strange to see you. I was just thinking about you the other day."

"Really?"

"Someone walking past the college gates. Someone with

just your kind of walk, you know, that hard little bounce, that really *guy* walk, and I thought, Evan. That must be him. But when I looked over my shoulder . . ." He shook his head. "Not nearly as cute," he said, with a nervous smile. "I like the hair-cut, by the way."

Something scratched behind the bedroom door. William hurried down the hall, and soon enough, the Dobermans were crashing toward me, bellies closer to the floor, tongues lolling, eyes crazed with desire. Their muzzles were sprinkled with white.

"Hey, Pedro, Hey, Mrs. Fox. Do you remember me?"

"It's Evan," said William. "Say hi to Evan. You certainly remember Evan."

"They're getting older," I said, looking up at his face.

"Like all of us."

"Not me," I declared, and then we both laughed.

I squatted, pressed my nose into their dusty scalps, and breathed. They gave me their weight as I gazed over their heads. It bore only a minor resemblance to the house of the past. The dull, tepid rooms were gone. In their place a huge white room with squat, tasteful furniture facing out toward the banks of bougainvillea. The pool looked profoundly blue, almost lunar, a gray-green life ring knocking about its surface. A single spoon glinted on a table.

"It's so peaceful," I said. "Orderly. How did you manage it all? It's barely the same place."

He pressed his palms together. "You don't like it."

"No, no, there's nothing *not* to like. It's really beautiful. I like the openness, the light. And the clerestories are pretty. It's just—" What was I trying to say?

"Well, the original plan was to do it one room at a time. But then I thought, do I want to breathe in sawdust and fiber-glass for the next two years? Why not get it over with while things are still fine?"

There were footsteps up the walk. A key jiggling in the lock, and the dogs started barking.

"Hey," someone said.

"Hey, you. Look who's here, it's Evan. You remember hearing me talking about Evan."

He was a young, wiry sort, mid-twenties, in orange drawstring shorts, with the most forbidding calf muscles I'd ever seen. He leaned over and kissed the dogs on the tops of their heads. He extended his hand up to me and smiled warmly, but with a remote, abstracted expression in his eyes. "Alfred," he said.

"Hello, Alfred."

"But my friends call me Laser."

He stood. Laser folded his arms across his thick chest, smiling, sidling up next to William. If only through their shared gestures (the smiles, the closeness of their stance), I could see that they were clearly a couple, inhabiting their lives with a fluidity and ease. How did any two people do it? How did any two people achieve a life, sharing each other's time with kindness, respect, and sexiness, without pushing each other away? I was troubled with the urge to say, *Do you fight? Are you in love? Do you still sleep together?*

"Excuse me for a minute," said Laser. "I have to take these two for their walk." Their eyes brightened at the word. "Walk? Walk? Do you want to go down to the beach for your walk?" Panting, the dogs scampered after him, nails clicking, down the hall.

"You guys are happy?" I said dully.

"You wouldn't think it would work, but it does, believe it or not. It's been almost a year and a half."

"He's in school?"

"He's still in school. Med school. A year to go before his internship."

I tried to compose my face, but I must have looked strange to him. I knew what kind of expression it was: it told anyone who was even halfway perceptive that my outer self, which was trying to maintain decorum at all costs, was at odds with my inner self, which was plunging downward like a kite. What did William's relationship with Laser have to do with me? I'd moved forward in my life. I'd had all sorts of experiences. I certainly did not want to come back here. *Do not take this in. Do not take this personally. At least give them that.* A thought: I was just as resentful and afraid of abandonment as my brother Peter.

What makes you think you're any more direct than anyone else?

"What's all this?" I said, indicating the orange plastic pill bottles on the kitchen counter. I picked up one and shook it gently beside my ear. It made a kind, pleasant sound like maracas.

His eyes fixed on the coffee pot beside him.

"Something wrong?"

"Evan—"

"Is Laser okay?"

He raised his face to me.

I said, "Why are you staring at me like that? Why so serious?"

"Have you been tested?" William said finally.

My attention still snared on those bottles, the miraculous capsules inside.

"I think you might want to get tested," he said, graver now, looking directly in my eyes.

I grimaced. "Are you—?"

I held myself still for a few seconds. Then I felt myself falling off a building, the ground close, closer, advancing like a bull's-eye, then *slump.*

I was still shaking after William came up to hold me.

Ash dusting now, sticking in our throats, the world colder, meaner, more ragged than before. I saw myself walking through jags of ice—dark, dark world, steam rising from my mouth.

"I know we've talked about this before. Frankly, it's not like it's a total surprise."

"Oh *God.*"

"I *feel* fine, though. I can't quite explain it. I haven't felt this optimistic and energetic in years." And I saw what I'd overlooked before: the flat, puttied color of his skin, the waxy hollows beneath his cheekbones. He stepped toward the window, not quite so confident on his left leg. "But I just talked to my doctor yesterday. My T-cell counts aren't good. They're on, as the professionals like to say, a downward trend."

"Oh," I said.

"But he says better drugs are on the way. Well, as far as I'm concerned, the sooner the better. We need them now. Right now."

I looked down at my fingers curling on my lap. I thought of my stomach—emptied, translucent, the ghost of a stomach—floating somewhere in the room, then out the window, floating on and upward through the palms like a soul. *I am twenty years old,* I thought. *I am twenty years old and I am going to die.*

"It's not like you have much to worry about," he offered. "I mean, it's not like we weren't using rubbers or anything. We were very careful together. You should be fine. Assuming you've been watching out for yourself." He raised his brows, tears filming his eyes.

But had I? I thought about my hands—nicks, cuts, abrasions, little openings. I thought about my teeth, brushing and flossing only seconds before sex. And of course there were those occasions on which we'd slipped. Had he forgotten all about them, purged them from his memory?

"And what about Laser?" I asked.

He nodded. "He's positive too, but his health is good, excellent actually. He's going to beat this thing. We have high hopes he's going to outlive the best of us."

The world torn in pieces, scattered on the ground like marble, broken bridges. I tried to think of William and Laser, of the difficulties that lay ahead for them, the infections and the doctors, how one would die before the other, leaving the survivor to spend his last months—years?—in loneliness, in a hospice, in pain, surrounded by doctors and strangers, but I couldn't. I could only think about myself, how I was going to die before I even had the chance to live.

I wasn't as generous as I should have been.

He came up behind me and massaged out the knot where my neck met my shoulder. For some reason that made me cry.

"I know it's a lot to take in at once. Are you okay? Let me

get you something to drink—some tea, some coffee? Or how about something to eat?"

I shook my head hard.

"I'm sorry," he said plainly. "I'd hate to think I'd . . ."

"Don't—"

"I'm sorry, I'm very sorry. I feel awful about what happened between us. This stuff's been on my mind for a long, long time. I think I must have known I was sick on some deep level, and I wasn't ready to acknowledge it yet. And then I didn't have any choice. One night I woke up, and all the sheets were drenched with my sweat."

He leaned backward into the woodwork and sighed, said *ahh*. Drops of moisture glistened on the tip of a fig leaf, holding on for as long as they possibly could before they fell to the floor. The ceiling fan clicking. A dog—a St. Bernard, I decided—barked somewhere in the distance, solemn, calling for his dinner. The sky over the trees went gray, the absence of color. Then everything in the room, the smallest details, seemed to glitter fiercer, brighter, until I thought they would pop: the bulbs in the chandelier, the violet irises in the clear glass vase on the table.

"Where are you staying tonight?" he said. "You're always welcome here."

"I have to be somewhere at six. I promised Ursula I'd meet her at Dadeland."

"I'm glad you're talking. That seems like a start at least."

"Well, I want to get to know her again. I don't have huge expectations, but you never know." I made a silly, stranded face. I didn't know where my words were coming from, but I tried to invest myself in them, if only for the moment.

We were stalling for time, fearful of our awkwardness, fearful of departure. Then, looking out the window, I thought about the dream I'd had on our fifth night together. We were standing by a riverside amusement park: PLAYLAND. Somewhere north. Maryland? An empty roller coaster surged down the track. The river surface shimmered in a pewter haze. Before I knew it I'd taken William's hand and walked into the water with him, feeling not a second of trepidation. Trust, hope, absolute confidence, and delight. The river splashed warmly against the backs of my legs, rising higher around us. Side by side, we started swimming across the river. The roller coaster struggled up the rusty track, cranking and ticking, as if for the very last time.

Was it the mere absence of our life together—and not so much William himself—that had pained me?

Would our time together always have such significance for me?

"So—" I gazed downward at my shoes, empty and full at once. I wanted to run as much as I wanted to stay, to move into the old den with its stacks of mildewing magazines.

"Take good care of yourself. Stay in touch, okay? Are you around for a while?"

I shrugged, smiled weakly. "We'll see."

"Just let me know how you're doing."

"I will."

I kissed him right on the mouth then, with all the tenderness I could muster, without understanding it, wildly alive, before leaving through the door.

Chapter 23

Ursula was already seated at the front table of the ice-cream parlor, her legs resting up on a chair, when I arrived.

How odd that we were in Dadeland, in the space once occupied by Farrell's, a short-lived chain for which our entire family—Sid, Ursula, Peter, and me—once managed to have affection. It had nothing to do with the menu (which challenged one to take on the "Zoo," an ice-cream project comprised of twenty flavors), or the atmosphere (hokey Victoriana with lots of screaming and hooting at birthdays), only that its presence coincided with an especially poignant time in our family life, when there was a period of relative peace in the house, when we knew that our outings as a complete family unit were numbered. We were already too old for this. Still, these excursions were the single activity on which we could all agree, and once they were mentioned as even a remote possibility, the four of us, sadly enough, would hurl ourselves in the car, forgetting our differences for an hour, convincing ourselves we weren't nearly as fucked up as we were.

"Look at you. What happened to all your hair? You look like something off a chain gang."

"Mom."

She rubbed the bristles of my scalp, then stared at the blue Icarus on my bicep. "What's this?"

"Tattoo," I mumbled.

"Tattoo? Where on earth did you get a tattoo?"

"Prison."

"*Prison?* Oh my God. Since when have you been in prison?"

I couldn't help but roll my eyes. "Hel-*lo*—"

"Well, don't do that to me. Don't get me all worked up like that."

We smiled wanly. In spite of our mutual cautiousness and fear of each other, I was relieved to see her. She appeared to be in good spirits—playful, even proud of me, and she'd spruced herself up for the occasion with a purple-pink scarf tied jauntily around her throat. Her hair was a complex of darks and lights, the color of nutmeg. She smelled of tea-berry, weeds.

In no time at all she gathered herself. I glimpsed at her hands—veined, brown, dry, with their fragile superstructure of bones—remembering how she'd once been so proud of them.

"You could have met me at home, you know."

I shrugged. Could I have told her that just being inside the house would have shaken something loose? Already I saw it all in my head: the oak door between the garage and the house—split, dented—which I'd kicked repeatedly after being locked out in my tenth year; the backyard toolshed, chewed to a soft pulp by termites; the hole in the laundry-room ceiling, still unrepaired after ten years, the tufts of pink insulation revealing the guts of the house.

"You look different," was what I said. "Something's changed. What is it?"

She tilted her head, inhaled, not without delicacy. Then she turned to the side, offering me her profile.

"Nose job," she said finally. "I just had a nose job."

I examined the new nose, the softer bridge, the flaring,

dilated nostrils. A bungled approximation of a WASP nose. "You're kidding me."

"I'm actually relieved. Julie Spivak thinks it's very, very natural. Some of the best work she's ever seen."

"But you had a nice, voluptuous, Eastern-European nose. It had character."

"Character, shmaracter. What do I care about character?"

"But—"

"Do you know what it was like to have been made fun of as a child?"

My tongue felt fuzzy and thick, a wad of cotton in my mouth. I had to remind myself it wasn't anything new, this will to remake herself. How could I forget the complete line of diet products, many of which were even then out of date, she'd stashed in the kitchen cabinet when I was young—Metrecal, Figurines, Carnation Slender, Instant Breakfast. Even something called Ayds, of all things.

"What's Dad think of this?"

She shut her eyes for a moment, then opened them. She looked hurt yet detached from that hurt. "Don't ask."

"What?"

"That son-of-a-bitch—"

"Mom—"

"That fucker—"

Her voice was rising. I glanced around at the other tables.

"Don't talk to me about that snake in the grass."

The waitress, a slip of a thing with a crest of hair like some rare tropical bird, pretended to be oblivious to my mother's mouth. She scribbled our order on her hand with a lavender-tipped ballpoint. All the while my mother frowned, her face pinking, staring down at her sunfreckled arms crossed tightly over her chest. She waited for the waitress to depart.

"Airhead," she mumbled.

"Shhh—"

"Bimbo."

"She'll hear you."

"I don't care," she said miserably. "If she doesn't have

enough decorum to know that you're supposed to write on a sheet of paper and not on your hand, then what do I care?"

I shook my head, exasperated. My neck felt hot in my collar. "But what about Dad? I'm waiting to hear about Dad."

She eased forward in her chair. She looked pained again. "You sure you're up for this?"

"What's the matter now?"

He'd been gone for some time now, almost three months. He was living in Huntington Beach, California, with a forty-three-year-old woman named Anita Burnell who had ironed, bottle-blonde hair all the way down to her ass—"right out of 1969," according to my mom. He'd met her six years ago at an academic conference at UC Irvine. Like my father, she was an assistant professor with a specialization in nuclear fission, and she and Sid had corresponded by letter, phone, and fax for years, so openly and casually, in an approximation of professional comradeship, that my mother hadn't once suspected there was anything between them. If anything, she'd convinced herself that Sid was put off by Anita's chumminess, that he quietly dreaded running into her year after year at conferences, that he imagined her pushy and coarse, always sniffing around for the next job opening (or "corpse-to-be") until she—my mother—found out otherwise. It happened on a quiet Thursday evening, moments after she'd finished up a *New York Times* crossword puzzle with the word "glossolalia." Sid walked up behind her in the kitchen, wrapped his arms around her waist—her "love handles," she said—then told her, not without tenderness, that he didn't love her anymore, that she'd be better off by herself, that he was leaving for Huntington Beach in the morning.

"I just never thought he had it in him. I mean, I never thought he'd leave. He never seemed particularly, I don't know—passionate? Is that the correct word?"

"Did you two still have sex?"

God knows what possessed me to ask such a thing.

"If you could call it that," she answered thoughtfully.

"What do you mean?"

"When a man—when a man can't—" She stared at me,

startled, and rubbed at her arms. "Why in God's name am I talking about this with you? I don't want to talk about this with you."

In the mall two teenagers, a boy and a girl, ambled in and out through the fountains, the figs, the ficus, grasping hands. Unlike us, they were the very picture of safe. It seemed incredible to imagine that they had any complexities swirling in their midst. When I looked back at my mother, she was staring at her new nose in her compact. Already she'd rolled on a fresh coat of coral lipstick.

"So next I'm going to get an Adrian Arpel makeover, then I'm going to get eyeliner tattooed around my eyes."

"No way," I said. "No tattoos around the eyes."

"What about you? You have tattoos."

"We're talking about your *eyes,* Mom."

She nodded. "You've convinced me. It's all because of you. I'm going to get my eyes done, and then I'm going to get myself a new boyfriend, and I'll show that"—she wrenched her head—"*ass*-hole he's made the most foolish mistake in his life."

A thousand thoughts were leaping concurrently in my head. I saw them luminous—dark and oily, like colored fish in an aquarium. The tips of my ears felt hot. I couldn't restrain myself any longer. "Mom," I said, "I hate to bring this up, but there was an actual purpose to my visit."

Her face dulled as if she'd been taken aback. I hadn't meant to sound cold or insensitive.

"Could I ask you a question?"

"Of course, dear."

"If I ever die, could you do a favor for me?"

She grinned darkly, addressing me as if I were eight years old again. "You're not going to die."

"Oh yes I will."

"You're not."

"*Yes.* We're all going to die."

Her mouth parted.

"It's not like when you were a girl. It's dangerous out there.

Young people die all the time. Tons of young people that I know."

She blinked once. She looked at me as if I were telling her that the world, as she knew it, was about to implode.

"I want you to give my CDs, the Joni Mitchells, to Jane. Take all my books to Herridges and keep the money for yourself. And pack up all my clothes and send them off to the Salvation Army."

Her face blanched with worry, hands twisting. "I'm not sending anything to the Salvation fucking Army. You're not going to die, okay?" Her voice carried, just loud enough for the women two tables away to hear. They halted their conversation, pretending not to listen. Quietly, she said, "You're not going to die."

"Mom—"

She smiled slightly. "I'm not going to listen to this. How dare you make me listen to this. There are a full range of beautiful topics in the world. What about your brother, for instance. Why haven't you said one word about your brother? What was it like?"

I didn't want to talk about him. I'd already made the decision not to go back. "Have you heard anything from him?"

"No, he's just like you. Both of you have deserted me. I don't even know what you look like anymore. I'll be lucky if I even get a Christmas card from him, sometime next June."

Something snagged into my stomach.

I watched her wiping her hands on her napkin. I knew she'd pictured her future differently. She'd lived her entire adult life as if its choices had been guided by a map, a paradigm: *Do these things right and you'll get your just reward.* Once she'd pictured both Peter and me living nearby, in Cocoplum or Coconut Grove, with decent jobs, dropping in on her every Tuesday night, bringing our pretty wives with whom she'd have coffee and talk about furniture. She'd have grandchildren, four of them. She'd have stayed married to my father, and though their lives would have been marked by silence and periods of retreat from each other, she would have had a vision to present to the world: *I am fine, I am not marked by grief, I am just like you.*

"I'm so lonely," she said. "I never thought I'd be so lonely."

"You have to be tough, Mom."

"What if I don't want to be?"

The breath left my lungs.

"Listen," she said, glancing at her wristwatch. "I have to go. I have to be somewhere at eight."

I faintly smiled. We both knew she was lying, but I understood: all this was more than she could bear at once. At home she'd fumble for her Halcion, or Valium—whatever was closest to her grasp—then go straight to bed, and for the next two days ponder over and over what we'd said to each other, weighing my words for their various meanings.

We stood. She stepped forward toward me, then held me close, if tentatively. I smelled the soap in her hair. "Mom?"

"Yes, dear?"

"Watch out of yourself."

She nodded. "I'm not as helpless as you'd think."

"I know."

"And no more tattoos," she said, smiling slightly. "Be *care-ful*. Deal?"

"I'll try."

"Stay in touch now. Bye, dear. Bye-bye." And with a quick peck of a kiss, she left the table, stumbling for a second, then righting herself, hurrying out past the kiosks of the mall.

———

The free clinic was in a pagoda-like structure with glass-block walls, so close to the beach that I heard the waves, the life-guard whistle, the joyous shrieks of tourists in the distance. Inside, I slouched in the waiting room with three other boys and a girl—all of us with sullen, vaguely bored faces—waiting for our names to be called. A TV monitor droned a message: "A positive result is not a death sentence." I didn't flinch as the health care worker pressed the needle into my vein and drew back a syringe-full of blood. I stared fully at my blood, its thickness, its rusty red potency. I wasn't as debilitated as I'd expected. I'd already prepared myself. There was no reason to assume the results would be anything but positive, anyway.

With the remainder of my money, I rented a room at the Hotel Lumiere for the week. It was no-frills simple, with single bed, TV, combination bureau/desk, and salt-pitted, dorm-sized refrigerator. And it had that scent, that inimitable fusion of cigarette smoke, mildew, cat pee, and chlorine bleach. I thought of the people for whom this place had initially been built—working-class Jews from Brooklyn or the Grand Concourse who'd anticipated their stay here for months, who'd envisioned their vacation on the beach as a little taste of Heaven. It cost a near mint now, more than I could afford, but I didn't care. I spent most of my days lying in bed, thinking, ordering pizza or Chinese food, listening to the many languages of the people on the street: German, French, Arabic, Japanese, Spanish. One night there was a loud crash, like a stack of falling plates, and I walked to the window to see a party revving up in the apartment across the street. A samba spun louder, and a good twenty or thirty people stumbled out onto the balcony, some in a conga line, some with cocktails in hand, before waving over to me, and I back at them.

A girl with large, soulful brown eyes cupped her hands around her mouth.

"*¡Anda ca!*" she cried.

"Come over," someone else yelled.

"Join the party," said a third.

Across the bay, a faint popping of fireworks.

"I can't," I answered.

◇ ◇ ◇

I waited until the following morning to leave the room. I walked up Collins Avenue out of the trendy, gentrified zone into the run-down section of South Beach that hadn't caught on yet, where the tourists weren't glamorous, but looked ashen, pockmocked, and haunted, dressed in their tight shiny fabrics, gold chains, and wide collars. It could have been twenty years ago, the Miami Beach of the late seventies, and I both loved it and was depressed by it. I walked into a T-shirt shop, checked out the gag gifts and souvenirs: oversized dice, Statue of Liberty pens, furred little beagles with nodding heads—stuff I hadn't seen since I was a kid. I thought about how much Jane would have gone nuts over these things, how she would have borrowed money from me, chattering excitedly, leaving the store with a full shopping bag and then some. Where was Jane? I missed her so much. It was time I made an effort to get in touch with her.

I couldn't have been in the store more than three minutes when I spotted a man in the aisle ahead of me. I didn't see his face, but I saw the back of his neck, a long thin neck, swan-like, though on the verge of gawky, atop which balanced a sweet head with ears that stuck out. He looked nearly perfect to me. I watched him picking up the very same things I'd picked up—snow globes, netted bags of bubble gum resembling lemons, tangerines, grapefruits, and limes—cupping them in his palm, eyes shining. I couldn't stop looking at that neck. The neck had always been the most telltale part of a man's body for me. Nothing could excite me more, not even muscles or big feet or big dick or large nose or dark hair or well-developed Adam's apple.

I followed him. He walked north on Collins, past the Sunoco and the Shelborne, before turning left on 16th. He strode down the street, looking straight ahead, taking long, athletic, supremely confident strides. My eyes watered. The wind crackled, purred inside my ears. He turned south on Meridian, glancing at a particularly beautiful cherry palm outside an apartment house—good sign—then started toward Lincoln Road. His walk seemed to have no destination or plan. Was he cruising? Lost? I decided he was lost. I decided I could bump into him, step down on the back of his shoe, ask if he needed directions, and he'd recognize something in me, something in my eyes, a shared spirit, a sense of humor, and we'd get to chatting, and soon enough we'd be drinking coffee together, talking about what we were doing tonight.

I kept following him. I kept looking at that sweet and luscious and vulnerable neck, and I wasn't about to let him go. I thought of his chest—firm, muscular, lightly matted with hair—and I imagined holding a melting ice cube over it and watching him shudder as I worked my tongue upwards from his belly button. The heat beat in my face. Outside the Night 'n' Gale he turned a bit to the side, not fully facing me, but just enough to see me out of the corner of his eye, and he knew who it was, and he knew I was after him, and I knew that he liked it. I pictured him smiling. My dick rustled, plumping the front of my jockey shorts. And then, just as I stepped closer to him, narrowing the distance between us, he crossed 14th, mere feet before a cargo truck, and the traffic light went red, and everything stalled. Horns. Curses. Heat. Gridlock. I tried to pass around the truck. I tried to sidestep to the left, to the right, but the seconds were ticking. The noon sun hammered my brow, blurring my vision. I banged my fist on the side of the truck twice, three times, before it moved forward. My fingers throbbed like a boxer's. The traffic loosened, I walked ahead.

He was nowhere in sight.

Something occurred to me: I didn't want to die.

Chapter 24

Three weeks passed at the Hotel Lumiere. I lay in bed, staring up at the rotating paddles of the ceiling fan. Checkout was 11:00 a.m., and I'd timed it so that I could pick up my results from the clinic upon my departure. I stood, shoved my possessions—jeans, T-shirt, contact-lens solution—into my backpack. My mouth was dry. My hand looked old. I kept staring down at the skin of my hand, asking myself how on earth could the hand of a twenty-year-old get to looking so old.

But who was I kidding? Already I felt it: that slight white heat, simmering inside the engine of my body, making me older before my time. Correct? Didn't anyone who'd ever lived through this recognize early on what had already possessed him, inhabiting his corpuscles on the deepest, most urgent level? It was as if one had never been anything but sick, that loneliest place, and it seemed astonishing that there were actually people in the world who'd never felt this: to have something burning inside you as intimate as a lover.

And yet I wondered whether I was cutting myself off from surprise. What if, to my good fortune, I was deemed negative?

What if I was told that my days weren't immediately pressured, that I most likely had decades ahead of me? Would I feel different? Negative: funny, awful word. What did it mean to call oneself negative, anyway? I was only negative until the next time I had sex with someone. Wasn't staying negative always the most demanding of efforts, and not a state of grace, not a protected, privileged zone?

Something became evident. This whole matter was about being handed two choices.

I stared at my reflection in the window glass. I looked fine, I felt fine.

I couldn't bring myself to believe that there were only two choices.

I walked to the window, not knowing whether I was copping out or not. I felt relieved and shaken all at once. I looked out toward the ocean and saw a cruise ship passing into the warm aqua of the gulf stream. It looked so small from here, the size of a toy. I imagined a couple—straight, young, still in their twenties—lounging on the deck of that boat, the sun shining on their faces. How would they have reacted if they'd been informed in hushed tones that a terrorist bomb had been planted aboard one of the ship's lavatories, that sometime within the next few minutes or the next few days they'd come to violent death? Would that have made them generous, wise, more responsible to one another, or would it have diminished and destabilized them, making them feel they were under the fist of something so much greater than themselves?

But even that wasn't the same. An instantaneous death—even a death that permitted a few days of preparation—seemed merciful compared to a death that lingered for years and years, where one got sick, better, then sick again. Where a simple sore throat could signal the onset of ruin. Where one's family and lover and friends were ever tempted to bail out. Where one had to push past the inevitable burdens of blame and shame—all the meannesses that people happened to attach to them.

Where one had to forgive. *Forgive.*

I glanced down at the appointment card in my hand and

tore it in two. I watched its pieces flutter down onto the people of the street.

It seemed that I'd already made my decision weeks ago.

Was I a coward? Was I selfish, irresponsible? It seemed that even now, I was suspended between the two worlds—the world of the living and the world of the dead. I would go on in the only way I knew. I picked up my backpack, walked down to the lobby, and handed over my money to the desk clerk. The lighting was milky. Outside, the people seemed beautiful, pale, their ghosts following close behind, already guiding them someplace.

◇ ◇ ◇

Three hundred dollars: enough to get me through the next two weeks, but barely. It wouldn't last the month, unless I was willing to subsist on rice and beans. I tried not to fret too much. I had the uncanny sense I was revisiting my days when I'd first moved out of William's house. I thought briefly about the nature of time, how it's always tricking us into thinking it's taking us forward, when, in fact, it's always coiling around like a spring, bringing everything we've known back to us.

I spent the days looking for work. I bought the *Herald* and checked out the various restaurants, clothing stores, gas stations. Everyone I talked to seemed wary of my lack of experience. It was all right; I would have screwed up those jobs, anyway. I was about to start lying, fabricating a history for myself—name: Vico Bakaitis, age: 24, place of birth: Seal Beach, California—when on one of my wayward afternoon walks I literally found myself within the fencing of a nursery. It was on a forgotten back road, west of the city. It bordered a canal filled with stagnant, olive-green water. Florida's turnpike rushed in the distance like a waterfall. Though the place was overgrown and past its prime and sadly disheveled, it yielded the most offbeat plants, the likes of which were impossible to find at bland, commercial nurseries: blood banana, surinam cherry, weeping fig. Immediately I felt possessed of a good feeling, as if I'd been here in another life. I needed a task if I was going to make it through. I wanted nothing more than to reinvent the place, to reclaim just a bit of its former glory.

"I'd like a job," I said to the owner.

He squinted down at the marl beside my shoes. His face was weathered, puffy. Above his shirt pocket: a blue patch that said Hickory Bob's. In the calmest, kindest voice, he said: "I never said I was hiring."

"I'm not asking for much money. All I want to do is help out. Get this place back into shape."

He squinted, only mildly threatened. "You're young. What would you know about plants?"

"A lot."

He walked me up and down the rows, expecting me to identify each variety he pointed to. Without pause, I said: loquat, maya palm, aurelia. I even named the dreaded pitch apple, a variety that had routinely stumped even the most knowledgeable of his clients. "What else? What else?"

He shook his head back and forth. He didn't know what to say.

"You think I'm a weirdo, don't you?" I said after a while.

"No." His face was clearly dazed. "We better sit down," he said ruefully.

I followed him down the path to a bullet-shaped trailer. Cattle egret scampered about the yard, in and out through the windbreak of Australian pines that bordered the Everglades. A pink sky rumbled over our heads. It turned out that Bob had been wanting to sell after his wife, Dorothy, had died, but had taken it off the market after receiving but two meager, demeaning offers. Things only worsened after Hurricane Andrew. Though managing to cut a swath a mere three miles north of the property, leaving the nursery virtually unscathed, it hurled the entire region into a real estate depression.

He fell silent for a full six minutes. He quoted a salary that was a full three dollars an hour more than I'd expected. He also offered me a place to stay in a second trailer out back. I'd tried to conceal my astonishment and disbelief.

"Do you think that's enough to live on?" he said.

I looked at the wall clock, a cuckoo clock in a shellacked box on which drawings of various minerals had been pasted. I hated to think that I'd be taking advantage of anyone in dire circumstances, but he was offering it to me.

"I guess we could give this a try."

I nodded avidly.

"Why not," he said as if convincing himself. "Let's give it a try."

"Done." My handshake was damp, feeble. "Done deal."

In only a few days I threw myself completely into the nursery. I told myself that my work was all that mattered, that contentment and peace were not to be found in the world of people, but in the world of vegetation. I dealt with my customers with patience, caution, and care, never raising my voice or condescending to them. The dirt blackened my fingernails. I walked to my little trailer every evening, welcoming the ache of my lower back, concentrating on the sting of cuts on my hands, if only because they told me in no uncertain terms that I was still alive.

One morning, I walked up and down the rows of plants, garden hose in hand, watering. I loved the plash of water on the leaves, loved the tuneless flat splat it made on the mulch. I walked to the cluster of shrimp plants, which Bob had virtually left for dead after a brief drought last year. Their leaves were healthy now, shiny and loose, with pretty saffron heads (ladies' swim caps!), and for the first time since my arrival (or "takeover," as Bob called it), I realized that my simple gestures were doing some good in the world. I squirted a squat wooden fence and glanced around at my little domain. I shivered inside. Soon I'd get to moving the cacti closer to the front, then cleaning out the old koi pond, stocking it with marbled, thick fish. Then more varieties of plants; weirder, stranger specimens, plants I'd never seen, names I'd never heard. I wanted them all. I wanted to stay surprised. *This is happiness,* I thought. *This is where I want to be.*

◇ ◇ ◇

And love?

What else is there to say on the subject? I wasn't quite bitter about it, but I wasn't hopeful either. I was in some vague, vaporous place that blended both of those worlds. If anything, I'd come to decide that relationships were best for other people, that my own longing and need had in the past gotten the best of me, and it was time to let that go. There was no reason to assume that I couldn't be comfortable by myself. All I really needed was a few close friends, a love for my work, and some occasional sex. I felt wary admitting to this, as if I were only deluding myself, trying to justify my failure, my giving up. But was I giving up, or growing up? Was I in some deep depression and afraid to deal with its causes? My answers wavered depending upon my state of mind.

And yet there were worse places to be. As the months passed, I looked at the people who came to the nursery regularly—my new friends—and saw how their notions of love had nearly wilted them. I saw how Nan, nearly thirty and still single, was willing to settle for a mostly mild-mannered man who occasionally flew into rages, striking her, because she needed more than anything to satisfy her demanding parents who wanted her to marry a graduate of an Ivy League school. I saw how Zack, the most loyal of my customers, had moved in with a man he suspected of being both heartless and mentally deficient weeks after breaking up with Ladd, the love of his life, only because he was afraid to be alone. I saw how Zack's friend Beth had fashioned herself into such a control freak that she wouldn't date any woman unless she was over six feet tall, dressed in fox stoles from the forties, spoke with the slightest lateral lisp, and knew inside and out the collected works of Jane Bowles. I saw how Thisbe—a sculptor, fresh out of a bickering, competitive marriage in which her painter husband continually sabotaged her work—kept rejecting each successive suitor, simply because he never measured up to her idealized image of her ex. It went on and on like this. Was there something wrong with all these people, or was it me? How could I not see myself as lucky when I looked at them, then looked at myself? How could I not stand in front of the mirror, stare into my cool, uncomplicated face, and not call myself one lucky son of a bitch?

◇ ◇ ◇

His name was Jesus. He was short, muscular, with blue-black skin, thickly lashed eyes, and a wet, enormous mouth curving upward. I'd met him in Lummus Park late one night, sitting on a bench beside the beach. The ocean scented the air with seaweed, tanker fuel. A reggae band thudded loudly in the distance. Soon enough we'd gotten to talking, then we were walking arm in arm up the street, laughing at things that weren't even funny, ambling toward his second-floor apartment off Meridian.

We were lying together in his bed, holding each other. "Man, you're sweet," I said, pulling away from him.

He smiled back at me. "You too."

We continued to make love. It occurred to me I'd leave early in the morning after a quick cup of coffee to be back at the nursery. I knew I'd never see him again. But it was possible, I believed, to enjoy a stranger's company, to be a little in love with somebody, even if it was only for the moment. A breeze stirred the leaves outside the window. Headlights flittered through the slats of the jalousies. I knew we'd never be boyfriends, but there was nothing sad about this.

"Think about it," I said afterwards, latching my hands behind my head. I gazed up at the splintered ceiling and pressed my head deeper into the pillow. He'd brought a bag of tortilla chips to the bed. "I can tell everybody I spent the night sleeping with Jesus."

He winced. "Watch your mouth." But then he smiled again, making love to me over and over.

Chapter 25

How expected that someone should be interested in me when I most wanted to be alone. Not long before we drifted apart, Jane had told me that this was the way it happened, that one only received what one longed for when one achieved perspective, when that desired thing ceased to occupy one's every thought. To me it sounded false, though, something sifted from some ghastly self-help book, and I never thought she fully believed it, the way she believed that you should pursue what you want with all your energy, heart, and affection until you gleamed like plutonium.

I didn't want to be in love now.

I should have sensed that something was up by the simple fact that he stopped into the nursery nearly every day, asking me questions about fertilizers and sprays, about the appropriate ground covers for his particular agricultural zone. He was about forty or so, tall, with red hair that receded in a point, full lips, and deeply blue eyes. Handsome, vaguely conservative in appearance. I'd been told by my friend Zack that he was one of the most successful surgeons in Dade County. He

listened to my answers with a feigned thoughtfulness, looking directly in my eyes, even though his mind was clearly elsewhere. For all I knew he was thinking about his latest triple
bypass or whatever, and he was one of those annoying, enti-
tled types who expected complete attention from service people, who needed to be chatted with and fussed over and appreciated just so he could feel good about himself.

One afternoon, after I'd spent six minutes describing
to him the fertilization procedures for sabal palms, I said,
"You're not listening to me."

"No," he said, and grinned, abashed. "I guess not. Could I
ask you another question?"

I thought, *Make it snappy, buddy boy.* To my left an older
man in a floppy golf hat was examining the wrapped roots of
an acacia, checking for the price tag. "Look, I don't mean to
be rude, but I have customers waiting."

"Okay. I'll let you alone in three seconds." He leaned forward on the counter and whispered something, his lips almost
grazing my jaw line. "Would you be interested in going out with
me sometime?"

My face must have contained within it an element of shock.
I'd been so absorbed in my own duties that it hadn't once occurred to me that he might be attracted to me. A pleasant,
though alarming surprise. "Of course," I answered.

Immediately I regretted the eagerness I projected.

"Let's do something tonight. What are you doing tonight?"

This wasn't what I wanted. I preferred keeping it open,
vague, in the distant, far-off future. The notion of spending
any substantial time with him did not sit well with me. All day
I'd been looking forward to going to bed early and finishing up
a book. "Nothing," I admitted.

He said something about dinner, something about picking
me up out front at eight.

"Okay," I blurted.

"I'm Perry, by the way."

"Evan," I said, and extended a hand to him.

I felt that peculiar combination of flattery and dread. Where was my backbone? How banal was my life. Watching him stride to his car, I thought: *Now you've done it, you fool.*

❖ ❖ ❖

It certainly wasn't his body, which was muscular and dense, from laps of hard swimming and years of working out. It certainly wasn't his voice—an important consideration for me—which was resonant and deep, commanding authority and projecting confidence. It certainly wasn't his taste in music—he loved Stravinsky and Poulenc and Joni Mitchell, especially the albums *For the Roses* and *Hejira.* It wasn't his height or his manner or his intelligence or his personal style or his sense of humor.

That thing called chemistry, that elusive connection and tension, what was that about? Why did we feel it for some people, for people who weren't necessarily good for us, who could even do us damage, and not for others? La Quan, who I'd met at one of Nan's parties, insisted it was deadly to fall into any relationship where the sparks weren't flying all over the place. She, after all, would know; she'd spent four years with an older man for whom she felt nothing only because he took care of her, putting her through school, literally rescuing her from her dismal life in Chicago's Cabrini-Green housing project. In the years following the breakup she'd coined something she'd called the boner test—"Does he give you a boner?"—and every time she'd dated she asked herself that question, even though, for obvious reasons, her experience was figurative.

Why was I getting so worked up about this before anything had happened between us?

We drove north on Collins Avenue, toward the Broward line, where Perry insisted he knew of the cheesiest restaurant in the world. "I think you'll like it," he said nervously. I looked out at the fountains of the Bal Harbour Shops, the high-rise apartment towers—the Avant Garde, the Seascape—to which the word "tony" had once applied, while trying to fill Perry in on my history. I didn't sound terribly interesting to myself.

How much I would have preferred staying in bed, reading; after all, I had to wake up at six-thirty to ready the nursery.

"Here it is," he said, easing the car into a parking stall.

I wasn't surprised to see it was the Speedboat—William's old favorite. I had an odd psychic sense, a kind of quasi-deja vu, which brought up a whole host of allusions and associations. I watched my knuckles whiten on the armrest.

"Isn't this great?"

Through the windshield, I stared at the incongruous window display: the bonsai trees, the felted grass sheet lining the floor. "Oh yeah," I said, not without sarcasm.

Instantly the enthusiasm went out of his expression. "We can go someplace else."

"No, it's fine," I said. "I guess I'm just a little tired. Long day."

Inside the waitress seated us beside a wooden wheel, through which a continuous stream of sudsy water kept pouring into its pitchers, keeping it turning. In the pool beneath, an orange carp floated beside a hunk of coral.

"Look at this," he said, gesturing around. "They built this place when going out for dinner was exotic, an event."

His manner was unsettling. At one point, I'd had that kind of energy and passion for things, but I'd worked it out of myself. Was I in mourning for something and hadn't admitted it? He made me nervous—truly, deeply nervous. "You haven't said very much about yourself," I said.

He went through the requisite details, telling me about his job, his patients, his hobbies and house—all with a genuinely humble bent. In all outward respects he'd be the ideal boyfriend. Still, that didn't make me any more comfortable. What was he doing at forty-one, single, alone? Maybe he wasn't alone. Maybe he already had a boyfriend and just wanted to have sex, just once, with me. If that were the case . . .

There was a lull. He stared at me with an increasing interest, and I found myself looking away, continually, in shyness.

I didn't have the energy to keep up my end of things. "So

what else?" I said, much too loudly. "Tell me about your love life."

His expression grew serious. Immediately, I regretted my flippancy. It turned out that he'd lost a lover within the past two years to AIDS, a lover with whom he'd lived since med school. His name was Andrew, and he spoke about him, a serious painter who'd been inspired by the original Arrow Collar Man ads and the covers of 1950s detective novels, with a quiet affection and longing that clearly indicated that the loss had shattered his life. Sometimes he wondered whether he himself had died with him. In the months since, he'd dated any number of men, a leather boy, a go-go boy, a personal trainer, a boat builder—all frivolous, insubstantial types, he acknowledged now—in an effort to make some contact again with the world. But he wasn't sure he was ready yet. He looked down at the tabletop, latching his fingers together. He'd barely eaten his dinner.

"And you?" I asked.

He looked up. "What do you mean?"

I looked away again. I was the last one to put him on the spot.

"Am I healthy, you mean?"

I nodded, flustered.

"Well, I'm negative, if that's what you're asking. At least the last time I tested. But that's been six months. Who knows? It's not like I haven't had sex since then."

I gazed downward at the stone crabs on my placemat. I felt like nothing but a coward. "I didn't mean to pry," I said quietly.

"Don't worry," he said, taking a sip of his water. "What about yourself?"

"I've been tested," I said. "But I never picked up the results."

I expected him to draw back from me, but his eyes shined with interest and understanding. "Do you have any reason—?"

"My ex-boyfriend's positive. Actually, he has AIDS. I just found that out a couple of months ago."

"I'm sorry," he said.

"Yeah," I said. "It sucks."

We were both quiet for a time, watching the waitresses scurry from table to table, setting down dinners like porterhouse steaks and lobster thermidor prepared from the same recipes the cooks had used thirty-five years ago. To our right a young white couple squealed delightedly at the yellow umbrellas in their drinks. Water plashed from the wheel. If only things were so easy. I expected Perry to be through with me, to call the evening to an awkward, ho-hum finish, but then I felt his shoe resting over mine under the table. There was a complicated smile on his face.

"Listen, I know how hard it is."

I didn't say anything.

"It happens all the time. When I saw what Andrew went through, the drugs, the doctors, all this . . . *shit* in an effort to prolong his life a few months, I'm not even sure it was worth it. I think it was the stress of knowing, the depression, that wore him down. I mean, wouldn't it be better not to know anything at all, and die—*boom*—just like that?"

"I don't know," I said. And I really didn't.

"Just as long as you're not putting anyone else at risk," he said. "I mean, aren't we supposed to behave like we're all positive anyway?"

I nodded.

"Ugh," he said, rubbing his face with his palms. "Enough already. I can't stand this anymore. Let's talk about something else."

"Shall we get out of here?"

He stood up, nodded, and paid the check himself, a gesture I appreciated. Walking to his car, I felt a peculiar wave of kinship with him, something I suspected should be resisted at all costs. Perhaps we'd just be friends. I assumed that that was where this evening was headed, anyway. He'd drop me off, stop by the nursery in a few days, call me once or twice before it was over. Maybe we'd even have coffee one day in the future if our schedules permitted it.

He stared at the dashboard for a moment without turning the key. On the pylon atop the restaurant's roof, the neon speedboat pulsed once, the deepest blue, in the night sky. "I don't know if I should say this," he said.

"What's the matter?"

He gave a heavy, measured sigh. "I don't mean to be presumptuous—"

"What?"

He turned to me, a vulnerable, scattered look on his face. The silence between us was as heavy as the damp air.

"You want me to go home with you?"

He nodded, relieved.

I looked over at him. It wasn't the worst idea in the world. It was clear, after our talk, that we were lonely, in need of connection, affirmation. We needed to leave our brains. So what if I had to get up early the next morning? Actually, I admired the intention. It seemed that everyone I'd ever dated without having sex with right away ultimately failed to seize my interest, and they'd fallen away from my memory, nameless and vague. But that was irrelevant, anyway. I wasn't looking to get hooked up with him.

His house lay hidden behind a thatchy grove of palms. I hadn't been inside more than two minutes when he started kissing me, eagerly, pressing the hard weight of his tongue into my mouth. It all seemed a tad fast. I hadn't even had a chance to glance around, to check out the floor plan and furnishings, but I thought, all right, if we're going to do this, we might as well get it over with. I was as ready as I'd ever be. Would I get a boner? I thought of La Quan.

We moved to the bedroom. In no time at all, he'd taken off his clothes, and he stood to the side of the bed. His was in much better shape than I'd anticipated; muscular and dense, a trimmed mat of reddish hair sprinkling his chest, leading down a thin line to his abdomen. It might have been the body of a twenty-five-year-old. But what really surprised me was his dick. How could such a gentle, mild-mannered fellow be hiding such a killer in his pants?

He lay on top of me, kissing me all over my face with an

intensity I'd never met in anyone else. It unnerved me, for all my life I'd always been more into sex than my partners, and this felt off-putting, as if my efforts to reciprocate were coming up short. I didn't want to disappoint. I closed my eyes and tried to think of Hector, his long lean body, his inky, close cropped hair, but all I saw were the scattered vague parts of him, and not the whole person, the disparate pieces never fusing into a soul. Same with William. He seemed remote, posed, a spread from *Honcho* or *Mandate*. I was trying too hard. Why wasn't this easier? I opened my eyes and watched Perry's face, his tightly shut eyes, his bitten lip, and thought, *You really died, didn't you? You really died along with Andrew and are coming back to life.*

He shuddered. He lay on top of me, wet, out of breath, burrowing his chin into the soft part of my shoulder. He opened his eyes and looked at me as if I might be a stranger. And then he grinned, recognizing me. "Yee ha," he said plainly.

I lay there, nodded. I didn't know what on earth we'd just done.

"Back in two seconds." He kissed me once on the forehead, then disappeared inside the bathroom.

I fell into a deep, dreamless sleep, not waking up once until the following morning, when Perry came in the room dressed in a business suit, carrying a cup of hot coffee to the bedside. I stretched my arms over my head and yawned. "What time is it?"

"Late," he said, his face a bit fretful now. "We overslept. It's"—he picked up the alarm clock—"it's twenty past eight."

"Oh God," I said, sitting up. "I need to be at the nursery. Bob's going to kill me. I have a delivery of cedar chips at nine."

"That's okay, don't worry. I'll take you," he said calmly.

He sat on the edge of the bed, watching me picking up my clothes from the floor. He sipped from his cup of coffee.

He hadn't said a word in minutes. "Do you think we should pursue this?" he asked.

I glanced upward at him as I pulled on my sock. I wasn't quite sure what he meant.

"I mean, should we try to see each other again?" He bit into the skin of his lip. "It's not like I don't have mixed feelings. I'm not even sure I'm ready."

I kept looking at him. I could have said anything at that point. If I'd said no, what risk would there have been? Instead, I said, "I don't see why not."

His face relaxed a bit. He walked over to me, led me to a standing position, then held me tightly in his arms. His chest felt warm and enormous next to mine. "There's something about you," he said cryptically.

I kept absolutely silent. *Sweet man,* I thought. *Don't you know who you're fooling with? Don't you know I'm only going to hurt you?*

Chapter 26

Three times a week Perry and I did the typical things—movies, dinners, walks, beach, gym—nothing unsettling or spectacular. Sometimes we just drove around when we managed to have a day off together. We'd spot an isolated road with a quirky name and turn onto it, only to find something waiting for us at the end: a Dalmatian sunning herself on a floating raft, a house painted with patterns of tulips. These odd little visions seemed to present themselves to us, and we stopped questioning them after a time, accepting them as a function of our being together. And always at night, there was the sex, sex that was playful and complicated and demanding, if only because Perry was putting so much effort into it.

Still, something bothered me about this whole endeavor. It was clear that he was much more committed to this than I was. I knew I could learn to love him. I could see that he had all the qualities that would make for a decent, stable boyfriend— patience, tolerance, compassion, brains, even an edge when need be. But I trusted my gut more than anything. I wanted to feel reckless, and it frustrated me that I was still questioning my involvement with him. Watching him make love to me, I thought nothing could be sadder between two people, that one could have such feeling for the other and not have any idea it wasn't being returned to the same degree.

In October I read in the *Herald* that a woodwind ensemble from the Richmond Symphony was to perform in South Beach, in the concert hall on Lincoln Road. A while back I'd heard that Jane had taken a leave from Savannah to play second chair in Richmond, and I thought I'd show up to see if she'd be a part of things. I arrived ten minutes late, carrying a box of Fannie Mae candies, a token from another era. I couldn't see all the players from where I was sitting, but I suspected she was in back, with a mop of tangled hair, her head lilting in time to the music.

When they stood to receive their applause I saw how wrong I was. She was sitting on the opposite side, her hair bleached silver, pulled back severely off her tanned forehead, with frosty lipstick, and green contacts. She'd appeared to have lost weight. She looked terrific, but oddly unapproachable at once. For a moment I was tempted to leave. Then I decided to wait for the crowd to disperse.

"Why didn't you call me?" I called out to the stage.

Jane looked over to me, distracted from her conversation with the piccolist. "Oh my God," she said, bringing her fingers to her mouth. "Don't move. Give me time to change. Wait," she said, pointing a finger at me. "Wait right there."

In no time at all she came out in leggings and an oversized T-shirt emblazoned with the Empire State Building. It was quite touching: Already I could see the kind of middle-aged matron she was to become—stepping gingerly through the lanes of Palm Beach with a Saks bag on her arm and a fretful look on her face. "What's all this?" I said, regarding her new look with a wary affection.

"Look who's talking." She rubbed the top of my shorn scalp, then pointed to herself. "Don't you think I look like a drag queen?"

"For you," I said, passing her the box of Trinidads. The gesture felt wrong suddenly, though I didn't know why.

"Oh honey," she said. "I can't. I try not to eat candy anymore."

"No?"

She wagged her head from side to side. "You meant well, though. Thanks."

We sat in a little deli, the last of its kind on a street that was rapidly being overrun with galleries, stores, and gay pride shops festooned with rainbow flags. "It's time for shame," I'd said on the walk over. "I'm going to start it, I think. The latest industry. Gay shame." Jane smiled slightly, but her mind seemed to be elsewhere.

She filled me in on what had been happening with her. To my surprise she'd gotten married last August. His name was Moon Lee; he came from a wealthy family who'd started up a successful carpet-cleaning business in Midlothian, Virginia, after their emigration from Seoul. She claimed to be in love with him, though I found that hard to believe. She adored her house, a center hall—"hip colonial" she called it. She was hoping that the current oboist would vacate her chair because she had no intention of returning to the "dingy backwater" of Savannah. Otherwise, she'd quit and go into retail if the chance presented itself. "I want to work," she insisted. "I don't want to sit around painting my toenails. And there's this, of course."

She tugged up her shirt, reached for my hand, and pressed it on her stomach. Beneath my palm I felt the sensation of something turning. "You're pregnant," I said.

"Mm hmm," she said, smiling. "He's due in July."

"It's a boy?"

"We don't know yet." She gazed longingly at the pastel-colored Sherman between the lips of a pretty young dyke. "Aren't you excited?"

"Of course."

Her eyes hazed over. "I'm a little surprised. I just thought you'd be more excited."

"But Jane—"

She blinked away some odd welling of emotion, embarrassed. "What is it? Something's bothering you, isn't it?"

I started talking about Perry. It was hard to get it all out at once, organized. I told her about his generosity and attention. I told her about his own difficulties, his struggle to regain himself after the death of Andrew. I told her of my doubts, my paradoxical feelings, which seemed to fluctuate with every hour of the day. I talked so scrupulously, covering everything in such minute detail, that it occurred to me why all my confidants and friends hadn't been returning my calls. I hadn't realized it was bothering me so much. Only one thing I left out: the burning, low-grade fear that I was dying.

"So I don't get it. What's the big problem here?"

"What do you mean you don't get it?"

"I mean, please, he's falling in love. It sounds like he'd bend over backwards for you."

"It's a matter of integrity," I continued. "I feel like I'm leading the poor guy on. Who knows what he expects from me?"

"It's not like you're married to him."

"Of course not, but—"

"Enjoy this time," she said evenly. "Enjoy this time, keep with it, and see how you feel in six months."

"I can't do that to anybody."

Her eyes sparkled green. "Just what the *hell* are you doing to him?"

"I mean, for all I know, he's in love with some image of me, and not me. He doesn't love me. I mean, what the hell would he want with me, anyway?"

My admission flustered me. My eyes darted toward the window, where I watched a rollerblader weaving, turning backwards, drawing figure eights in and out through the pedestrians. He was shirtless, sinewy, in amazing shape, a crazed, ecstatic look in his eyes. Cocaine? Crystal meth? I looked back at Jane. She appeared to be completely entrenched in her thoughts.

"You know what I think."

"What?"

She gazed down at the tabletop. "I think you're so used to being treated like crap that you don't know what to do with someone who's actually decent and responsible."

"*What?*"

"Shhhh—"

"Listen—"

I dug my fingernails into my palm.

"It's not all that easy to be with someone who's kind. You have to have a certain sense of yourself. You have to be able to say, 'I deserve to be with someone who's good to me.'"

"You sound like you're talking about yourself."

She shrugged her left shoulder. "Anyway, that's all I have to say on the subject. Enough already." She folded her hands on the Formica. She glanced at the dessert menu, returned it to the aqua wire stand. Then in a hushed voice she said, "Don't fuck things up."

"No?" But I didn't feel any better, and I didn't think she'd heard one thing I'd said.

◇ ◇ ◇

It happened weeks later. I was driving the pickup to Perry's house, where I planned to tell him that I didn't want to see him anymore. Things had been so much easier once I'd admitted this to myself, and my life had opened up again, allowing me to relax and to concentrate on the things that were important. The trick was to do it kindly, without menace, without making him feel I was deserting him forever. He'd been through too much. Perhaps I could tell him I needed a break for a while; perhaps I could tell him I only wanted to see him once a week, for a while at least. I'd play it by ear. In any case, what I had in mind would hurt him like hell, but it would be best in the long run, and he'd thank me one day for my brutal honesty, I knew it.

He stood outside the house, watering the bottlebrush with his shirt off. His nipple ring glinted in the sun.

"Aren't we bold?" I stepped out of Bob's pickup. I pointed to his bare chest, on display for all the suburban mothers to see. A grassquit flew over our heads.

"Hey, sexy." He dropped the hose, grabbed me to him, and attempted to wrestle me to the lawn.

"Not here. The grass is all wet."

"What's wrong with wet?"

Not five minutes later we were in his bedroom. God, I thought. This was going to be harder than I'd imagined. I'd have to tell him after we were finished, and that would hurt even more, feel more like a betrayal. I heaved a huge sigh then stiffened my limbs. I heard him squirting lotion into his hand.

"What's that?" I said, and clenched up, resisting his touch.

"Shhh—" he said. "I'm going to rub your back."

I lay there, trying to relax as his hands, strong and pressured, kneaded the muscles of my shoulders. I hadn't realized how tense I'd been. It felt terrific actually, although it hurt like a blowtorch, like he was writing his name onto my skin. Little utterances emanated from my mouth. After a while I moved into a place beyond thought. It only took minutes. I found myself floating, backstroking through a pool the size of space. Stars fizzled out, and I looked over my shoulder and saw a little earth turning in the darkness, silent. Even from this place I could see it diminishing. Even from this safe place I saw great forests burning down, towers crumbling, vast countries of people scrambling for food. I saw that there wasn't very much time. I didn't believe in epiphanies or easy answers or sudden revelations, but all at once Jane's words came flying home to me, a hail of pellets flung against a wall. I turned over on my back. I looked up at Perry. I saw him at six, waiting to be photographed with his mother and sister, staring sternly at the wolf puppet waving in the assistant's hand. I saw him at twenty-six, arm in arm with Andrew, in black robe and mortarboard, grinning upon his graduation from medical school. I saw him at ten, walking alone through Disneyland after his father left him off with a twenty-dollar bill, not knowing what else to do with him. I saw him at thirty-nine, feeling the heat gathering in Andrew's stomach as his body went cold. I saw him in the future, older, with a head full of white—all of these images stacking up at once, projecting themselves simultaneously onto a screen. A door might have fallen open beneath my feet, and then another. What had I been resisting? What was my strength? Had the thing I'd wanted all along been right here with me, for months, and I hadn't even seen it?

He turned me over on my back.

"Why are you crying?" he said.

"I don't know," I said, and then I held him close to me.

◇ ◇ ◇

It wasn't something I'd expected. I walked into the nursery one morning, spilling coffee on myself, rushed as usual, to find Bob sitting in his chair, eyes opened, a glassy, bemused smile on his face. I wouldn't have known as we weren't in the habit of exchanging greetings, and he'd always said hello the first thing in his gruff, kind voice. I had no idea how long he'd been like that, but I stayed with him, so calm I surprised myself, holding his hand until the medics arrived with the ambulance. Two days later, I helped with his funeral. A motley crowd showed up at the Methodist church, comprised of police officials, our regular customers, and Dorothy's twin sisters, Muriel and Lu, both of whom had flown in from Las Vegas. The floral arrangements were the most screwy and peculiar I'd ever seen— canistel, tamarind, sapodilla, ginger lilies, firebushes, coral vines, Brazilian plumes—most of which were trucked in directly from our nursery. A silver banner draped across his closed casket—HICKORY BOB, in the darkest blue letters.

One rainy morning, a few months later, the phone rang. A lawyer identifying himself as Sam DeSears called at 8 a.m. to tell me I owned a nursery. I listened intently, quietly astonished, barely mumbling a reply, as he read off the clause from the will.

I told everyone I knew. I told Perry, whom I'd moved in with only a few months before. I told my friends Zack, Nan, and Jane. I went through the whole list of people, everyone I ever knew—Hector, William, Ursula, even minor customers—with the curious exception of a single person.

When I called the King Cole, a recording told me that the number had been disconnected. I called two more times, if only to make sure I hadn't dialed wrong. It took a while for me to admit that Peter had left, and that the resort had finally closed its doors.

I thought of him often, late at night, lying in bed with Perry. He might have been anywhere, but no one knew, not my mother, not Holly, who'd called me once or twice. I made a place for him inside my head. I put him somewhere in the Yucatán, close to the shoreline, in an aqua house with butterfly chairs out front. He had parrots, cats, mice, and a mule, and a large garden in which he grew plantains. He was utterly alone. He swam in the sea every day, after four, only after the last tourists had left. He watched the sunset—a gaudy, overblown event—from his kitchen window nightly. He even shaved off his hair and taught himself Spanish, giving things he'd made to his neighbors on the street: bread, enchiladas, cups of coffee rich as the blackest loam.

Or maybe he didn't.

◇ ◇ ◇

I picked up my test results one morning without intending to. The receptionist, a pretty red-haired woman with a cast in her eye, smiled faintly as she returned from the lab, and told me I could leave. I stood in stillness for a moment. The sunflowers blurred before me in their vase. Then I walked miles and miles through the buzzing city, grateful and melancholy all at once.

◇ ◇ ◇

We stood upon the beach at Biscayne National Park, a deserted preserve, barefoot and parched, while forest fires ransacked the Everglades. A flamingo straggled on the mud flats. Oyster shells clung to the roots of the mangroves. Earlier, we'd driven across the county, inspecting hurricane damage, seeking out the gardens and plants that interested us. At one point, I took Perry to the concrete pipe in which I'd spent so much of my childhood. The ditch that passed through it was filled with thick, sludgy water, clogged with melaleuca roots, and it was hard to imagine how anyone, man, woman, or child, would fit into that cramped cylinder without drowning.

"That's it," I'd cried, pulling hard on his sleeve. "That's the pipe I told you about."

Perry looked more than a little perplexed. "You hid out in *there?*"

"Yes, as a matter of fact, I did. But it was safe. That concrete pipe got me through my childhood."

He looked even more perplexed. He made a face now.

"What's the matter?"

"You know what I think?"

"What?"

He mumbled, "My boyfriend's a lunatic."

"Shithead," I said, and socked him in the arm.

We continued up the beach, rested, though half the world was burning down. The smoke spun higher in the distance. I stared hard at the horizon, picturing everyone I'd ever lost scorching, coalescing in that pyre, their spirits melding, turning yellow, green, copper, red. Was it too much to bear? It was hard to say no. For all I knew the worst would still happen: Perry would get sick, my mother would wither, Peter, my father, William, Hector, Laser, Jane, Arden, Holly, Ory, Stan Laskin, Todd, Douglass Freeman—all of us leaching white until there was nothing left but alkali, little crumbs of salt blowing up into the void like sand. Or maybe not. Maybe we'd all pass through the door, ruined, yet wiser. The ocean murmured. The kingbirds glided above the mangroves. The flames were still distant, rumbling, not quite advancing. At least the two of us were here, together, the sky over our heads ferocious, harsh, beautiful.

PAUL LISICKY is the author of *Lawnboy, Famous Builder, The Burning House, Unbuilt Projects, The Narrow Door: A Memoir of Friendship,* and *Later: My Life at the Edge of the World.* His work has appeared in the *Atlantic, BuzzFeed, Conjunctions, Fence, Foglifter,* the *New York Times Book Review,* and the *Offing,* among other magazines and anthologies. He is a graduate of the Iowa Writers' Workshop, and his awards include fellowships from the Guggenheim Foundation, the National Endowment for the Arts, and the Fine Arts Work Center in Provincetown, where he has served on the Writing Committee since 2000. He has taught in the creative writing programs at Cornell University, New York University, Sarah Lawrence College, the University of Texas at Austin, and elsewhere. He is currently an associate professor in the MFA Program at Rutgers University–Camden, where he is the editor of *StoryQuarterly.* He lives in Brooklyn.

Acknowledgments

Sections of this book have appeared in *A&U, Blithe House Quarterly* (www.blithe.com), *Cosmos, Global City Review, Province-town Arts,* and in the anthologies *Best American Gay Fiction 2* (Little, Brown, 1997) and *Men on Men 6* (Plume, Penguin, 1996).

❖ ❖ ❖

I'd like to thank my good friends Stephen Briscoe, Polly Burnell, Michael Carter, Denise Gess, Elizabeth McCracken, and Katrina Roberts for their careful, wise feedback. I'd also like to thank David Bergman, Brian Bouldrey, Karen Brennan, Chris Busa, Patricia Chao, Bernard Cooper, Michael Cunningham, Robert Jones, and Ann Patchett for their encouragement. Thank you to Ruth Greenstein for her astute editorial sugges-tions. Thanks, too, to Jonathan Rabinowitz and Turtle Point Press for kind, immeasurable support. Thank you and love to my parents and brothers—Anton, Anne, Robert, and Michael Lisicky—for their generosity, patience, and good spirit.

I'm grateful to the National Endowment for the Arts, James Michener and the Copernicus Society, the Fine Arts Work Center in Provincetown, the Corporation of Yaddo, the MacDowell Colony, the Djerassi Resident Artists Program, and the Ragdale Foundation for much needed assistance.

And finally, deepest thanks to Mark Doty.

◇ ◇ ◇

The new edition of this book invites me to thank the incomparable staff at Graywolf Press: Fiona McCrae, Anne Czarniecki, Janna Rademacher, Katie Dublinski, Mary Matze, and Jeff Shotts. And thanks to Kyle Hunter for the brilliant cover.

—*P.L., New York City, December 2005*

Paul
Lisicky

Lawnboy — Paul Lisicky (12/05)
Frequently Asked Questions

Your book expresses an ambivalent attitude toward Florida. How is the setting central to the book?

PL: I think of the South Florida of the book as a kind of a stage set. It's a Florida of the imagination, even if it makes reference to real cities and streets. I'm interested in the tension between nature and artifice. I think of the seagrape hedges of Palm Beach, surgically clipped to look like stone walls. Or plants that look like hats or wigs. You can convince yourself that the man-made has the upper hand in a place like that, but we all know that South Florida is a hurricane or drought away from being done in. I think of Elizabeth Bishop's great poem "Florida," in which nature is just lying in wait, ready to swallow up the whole grand scheme. She calls Florida the "poorest postcard of itself."

So the tensions within that landscape mirror Evan's imagination. I'm reluctant to pin down the metaphor, but I'd say that Evan's perception of that setting—his simultaneous love and resistance—is crucial to understanding him.

What were the special challenges in writing a book with a gay narrator?

PL: I wanted him to be both a representative character and completely himself at once. The struggle of trying to balance those two desires pulses behind every scene. If he was too much of a representative, he'd be dull and washed out, too externally conceived, a type. If he was too peculiar, he'd put off readers. It often put me in a quandary. For instance, I didn't know if I could get away with a sentence like: "How I wanted to lift the bowl in his moment of peace and kill him." All the same, I wasn't interested in writing a role model. I thought it was important for him to be fallible, wrong, even stupid at times. But he's also smart, sensitive, loyal to a fault, and capable of a huge, beguiling sweetness.

How are style and self-presentation important to the book?

PL: Evan's sense of himself as endlessly mutable worries him at first. At one point he wonders whether he's merely the sum total of "everyone who'd passed through [his] life" and nothing more. Hector teaches him, if only through example, that it's not necessarily awful to be one thing one day and something else the next. You can give form to that mutable self through your clothing, through how you make yourself up every morning.

I think we too easily conflate style with consumerism these days, but they're two different things in the world of the book. Style is constructed in the face of despair. It defies death and loss; it's an emblem of persistence, of faith in the world. And it's even better when it involves some act of reclamation. I'm thinking of Hector's thrift-store clothes, or Peter's doomed attempt to fix up the King Cole.

What is the significance of all the ruined buildings and places in the novel?

PL: They're all over the place: Golden Gate Estates, the ghost city of Boca Bay, Douglass Freeman's house and neighborhood . . . all cases of dashed hope, failed optimism. All originally conceived as points of pleasure. You could say that all this ruin stands for the fortunes of Evan, Peter, and Hector, who are all struggling against disillusionment and fear. And then again I hope that my metaphors resist easy explanation. You want them to be wilder than any attempt to cage and tame them.

In what ways is Lawnboy *a novel about the age of AIDS?*

PL: The dread of AIDS—and the stigma associated with the disease—is everywhere in the book. The body out of control, a limited sense of time, imminent loss—all these things haunt Evan, even though he hasn't tested positive. He has such a compromised sense of the future that even the prospect of going to the dentist seems futile. Hence, his urge to find someone *now* because he might not be around in three days. Every wish is intensified to the burning point. Life ablaze on the precipice.

What do you say to those who read the ending as happy?

PL: Sure, it's happy. Just as Evan tells himself that he's better off on his own, he gets the relationship he's wanted all along. But Evan's happiness lives with his knowledge that relationships are fragile. Even if he and Perry manage to make a long life together, Evan knows that he might outlive his new partner. The book closes with suggestions of terrorism and environmental collapse—"towers crumbling," "forests burning down." So any personal joy is cut through with melancholy and loss—my usual ambivalence rearing its head again!

Lawnboy is set in the early 1990s. How would Evan's story be different if you were a young man now?

PL: It's almost too obvious to say it, but we're the products of our time. Protease inhibitors, cell phones, September 11th, "The War on Terror," our disastrous president and his cronies, the Internet, online cruising, crystal meth, Friendster, MySpace, blogs, the widening gap between rich and poor: none of these was a factor in the early 1990s, and every last one—good, bad, or both—shapes daily experience in ways vast and small.

I'd like to think that Evan would feel less isolated, a little less afraid of dying before his time. But even the most open-minded parents don't raise their children to be homosexual, and the process by which gay kids come into their own is still traumatic. They often learn to efface themselves out of simple self-protection. What young kid wants to be called "gay," which still stands for "freak" or" loser," on the schoolyard? I think that any young man of Evan's intensity—his loyalty to his family and his contradictory pull toward a life of desire—would have a hard time of it. We're living in an era that's hostile to originality, to those who make their own path. There's a tremendous pressure to conform, no matter how you understand yourself.

Still, it's sort of fun to imagine him standing in line to see *Brokeback Mountain* for the tenth time, listening to the Hidden Cameras on his iPod.

Reading Group Guide for
Lawnboy by Paul Lisicky

1. Evan senses "a wall between himself and the world," and
   describes a "low-grade fear and rage burning" beneath all
   his decisions. He is torn by contradictory impulses and
   sometimes experiences himself as "a puppet" or only a
   compilation of people he has known. How much of these
   feelings have to do with his age and how much with simply
   trying to live in contemporary society?

2. Landscapes and settings play a tremendous part in the
   story. How does the King Cole reflect both the inner life
   and the desires of Evan's brother Peter? How are the brothers alike? How are they different? Why does Evan feel a
   need to visit the hurricane-ravaged home where Douglass
   Freeman once lived? Finally, what is the significance of
   Evan's love of plants and what they become for him at the
   end of the novel?

3. After Evan moves out of his parents' home and in with William, he runs into his mother one day and tells her that she's never looked so good. She replies, "I'd come to the point in my life where I realized I had two choices. I could either shoot myself in the temple or reinvent myself." In what way is her life a continual act of self-invention? A continual coming of age?

4. In her letter to Evan at the beginning of Chapter 10, Ursula Sarshik demands that Evan choose between William and his parents. She remains staunch in her decision not to let Evan come home for just a few days. She accuses Evan of turning his back on his parents. Is Ursula justified in her demand? Or have she and Evan's father turned their backs on their son? Does the Sarshik family strike you as typical or unique?

5. In Evan's childhood recollection of taunting the gay man, Stan Laskin, the hardware storeowner, Stan asks the boys, "Why are you so hateful? All of you, I don't get it. Tell me how you live with yourselves?" Are people meaner today? Are children meaner? Why? At the other end of the spectrum is the notion that sometimes difficulty makes people larger, better . . . Is this the case with Perry at the end of the book? Do you think that his kindness and thirst for life have to do with the loss of his partner, Andrew?

This book was designed by Rachel Holscher. It is set in Calisto MT type by Bookmobile Design & Digital Publisher Services.

Printed in the USA
CPSIA information can be obtained
at www.ICGtesting.com
LVHW091139150724
785511LV00005B/429

9 781555 974480